### *"Did you bring me here to seduce me?"*

Jessy asked.

"I want to make love to you very much," Dillon told her, "but I won't lay a hand on you until you want it."

"I have to be in Austin by Sunday evening."

"That gives us three days."

"Less than forty-eight hours," she corrected with a shake of her head. "That's not enough time to start a good friendship, much less an affair."

"We have to start somewhere, Jessy."

"I've—" She stopped herself just as she was about to confesss that she'd never been with a man—any man. Instead, she squared her shoulders and lifted her chin. "No. I won't be a one-night stand for any man. Not even you."

Dear Reader,

Welcome to Silhouette **Special Edition**... welcome to romance. Each month, Silhouette **Special Edition** publishes six novels with you in mind—stories of love and life, tales that you can identify with—as well as dream about.

April has some wonderful stories for you. Nora Roberts presents her contribution to THAT SPECIAL WOMAN!—our new promotion that salutes women, and the wonderful men that win them. *Falling for Rachel,* the third installment of THOSE WILD UKRAINIANS, is the tale of lady lawyer Rachel Stanislaski's romance with Zackary Muldoon. Yes, he's a trial, but boy is he worth it!

This month also brings *Hardworking Man,* by Gina Ferris. This is the tender story of Jared Walker and Cassie Browning—and continues the series FAMILY FOUND. And not to be missed is Curtiss Ann Matlock's wonderful third book in THE BREEN MEN series. Remember Matt and Jesse? Well, we now have Rory's story in *True Blue Hearts.*

Rounding out this month are books from other favorite authors: Andrea Edwards, Ada Steward and Jennifer Mikels. It's a month full of Springtime joy!

I hope you enjoy this book, and all of the stories to come! Have a wonderful April!

Sincerely,

Tara Gavin
Senior Editor

# ADA STEWARD

## LIVE, LAUGH, LOVE

*Silhouette*®

SPECIAL EDITION®

Published by Silhouette Books New York

**America's Publisher of Contemporary Romance**

**SILHOUETTE BOOKS**
300 East 42nd St., New York, N.Y. 10017

LIVE, LAUGH, LOVE

Copyright © 1993 by Ada Sumner

ISBN: 0-373-09808-1

First Silhouette Books printing April 1993

Printed in the U.S.A.

**Books by Ada Steward**

Silhouette Special Edition

*This Cherished Land* #227
*Love's Haunting Refrain* #289
*Misty Mornings, Magic Nights* #319
*A Walk in Paradise* #343
*Galahad's Bride* #604
*Even Better than Before* #680
*Hot Wind in Eden* #759
*Live, Laugh, Love* #808

---

## ADA STEWARD

began writing a novel at the tender age of twelve, when romance and romance fiction were the farthest things from her mind. As a preteen, she favored the fast-paced action of Westerns, war stories, even science fiction. As she matured, however, she realized that what fascinated her the most in life *and* in writing were people, and she turned her attention more fully to character. Since she was drawn to travel, the particular flavor and history of settings also became important. Romance fiction provided the perfect opportunity to combine the richness of place with the drama of people and possibilities. An Oklahoma resident, Ada Steward parcels most of her time into working, writing, traveling and exercising.

## Chapter One

Wearing only a roomy fisherman's sweater that covered her from neck to midthigh, Jessica Carder stood in the shelter of two parked vans and hurriedly tugged on a neon orange swimsuit that was tight enough to double as a tourniquet.

"Hurry, sweetie," Patrice called out as she approached. "Tony's almost ready for you."

Jessy pulled harder, working her hips from side to side while she edged the strapless suit higher.

Patrice, the senior editor on the shoot, peered around the corner of the van. "Is that the orange one?"

"Yeah." Jessy's muffled voice came from inside the bulky sweater as she peeled it off over her head. "And I'm hurrying." Tossing the sweater onto a canvas bag at the back of the van, she smoothed a hand over the high-cut fabric across her hips. "Are you sure this isn't too revealing?"

She and Patrice had decided on the suit the day before, and Jessy had been worried about it ever since. At twenty-nine, she had been modeling for fifteen years and still hadn't overcome the basic modesty that left her uncomfortable with the swimsuit and lingerie shots which, unfortunately, were the mainstays of her career.

"Turn around." Patrice twirled her finger.

Even as Jessy slowly turned for inspection, she knew the verdict didn't matter. Except for a strip of orange down one side, her midriff was bare, and with the mesh-covered cutouts splashed liberally over what fabric remained, the one-piece suit left little to the imagination. But she would wear it anyway, because that was her job.

"Well, it *is* revealing," Patrice agreed. She guided Jessy back around half a turn and adjusted an edge that was tucked under in the back. "But then, if swimsuits weren't revealing, magazines wouldn't be bringing out issues dedicated to them, and you and I wouldn't be here now."

Just as Patrice released Jessy and stepped back, the sun went behind a cloud and a chill breeze whistled past, kicking up sand.

"We're losing the light." The calm voice of the photographer's assistant rose over the low hum of conversation that filled the lull in shooting and blended with the gentle *shush* of the Gulf of Mexico as it broke against the shore of Padre Island off the Texas coast.

"Let's get some more lights up. Hurry." Tony, the magazine's photographer for the assignment, looked up from setting up the next series of shots. "Is Jessy ready yet?"

"Almost. What about her hair?" Patrice set off at a jog. "Do you want it wet?"

Jessy shivered as she left the shelter of the vans. "Brrr." She had to be out of her mind to have stayed in this business for so long. The first five years she had enjoyed it. The second five years she had tolerated it. And the past five years—well, the past five years she'd been deciding what she wanted to do with the rest of her life.

"Over here, Jessy." Patrice waved to her from a table where the hairdresser stood with a spritzer of water in hand.

Jessy picked up her pace and smiled through gritted teeth. An hour earlier the same hairdresser had put curlers in her hair to add body. Now he was going to take the curlers out and wet down her hair. For only an instant, Jessy gave in to the flash of irritation that went through her. Her life was no better than a paper doll's, being dressed and undressed, posed and unposed, shuffled from place to place. It was a life filled with empty hours and empty actions—and it wasn't much of a way to live.

By the time she reached the table her temper was under control again and Jessy stood obediently while the curlers were removed and her hair was brushed out. Then she leaned over with her long, tawny mane dangling in front of her while the hairdresser alternately sprayed and crunched the curls in his hand, maintaining the bounce and the wave in each perfectly moistened lock of hair.

As she stood there doubled over, a knife blade of pain came without warning, piercing her side and slicing across her abdomen. Jessy gasped and froze while seconds stretched like hours until, as quickly as it had come, the cramp released its hold and was gone. Almost dizzy with relief, Jessy let out a slow sigh and relaxed her tensed muscles. Cramps were nothing new. She'd been having them for years, every other month, like clockwork.

Running a hand gingerly over her stomach, she consoled herself with the thought that she had only one more day to get through before her part of the assignment would be done. One more day before she could go in search of her new beginning, before she would go in search of Stephen.

At the thought of him she sighed again, quietly so that no one would notice, and cradled the warm rush of happiness close to her heart. Stephen—he had been the love of her life, and her secret shame. Now he was her hope for the future.

"We're ready!" Tony called from the beach where the camera had been moved closer to the edge of the surf.

"Almost done!" Patrice answered. "That looks good, I think," she said, shooing away the others while the makeup assistant dabbed one last touch of clear gloss on Jessy's unadorned lips. "I think these are going to be our last shots before we lose the sun for today, sweetie," Patrice said, turning Jessy toward the beach. "Let's make them good."

Jessy shook herself loose and jogged in place for a second, limbering up while she kept herself warm. "Is it just me, or is it getting really cold out here?"

Patrice patted her arm. "Just a little while longer. Are you feeling okay?"

"Cramping a little. Nothing much," Jessy said with a shrug.

The rising November wind whipped around her more strongly than ever, threatening to raise gooseflesh on whatever wasn't covered by her swimsuit, which was almost everything. Ready to focus on the job at hand, Jessy turned and jogged toward the water.

"Tony, what do you think?" Patrice called out, following behind at a brisk walk. "You want to go for a cover on this one? I think she could be a cover. The suit is definitely hot looking, don't you think?"

Staying in motion to keep from turning blue, Jessy did jumping jacks on the smooth, wet sand at the edge of the water while her editor and photographer discussed her cover possibilities as if she were a windup Barbie doll. She could feel a pain building again, low in her abdomen, and wished they would get on with the shoot.

Working since before dawn, she'd been bitten by insects, shriveled by water, chafed by sand and chapped by the wind. She was hungry, tired and increasingly ornery. All she wanted now was to get the day over with. A hot shower and a good night's sleep was all she needed before she had to start the whole thing all over again tomorrow morning.

"Okay, Jessy, I'm going to try some different things," Tony called out. "I want you to walk into the surf a little, then turn around to me where there's nothing behind you but water and sky, with the colors changing as the sun begins to set."

Warmed by her exercises and sparked by the image Tony had described, Jessy walked into the gulf until the water washed over her calves. With each shove of the surf, she was grateful for the pale gray sand that rose almost to her ankles and held her firm.

"Great," Tony said. "Now give me a leap."

She laughed. "A leap?" She could barely move, and he wanted a leap.

"Like this," Patrice said, and launched herself into the air, arms and legs spread, in an ungainly imitation of a ballerina.

"Oh, well." Willing to give it a try, Jessy shrugged and shook herself loose again. Then she drew up her body, spread her arms gracefully on either side and leaped.

With a loud, sucking *pop,* her foot pulled free of the sand and her leg stretched out in a high split that jerked to a sudden halt when her second foot refused to budge, remaining firmly mired in the sand.

Jessy lurched forward with a strangled "Ach!" and went down to her knees. Catching herself with her hands, she tumbled onto her side and collapsed in laughter. While the surf washed around her, she rolled onto her back, gasping for air and laughing again each time she thought of how she must have looked. She just hoped Tony hadn't caught any shots of it.

"Maybe if I wasn't standing so deep in the water," she suggested between laughs. Rolling from her back onto one elbow, she twisted toward Tony, who was still behind the camera. "What do you think, Tony? Want me to move up a little and try it again?"

The surf rolled in behind her, nudging her over almost onto her stomach. Sand washed around her. Water tugged at the ends of her hair as the tide swelled and withdrew.

"No." Tony motioned with his hand. "Move down a little. Deeper into the water. And turn more this way." His other hand beckoned, arranging her body without touching her.

Shoulders back. Head up. Hips turned. Knee outstretched. A nymph crawling from the sea. Orange and gold like the setting sun and the sky behind her.

"Give it to me now," Tony coaxed. "With the eyes, Jessy. Those knockout eyes. More. Yes! Beautiful, just beautiful. Now this way."

Jessy snuggled closer to the wet sand and fixed a come-hither gaze on the camera. She always felt a little silly at times like these, as if she were doing the beach scene in *From Here To Eternity* as a solo. Deborah Kerr without Burt Lancaster. And as always the thought made her a little sad. Everyone needed someone.

She listened to Tony without really hearing him. He spoke and she moved, without thinking, this way and that, never taking her eyes off the camera.

With each shift of her body, her hazel eyes spoke of mysteries, promises, sensuality waiting to be explored. Innocent and knowing. Sweet and seductive. Emerald ice and amber fires. Lost in her private thoughts, Jessy reacted instinctively, no longer seeing or hearing the others around her.

The surf curled over her legs and trickled along the outline of her body. The sand shifted beneath her, creeping under the edges of the thin fabric that stood between her and nudity, grating softly against even the most tender flesh.

Water swirled over the hair that spread out behind her and tugged gently, like the fingers of a lover—unseen and yet near, embracing, teasing and then withdrawing. Like a mermaid born to the sea, Jessy lost herself in an imaginary dance with a dream lover, a lover more real than any she had known.

She tried to recall Stephen's face, the face she would see again in two days' time, but he was indistinct, his features blurred by too many years. His hair, a wiry, sandy brown she remembered so well, grew darker with each second she thought of him until what little of Stephen she could remember was replaced by a phantom lover with hair black and glossy as a raven's wing.

His dark eyes smoldered with the heat of an August night, this midnight man who invaded her dreams and stole into her thoughts until all that remained clear and untouched of Stephen was the one kiss she could never forget, a kiss filled with such sad, sweet longing, such unfulfilled passion, that no man had been able to take his place, not even the midnight man who lived only in her imagination.

"Okay, it's a wrap." Tony stepped away from the camera and clapped his hands loud enough for everyone to hear. "That's a wrap, folks. Jessy, you were fabulous." He patted the tripod-mounted camera that his assistant was waiting to retrieve from the advancing surf. "We got some shots today that were pure gold."

"I'll race you all to the van," Patrice called out.

Cold and exhausted, Jessy rose from the water, leaving behind her dream lover but carrying with her a lonely heart that ached for someone real. She made her way slowly among the small forest of lights set up on the beach to amplify the waning sun and through the crew of assistants who were tearing down and packing away equipment.

Somewhere there had to be a better life, a life filled with things that were lasting and with feelings that didn't disappear when the camera stopped clicking. Almost to the van, Jessy lagged behind the others, struggling to contain a surge of longing so fierce that she ached.

Somewhere out there was the kind of love she had known only once before. Somewhere out there, in the little border town of San Miguel, there was Stephen, waiting for her, the way she had waited for him, even after almost ten years. And when she found him she wasn't going to lose him again, not this time.

"Hey, Jessy, step on it. I'm starving."

Jessy looked up to find Tina, one of the other two models on the day's shoot, standing at the open door of the van, her blond hair spilling over the shoulders of a down jacket, her long, long legs encased in leg warmers and disappearing into boots.

"Sorry." Jessy looked around for the canvas bag and pile of clothes she had left at the side of the van. "Did somebody pack my stuff?" She shivered, wanting to get out of the wet, sandy bathing suit and into her warm, heavy sweater.

"Here." Cindi, a blue-eyed brunette with a pixie face, leaned out of the van with Jessy's sweater in her hand. "I didn't think you'd feel like gathering everything up after all that time in the water."

"Bless you." Jessy pulled on the oversize sweater and shimmied out of her bathing suit the same way she had shimmied into it. The only pants she had were cutoffs, but they were better than nothing, and by the time the van was loaded Jessy was dressed and ready to ride back to the hotel, warmer and happier, her spirits buoyed by the knowledge that tomorrow at this time she would be packing for San Miguel and a new beginning with the man of her dreams.

Two days later the sun was high overhead when the taxi's screeching brakes ground it to a halt in front of a squat, crumbling building in a run-down section of San Miguel, a dusty little town just minutes from the Rio Grande and Mexico.

"This is it, lady," the cabbie said. Turning to look at her over the seat, he didn't try to hide his misgivings, or his own eagerness to be gone. "You sure this is where you want to be?"

Jessy unfolded the crumpled piece of paper she held clenched in her hand and tried to crush the flutters of panic inside her. The street number on the paper matched the faded lettering over the dingy doorway of the building.

The windowpanes were papered over on the inside, with the words Free Clinic hand printed in English almost as an afterthought under larger lettering in Spanish. Jessy didn't know which scared her more, the thought that she wouldn't find Stephen in this makeshift clinic or the fear that she *would*.

"This must be the place," she said without much conviction.

"I hope you know what you're doing."

Almost to herself she answered, "Me, too." With trembling fingers she counted out the money she owed.

"You want me to wait on you?"

His offer was grudging. The taxi was already in gear, ready for a quick escape. And as much as she wanted to, Jessy wouldn't let herself accept an offer so clearly reeking of pity.

"No, thanks. I'll be just fine." She gave her hair a confident toss, flashed her best having-fun-now smile and exited the taxi with no sign of the reluctance she felt.

Her feet had hardly hit the pavement before the taxi zoomed away, leaving her alone and uncertain, a foreigner in a land of misery. Her heart fluttered inside her chest like a bird fighting a cage when Jessy took her first, shaky step toward the door of the clinic.

Moving from the hushed sunshine outside to the noisy gloom inside only made her feel worse. As her eyes adjusted to the new light a grim scene came into focus. Row upon row of flimsy plastic chairs were filled with mothers holding children and infants, some crying, some too terribly quiet. Intermingled with these were others—men and women, young and old—waiting patiently and impatiently, some silent, some loud, and over all hung a cloud of fear, pain and despair.

Feeling out of place in their world and intensely conscious—if not ashamed—of her own comfortable life, Jessy turned to go before anyone noticed her. Then, with her hand on the door and her back to the room, she stopped, realizing that she had nowhere to go and no way to get there. Her taxi was gone, and even if it wasn't she had come too far to turn back now, not without seeing Stephen, without knowing for sure if there was anything left between them, without hearing him say if he still thought of her the way she thought of him.

Nearly ten years ago Stephen Barlow had walked out of her life without an explanation or even a goodbye, but she had never stopped thinking about him. Since she was fourteen he had been her secret love, the boy she had saved herself for, the one all others had been measured against, but most of all, Stephen had been the one boy she could never have, because he was dating Jessy's twin sister, Rebecca, the one person in the world Jessy could never hurt.

"Can I help you, miss?"

"Oh!" Startled from her thoughts, Jessy clapped her hand to her mouth too late to stop the outcry. Turning, eyes wide, she stared into the flushed face of a gray-haired woman clad in white. Without removing the fingers that still covered her mouth, Jessy muttered, "I'm so sorry."

"Did you need something?" the nurse asked more sternly.

Feeling as if she were about to face a firing squad, Jessy lowered her hand and said with as much dignity as she could salvage, "I'd like to see Dr. Barlow, if I could."

The nurse's gaze went from cool to icy as it flickered over Jessy and, in an instant, recognized someone who had no business using the services of a free clinic. "If you'll just sign in at the desk, the doctor will get to you." With a huff of disapproval, the woman turned on her heel and prepared to go.

"Oh, no." Realizing that the nurse had mistaken her for a patient, Jessy caught the woman by the elbow and turned her back around. "You don't understand."

While the nurse's pale blue eyes turned from icy to openly hostile, Jessy explained quickly, "I don't need to *see* the doctor. I just want to say hello. I'm a friend of Dr. Barlow's from many years ago. My name is Jessica Carder, and I'd only take a moment."

The nurse's chin lowered a fraction and a bit of the iron went out of her stance. "I'll see."

"Thank you." Jessy breathed the words out with a sigh of relief and tried to ignore the watery consistency of her knees as the older woman nodded and walked away.

With the moment she had been waiting for approaching and her heart hammering in her ears, Jessy no longer heard the noises around her. Instead she remembered the last time her heart had pounded this way, the one and only time Stephen had ever kissed her, on an autumn night under a full moon. The heavens had roared. The oceans stood still. And she had never seen him again.

The next morning he had phoned Rebecca to break off their engagement, with the wedding only weeks away. And then he had disappeared, leaving Jessy torn between her guilt and a hopeless yearning that left no room in her heart for another man.

She had kept the secret of her betrayal for almost nine years before she had finally confessed everything to Rebecca. And it was at Rebecca's urging that Jessy had finally gotten up the courage to find Stephen and give whatever was between them one more chance.

Any moment now she would see him after almost ten years of waiting and wondering. Jessy put her hand over her racing heart and took a deep breath while the background noises slowly filtered back into her consciousness. Surely Stephen would still remember her. Surely he would still care, even after so many years.

The shuffle of restless feet, the insistent cry of a baby, the excited murmur of voices, a loud, thick cough, were all magnified by her heightened senses. When the rapid clicking of high heels across the tile floor cut through the other sounds and focused Jessy's attention, she lifted her gaze and saw a woman in a doctor's white coat coming across the room.

The woman was young, with black hair pulled up and back in a knot that was sleek, simple and sophisticated. Her skin was a soft, glowing olive, and her dark eyes were warm and welcoming. With a trained eye Jessy automatically registered that the woman's exotic, Latin beauty was the kind that would photograph well.

"Hello." With a smile as warm as her eyes, she extended her hand to Jessy. "I'm Dr. Barlow. Have we met?"

At the unexpected statement Jessy felt the world tilt ever so slightly off its axis.

"You're—?" she began and then stopped, trying to gather her thoughts, which were anything *but* cool, calm and sophisticated. For the briefest instant she almost wanted to cry. "But, uh, I—" She tried again and stopped, with no better success.

"I'm Dr. *Lita* Barlow," the woman said, still smiling, still gracious. She paused for Jessy to absorb the information and then asked, "Were you looking for Stephen?"

Jessy nodded while a certainty of impending doom settled over her. She hated to jump to conclusions, but this woman was either Stephen's wife or his adopted daughter, and she wasn't betting on the latter.

"Stephen's out on an emergency right now," Lita continued in her soft, almost musical tones, "but he should be back soon if everything goes well. Would you like to wait for him? I believe Celia said you were a friend of my husband's?"

*Bingo.* Jessy would have laughed out loud if she hadn't felt so sick. If only she would learn to stop and *think* before acting on her impulses. She should have at least tried to phone before showing up on Stephen's doorstep. It would have been the sensible thing to do.

"Would you like to wait?" Lita asked again, nodding her encouragement.

Jessy took a deep breath and tried to focus not on herself and her own turbulent mix of emotions but on this poor, gracious woman whose husband it was Jessy had come to steal away.

"This is a little embarrassing," Jessy said, instinctively opting for honesty. "I haven't seen Stephen in so long. I *would* like to say hello, but I have to confess that I didn't know he was married when I came here."

Lita smiled the smile of a woman confident of her husband's love. "I had suspected that. You're Jessy, aren't you?"

"Yes." Jessy tried hard not to show her surprise, but it wasn't easy. "You know me?"

"Stephen's shown me pictures. Yearbooks, things like that." Lita hesitated almost shyly. "I've always felt that I owed you a debt of gratitude."

"Gratitude?" Totally mystified, Jessy wished she could sit down over coffee and really get to know this woman, who was not doing or saying any of the things Jessy would have expected under the circumstances. "For what?"

Lita laughed. "For stopping that wedding." Her cheeks flushed a gentle pink. "I hope I don't sound ungracious, but you changed the course of history, at least my history. If it wasn't for you, I would never have met Stephen."

Jessy shrugged, not really knowing what to say. For too many years she had chased after a fantasy while Stephen was busy building a new life with someone else. Of course, anyone with half a brain would have known that he would go on with his life. Only a moonstruck dreamer would have wasted so many years on something that was never more than wishful thinking to begin with. Stephen had never loved her.

"I used to be jealous of you," Lita continued. "When I first met him, Stephen was still carrying such a torch for you he wouldn't look at anybody else."

"He was?" Jessy felt a fleeting moment of happiness, followed by pain, and then she thrust it all behind her. The Stephen she had known was gone, replaced by a man who was married to another woman, a Stephen who was nothing more than a vague memory with sandy brown hair.

"He was crazy about you, but—" Lita hesitated and lifted her shoulders in a silent shrug that said a lot.

Jessy knew, because she had used that same shrug herself many times when words had failed her, and words had failed her often whenever she thought of the hopeless mess she had created the night she had kissed her sister's fiancé.

"But because of Rebecca," Lita continued, "it could never be, so eventually Stephen stopped wanting what he couldn't have, and then—" She spread her arms and smiled brightly. "He noticed me, and the rest is history. You know, Jessy, I've always hoped that we would meet someday, because I've wanted to thank you for a long time, and—" Her smile softened, and she laid her hand lightly on Jessy's arm. "I wanted to know that you've found someone else, too."

Trapped, Jessy tried to smile, but it wasn't easy. "Well, actually, I haven't, but then I've been pretty busy and I haven't really been looking very hard."

"And you didn't know Stephen was married," Lita said quietly.

At the understanding sympathy in the other woman's eyes, Jessy gave in. Denial was too hard. "And I didn't know Stephen was married," she admitted.

"Do you still love him?"

"Boy, you get straight to the point, don't you?"

"I'm sorry. I know this isn't fair to you. I've seen pictures of you and Rebecca both, all the way back to junior high. And I've heard so many stories I feel like I know you, but I'm a total stranger to you, and if you want to tell me to go jump in a lake, feel free."

"No, if you can be mature about this, so can I," Jessy insisted.

Strange as it seemed, she could almost feel the same vague sense of kinship that this woman apparently felt toward her. Maybe it was because Lita reminded Jessy just a little of Rebecca, or maybe it was because Lita reminded Jessy just a little of herself.

"In all honesty," she said finally, when she had conquered her urge to turn and run, "a part of me will always love Stephen, but to what degree, I have no idea. Maybe I won't know until I see him. Maybe that's why I'm still here."

"Well, he should be returning any minute."

"Oh, I don't know." Jessy shook her head, as confused by her own feelings as she was by the unexpected turn of events. "Look, maybe I should just leave. I know you're busy here, and I'm sure Stephen doesn't need to spend his time reminiscing with me."

"Oh, no." Lita caught Jessy by the hand when she tried to back away. "Please. Stephen would be sick if—"

The door opened and an excited, laughing jumble of voices interrupted before Jessy had a chance to extricate herself and exit gracefully. She wanted to groan when the instant glow in Lita's eyes left no doubt that Stephen had returned.

"Look," Lita whispered, looking past Jessy to the open door. "It's him."

Giving in to her own curiosity, Jessy turned toward the entrance. Her heart pounded with a mixture of anticipation and dread as she glanced quickly over the exuberant trio in the open doorway. At the back was a tall, dark presence, hardly more than an outline against the halo of sunlight. In the middle was a small, bedraggled boy who instantly touched a chord in Jessy's heart. But the man in the lead, with the sandy brown, thinning hair and the stocky, well-fed body, was the figure that riveted her attention.

Stephen had changed from the boy she had known, but Jessy's heart filled with bittersweet memories at the sight of his kind and gentle face, lined from long years of too little sleep and too much worry. Like a rock worn smooth by the years, the sharp-edged youth he once was had been mellowed and molded by time.

Realizing that she might as well be invisible, she watched Stephen's eyes go straight to his wife, and Jessy's own beginning smile faltered. She stepped back as he walked by without a glance in her direction and pulled Lita into his arms for a hug. The sudden image of a child gazing in through a candy-store window, her nose pressed to the glass, flashed through Jessy's mind. She turned away, startled by the naked hunger she felt for something in her own life that could even come close to the kind of devotion Stephen and Lita so obviously shared.

Embarrassed by her own emotions and afraid that someone else might have noticed, Jessy glanced toward the other man who had entered with Stephen. No longer haloed in the open doorway, the man seemed even taller and darker than before as he watched her from the shadows. His unblinking gaze, dark as midnight, burned through her with cold disapproval.

She stared back at him while her embarrassment faded and the slow heat of defiance flared inside her. Whoever this man was, he had no right to *any* opinion of her, least of all disapproval. While her anger simmered toward a white-hot glow, Jessy tilted her chin to a haughty angle and returned his gaze with bold challenge in her eyes. Then she gave her head a flippant toss and coolly turned away, dismissing him and his opinion without a backward glance.

Finding herself facing Stephen and Lita again, Jessy watched while Lita took a half step back from Stephen's embrace and said, "Darling, there's someone here to see you."

With a gentle nudge she turned Stephen toward Jessy, and Jessy froze like a deer caught in headlights. From beginning to end this entire trip had been one long mistake, an ill-conceived attempt to rekindle adolescent flames, and Jessy had never felt so awkward and out of place in her life.

But her discomfort turned to delight when Stephen's expression went from puzzlement to recognition and then to joy. And when he swept her into his arms with a whoop and squeezed the breath out of her in a mighty bear hug, she had to admit that the whole awful morning had been worth it all, especially when she could see Lita's indulgently smiling face only a few feet away.

Over the years Jessy had almost forgotten that she had loved Stephen as a friend long before she had loved him as anything more. He was one of the sweetest, kindest, most admirable people Jessy had ever known. And with one kiss, she had lost more than the man she loved, she had lost one of the best friends she'd ever had.

With her heart so full she could hardly breathe, Jessy lifted her head from Stephen's shoulder and said in a choked voice, "It's so wonderful to see you again, Stephen. It really is."

"Jessy, I can't believe it." He gave her another squeeze and the breath went out of her in a huff. "You're as beautiful as ever. How have you been?"

"Oh," she squeaked as she twisted to gain a little breathing room inside his arms. "Pretty much the same."

Without conscious intention, her wandering gaze stole across Stephen's shoulder to the doorway and collided once again with the dark, unsmiling eyes of the second man. Still watching her from the shadows, he seemed to peer into her heart and shine a spotlight on every fleetingly selfish, self-serving thought that had ever dwelled there. Jessy blushed fiercely in spite of her determination not to.

Wishing passionately that she could march over there and tell him what she thought of his suspicious mind, she nevertheless disengaged herself from Stephen's embrace and stepped back.

Her angry eyes flashed one last time toward the door, and the dagger look she shot the man in the corner was designed to wound severely, but her efforts were wasted. His head was lowered and his attention was focused on the little boy who tugged at his hand. Their conversation was in rapid, whispered Spanish, which only served to remind Jessy once again that it was she who was the interloper on the scene.

"So, Jessy, did you and Lita get a chance to meet?" Stephen asked, bringing Jessy's wandering thoughts back to him.

"Yes." Jessy exchanged glances with Lita and knew that much of what they had said would remain between the two of them. "She seems pretty special."

"She is to me," Stephen said with pride. He slipped his arm around Lita's waist and tucked her against his side.

She snuggled even closer while gently protesting, "Oh, Stephen."

Once again stabbed by the open affection between the couple, Jessy glanced away toward the unnamed man who seemed determined to think only the worst of her. As if sensing her pain he looked up from the boy and took a half step forward, which brought him out of the shadows and into a narrow slice of light.

Confronted by obsidian eyes as piercing as any she had ever seen and a face as bold as it was handsome, Jessy caught her breath. Forgetting to hide her wonder, she stared openly at the high, broad cheekbones and bronzed face of an Aztec warrior. Proud and sensual from his hawklike eyes to his chiseled-in-stone jaw, his every feature was carved with strength, determination and challenge.

With hair black as a raven's wing and eyes smoldering with the heat of an August night, he collided with her senses and set her pulse to pounding. The lightweight cotton of her sweater did nothing to control the shiver that crawled over her shoulders and down her spine. Jessy closed her eyes against the powerful response she seemed unable to stop.

"And this is Dillon," Stephen said, oblivious to all that had passed between Jessy and the other man. "Lita's brother."

Almost afraid to look at him again, Jessy forced her eyes open and found Dillon watching her. The ghost of a smile tugged at the corner of his mouth.

She watched his smile spread slowly and knew that he had seen her reaction to him. He knew that the tremors coursing through her were not born of revulsion. Jessy forced her gaze higher until her eyes met his, and her stomach twisted at the confirmation she saw there.

And once again her embarrassment was followed by defiance. He might have a name now, but he was still a stranger she wouldn't see again after today. And if he had stirred something in her that few other men had, that was something he would never have the satisfaction of knowing.

Once again, with a toss of her head that was more in spirit than in fact, Jessy dismissed him and turned away just as Lita said, "So, Stephen, tell me all about it. How did the delivery go? You seemed pretty happy when you walked in here."

Stephen's smile spread until he seemed to glow, and his voice grew soft. "Mother and son are doing great. I'll check in on Blanca and the baby again tonight. But I couldn't have done it without Dillon. He coached her through it and kept her calm."

When Dillon's obviously proud sister turned toward him, Jessy turned, too, eager to know more about this man, and at the same time resentful that he could rouse her interest after he'd made no attempt to hide his hostility toward her. No man should have that power of fascination, and certainly not over her.

"Poor Dillon," Lita teased with a mischievous laugh. "And you didn't even get to have lunch first."

Dressed in chinos and a short-sleeved black polo shirt badly smeared across the front with rusty brown streaks, he looked like someone who had been pressed into service on his day off, and Jessy wondered if he might be yet another doctor in the family.

Dillon's gaze flickered from Jessy to his sister and back again, his thoughts hidden in the dark depth of his eyes, while his hand tightened protectively on the shoulder of the little boy whose torn jeans looked too authentic to be a fashion statement.

"It takes me back a few years," Dillon said in rich, deep tones that were devoid of the Spanish accent Jessy had expected.

Lita laughed again and tilted her head toward Jessy. "Dillon was only here to take me to lunch, and when the emergency call came in, Stephen dragged him along just because poor Dillon's spent so many years as a paramedic."

Joining in the ribbing, Stephen added, "I think he got to set a fractured leg the last time he stopped in to visit."

Beneath the smooth bronze of Dillon's skin, Jessy thought she detected a faint flush across his cheeks and wondered if the cause was embarrassment or temper. Either way, she hadn't learned much more about him than she already knew, except that he was a paramedic, not a doctor, and he didn't particularly enjoy being teased.

"If you'll permit me," Dillon said unexpectedly in the velvety baritone that made each word a pleasure to hear. His strong fingers curled over the shoulders of the little boy he held in front of him like a shield. "My young friend here would like to be introduced to the lady." With a nod toward Jessy, he said, "May I present Mr. Emilio Suarez."

Tousling the boy's hair affectionately, Dillon looked down at him and conducted the second half of the introduction in Spanish, ending with "Señorita Jessica Carder," the only words Jessy could understand.

The boy's dark eyes danced with pleasure and mischief as he took a step toward her and extended a small, grubby hand. Thoroughly charmed, Jessy returned his handshake with a smile of delight, but when she clasped the fragile strength of his thin hand in hers, her mood grew poignant.

While unexpected sadness blossomed inside her she fought the urge to sweep the little boy into her arms and hold him with a rampantly maternal ardor that would almost certainly have shocked and mortified him. Releasing Emilio's hand in self-defense, Jessy forced a smile as she stepped back, shaken to the core by emotions that had arisen out of nowhere. Avoiding Dillon, whose gaze seemed to miss nothing, she turned to Lita.

"You've been so kind, but I've taken up far too much of your time."

"You're not leaving already?" Stephen protested.

"Oh, Stephen, you're a busy man." Impulsively Jessy clasped his hand in hers. "I just wanted to see how you were doing, and I can tell you're just doing fine." She looked at Lita again and smiled while Stephen's fingers slipped through her own.

"But this isn't a visit," Lita said with a frown. "You two still have so much to catch up on. Please, come to dinner tonight."

"Oh, no," Jessy said, shaking her head finally. "Really, no."

"Dillon." Lita turned to her brother, her faith in his power naked in her eyes. "Talk to her."

Polite reluctance became defiant determination when Jessy swung her gaze from Lita to Dillon, challenging him to say anything that would make a difference. But Dillon only shook his head. Looking from his sister to Jessy and back to Lita, he spread his hands helplessly.

Stung, though she should have known better, Jessy took a step backward. Dillon didn't want her to stay, Jessy realized with a disappointment that hurt much more than it should have. He didn't want her anywhere around.

## Chapter Two

"But of course she will." Stephen reached out and caught Jessy's hand and her attention, pulling her startled gaze away from Dillon. "We have two sons you haven't met. And you haven't told me a thing about Rebecca. Just tell us where you're staying, and we'll pick you up. About seven?"

"Please," Lita echoed.

Feeling trapped, Jessy looked to Dillon for support this time, but she was greeted by a shrug of his brow and a sardonic smile of defeat.

"Tell me where you're staying and I'll pick you up," he said in his deep, caressing voice. "You'd starve to death waiting for Stephen or Lita. They can barely manage to get themselves to dinner on time."

"What a wonderful idea." Lita's purr of delight sounded suspiciously as if she had just gotten what she had wanted all along. "Well, I'll leave you two to work out the details. I'll see you tonight, Jessy."

Smiling at his wife's retreating figure, Stephen shook his head. "Such a matchmaker." He leaned forward to give Jessy a peck on the cheek. "Don't let her bother you," he whispered with a nod toward Lita. "She can't help herself." Still smiling, he turned and followed his wife toward the back of the clinic.

"I'll walk you to your car," Dillon offered.

"Thank you." Thoroughly dazed by the events of the day Jessy needed to get away, to spend some time alone, to regroup. As she drew even with Dillon in her flight toward the door and freedom, he cupped his hand against the small of her back and fell into step beside her.

"Oh, Dillon," Lita's voice called.

He stopped and turned, catching Jessy by the arm as he did so and turning her with him so that her shoulder nestled against the hard cushion of his chest. "Yes, Lita?"

Pausing in the doorway to the corridor, like a bird about to take wing, his sister said, "If you're still hungry, I don't think Jessy's had lunch yet, either. And she probably doesn't know anyone else in town. It was just a thought." With a smile and a wave, Lita turned and disappeared.

"Well—" Dillon began, then stopped when Jessy pulled her arm free.

"I've got to get some fresh air," she muttered and practically lunged through the doorway and into the sunshine.

Once outside she kept walking the half block to the corner. All she had to do was find a pay phone, call a taxi and make her getaway before these people tried to take over any more of her life. She had absolutely no intention of being set up with anyone, especially not someone like Dillon, who so clearly couldn't stand her.

"A simple no would do," Dillon said, the velvety caress of his voice coming from directly behind her.

Startled that he could be so near so quickly and resentful of the jolt that his proximity alone could deliver, Jessy turned on her heel and confronted him. Her flashing eyes dared him to come one step closer.

"I'm sure Lita didn't mean to upset you," he said. "She wouldn't be so insistent if she didn't like you."

"I—" Her temper cooling as quickly as it had flared, Jessy stared up at him and wondered what she could say in her own defense. That her prickly independence had long since caused her own family to leave her to her own choices? That she wasn't used to being the target of someone else's caring interference? Or that just being near him made it hard for her to think straight?

Not ready to admit any of that, Jessy capitulated with a sigh and a smile so grudging as to be almost invisible. "I guess I might have overreacted."

"I know how you feel. Between my sister and my mother, I get pretty tired of it myself sometimes." Dillon broke off his mesmerizing gaze finally, to scan the area behind her. "Where's your car?"

Jessy momentarily considered lying, then realized the desperation inherent in the thought. "In Austin."

"Oh?"

"I took a taxi from my hotel this morning."

"Then you need a ride."

She shook her head. Attractive as he might be, she wanted to get away from him, and everything that would remind her of this day, as quickly as possible. "I can call a cab."

Dillon laughed. "Yeah. Sure." Still chuckling, he slipped his arm around her waist and turned her toward the clinic. "I'll give you a ride."

"Excuse me." Jessy put on her brakes and sidestepped out of the circle of his arm. "I took a taxi to get down here, and I can take one to get out of here."

For a moment they faced each other in a standoff, a man who was clearly accustomed to giving orders, and a woman who was clearly *not* accustomed to taking them.

"You will never get a taxi to come into this neighborhood," Dillon said slowly and distinctly.

"I might."

"You can give them a call and see. But the only phone around here is inside the clinic."

*Damn.* The last thing in the world she wanted to do was to go back into that clinic, for any reason. Trapped, doomed to spend more time alone with a man who made her feel vulnerable, excited and uncertain in a way she could never remember feeling before, Jessy gave in. "Okay. Thank you."

Reluctantly she lifted her gaze from the sidewalk to Dillon's face. He wasn't smiling, but in his eyes shone the same darkly cynical, vaguely amused light that had been there off and on since they had met, as if he shared a secret with her, but she was damned if she knew what it was.

"My car's this way." He motioned down the street past the clinic.

Looking in that direction, Jessy saw Emilio waiting patiently by the curb, watching them. When his eyes caught hers, he smiled and waved, and once again Jessy felt her heart reach out to him.

"Is Emilio going with us?" she asked Dillon, careful to stay one step behind him, just out of reach, as they walked. It was too easy to enjoy the light touch of his hand on her back, too easy to feel drawn into the magnetic circle that seemed to surround him.

"No, he's going back to help his grandmother take care of Blanca and her new son."

"Shouldn't he be in school?"

"Yes, but he won't stay." A very personal blend of anger and sadness crept into Dillon's voice with the statement.

Surprised by the sense of helplessness that he conveyed, Jessy took two quick steps to draw even with him and allowed herself a small concession to the curiosity that burned inside her. "Is Emilio part of your family?"

"No. He's just a friend." Dillon broke off his conversation with Jessy to call out in Spanish to Emilio, who laughed and danced away several steps before answering in light, teasing tones.

Smiling, Dillon gestured as he spoke again, shooing Emilio on his way. The boy backed away, talking as he went. A wide grin spread across his face when he motioned toward Jessy. Then he turned and ran away down the street, his teasing laughter trailing behind him.

"What was that about?" Jessy asked, her curiosity once again overcoming the inner voice that told her not to ask.

"I'm not sure you want to know." Still grinning, Dillon leaned nearer. "Emilio thinks you are very beautiful."

"Well." Touched by the little boy's compliment, Jessy broke into a smile. "That's so sweet."

"He also thinks I should marry you quickly before you get away."

Jessy halted in midstep. "What?"

Eyes dancing, Dillon explained. "He wants me to adopt him, and he thinks that if I get married I'll be able to do it easier."

"Oh, so I could be just any woman. It really wouldn't make a difference." Ridiculous as it seemed, Jessy realized that she was disappointed.

"Well, yes, but he really likes you. He usually waits until I've at least dated a woman before he tries to get me married to her." Stopping next to a car distinguished only by its faded blue paint and lack of hubcaps, Dillon said, "Well, here we are."

Faced with the reality of a cozy drive alone with Dillon, Jessy wondered if she hadn't made the wrong choice. "Really, I could just take a taxi back to my hotel."

Dillon opened the door and waited for her to enter. "It's no trouble."

Jessy took a step toward the car while her body set off clarion signals of danger. Not daring to look to the side where she knew Dillon's steady gaze waited, she moved past him and into the passenger seat. As she sat, her sweater-knit skirt slid from just above her knees to well up on her thighs.

When she was safely settled inside, he slowly pushed the car door closed behind her. As it clicked shut she couldn't take the suspense any longer. Against every better instinct she possessed, Jessy turned and looked up to find Dillon's intense gaze locked on her just as she knew it would be.

His eyes, dark and mysterious as a moonless night, caught her own, a soft hazel with a light sprinkling of gold, and for a long, breathless moment they held each other motionless. Then Dillon stepped back, the spell was broken and Jessy's heart began to beat again.

Facing forward, she steeled herself against the sensuality he seemed able to turn off and on at will. She tried to find the anger that seemed to be her only defense against him, but it wouldn't come. She was torn, not knowing which Dillon to believe—the one who was warm and charming one minute, disarming her with his laughter, or the Dillon who could send her reeling the next minute with the impact of a glance so unreadable she couldn't even tell if he liked or despised her.

"Are you hungry?" Dillon slid gracefully into the driver's seat and turned the key in the ignition. "Because I'm starving." The whining engine sputtered, coughed and finally caught, roaring to life with a surprising energy. Triumphant, Dillon turned to her with a coaxing smile that set his black eyes to dancing. "And I hate to eat alone. I really hate it."

Knowing that he was doing it again, Jessy melted anyway. "When you put it that way, I do feel a little hungry myself."

"Good. I was hoping you would." He pulled away from the curb and began the long, slow drive through the narrow, busy streets of the neighborhood.

While he concentrated on the traffic, Jessy was left alone with her thoughts, which circled back to Dillon no matter how hard she tried to stop them. Hot and cold, fire and ice, he was as mercurial a man as she had ever met, and when she was with him she was just as bad.

She'd been turned topsy-turvy by a man who aroused her temper as quickly and easily as he touched her heart, but he was nothing more than a stranger. After this one brief drive she'd never see him again, and she was glad because he was dangerous. He was the kind of man who would be much too sure of himself and far too hard to forget.

"Jessy," Dillon began quietly, "I'd like to apologize if I seemed rude earlier."

His hand brushed her arm in just a whisper of a touch that was enough to set Jessy's heart pounding and reaffirm her instinct of danger in just being near him.

"Spanish is the language of the barrio," he continued with no sign that the brief contact had affected him. "And when I'm here, it's too easy for me to forget that not everyone speaks the language."

"What?" Caught off guard, she turned to him with confusion visible in her eyes. She had expected him to apologize for his hostile attitude when they first met, not for his Spanish. "I mean, I wish I did. Speak Spanish, that is."

"But you don't." He smiled the gentle, warm smile that always surprised her and seemed increasingly able to turn her bones to taffy. "And from now on, my conversations in front of you will be in English. Am I forgiven?"

"Well, of course, but this is your home, Dillon. You can speak any language you want." She felt awkward accepting an apology that only seemed to emphasize the glaring error that had been her entire day.

Luckily Lita was an exceptional woman. Most wives wouldn't have been so understanding if an old flame turned up on their husband's doorstep. If Stephen had been married to a different woman, Jessy might have succeeded in accidentally wrecking his life once again.

"I'm the one who was out of place down here today," she said, making an apology of her own. "I had no business coming here. It was a stupid idea."

Dillon's smile unexpectedly flattened into a straight, hard line, and a wintry chill crept into the close confines of the car. "Why *did* you come here today?" he asked in a voice that was menacingly soft.

Not missing the change in Dillon's attitude, Jessy stiffened. The hostile man who had watched her from the shadows of the clinic doorway was back. "It's a long story," she answered firmly. It was one she had no intention of sharing.

"Maybe I should tell you that I was Stephen's roommate after he switched colleges," Dillon said in that same, too-quiet voice.

The statement dropped between them like a cement block and lay there with all its implications slowly filling the silence. Jessy felt almost undressed by all the things this man could know about her, and about Stephen—things that she would have given anything to hear only yesterday, things that she would give anything not to hear today.

"You—"

"He was pretty confused those first few months I knew him," Dillon said when she choked to a halt. "He was upset, and I know he said a lot of things that he wished he hadn't later. But at the time he needed to talk, so I let him."

Shame and misery welled inside Jessy. Of all the things she had done in her life, one of the few she genuinely regretted was letting her feelings for Stephen lead her to betray her sister, even for one stolen kiss. Even after Rebecca had begun to doubt her own feelings for Stephen.

The fact that Stephen and Rebecca had both gone on to happier lives didn't excuse Jessy in her own eyes. She had set out to do a good deed and had allowed her own selfish, headstrong nature to take over, and for that she had ended up paying a far greater price than either Stephen or Rebecca.

"Stephen didn't think too much of himself in those days," Dillon said, breaking into her thoughts. "Personally, I never thought *he* was the one who needed to be ashamed.''

Jessy's head came up and anger surged past the shame and misery, burying the lesser emotions in its wake. What happened with Stephen was something she had never totally forgiven herself for, but it wasn't something she needed to be lectured about by a virtual stranger. She could call herself every name in the book if she wanted, but nobody else was going to do it while she had life left in her body.

Drawing a deep, steadying breath, she answered in dulcet tones that would have alerted anyone who knew her better. ''If you have something to say, Dillon, why don't you just say it?''

Without waiting for a second invitation, Dillon stomped on the brakes and shifted the car into Park in the middle of the street, blocking one of the two narrow traffic lanes. He seemed to expand in size as he twisted to face her.

''Why are you here?'' he demanded.

Uncowed by his anger, Jessy grew cooler as he grew hotter. ''That's not really any of your business, is it?''

''Lita's my sister, and that makes it my business.''

''Why don't you let Lita take care of herself? She doesn't seem very worried.''

''Maybe she's just too trusting.'' He paused and stared straight into Jessy's eyes. ''The same way your sister was.''

If he had tossed a bomb into her lap, Jessy couldn't have exploded any faster, and before she realized she had moved, Dillon caught her swinging arm in midair.

''Watch it,'' he warned.

Probably more shocked than he was by her actions, Jessy looked up at the strong fingers that gripped her wrist, keeping her arm stretched to the side.

''Let me go.'' She jerked against his grasp, but Dillon only raised her arm higher, pulling her closer to him at the same time.

His scorching eyes clashed with the blazing anger in hers. "Why are you here?"

Too furious for caution, Jessy shot back, "What do you want me to say? That I came for Stephen? Okay! I came for Stephen. There, are you satisfied?"

"No." He dropped her arm abruptly. Then his hand cupped the back of her neck in a seductive caress while the warm, whiskied tones of his voice washed over her. "No, I am far from satisfied, lady. Very far from satisfied."

The wild pounding of Jessy's heart was no longer from anger, but she refused to be moved. She would not be drawn into his web. He was only trying to manipulate her, to keep her away from Stephen any way he could.

Dillon's face lowered toward hers almost imperceptibly. The light burning in his eyes was a warm, sultry glow, and whatever his reasons, Jessy couldn't deny that the passion he ignited in her was starkly real. But she would be damned if she would give in to him now.

"Don't you *dare*," she whispered, forcing a coldness into her voice that was nothing but bravado.

Dillon stopped and drew back no more than an inch. "Why?" The word was a challenge that held no sign of retreat.

"I wouldn't kiss a man who insulted me the way you just did."

"Did I say anything that wasn't true?"

"You seem to have taken a conveniently simple view of the whole incident."

"Incident?" He drew back indignantly. "You seduce your sister's fiancé, and you call it an incident? Then ten years later you come after him again, without no doubt that he's yours for the taking, not even caring that he's married to someone else? You must be very sure of yourself, Jessica Carder." As he spoke he pulled her closer to him, stopping when she was just a breath away. "You must be *very* sure of yourself."

At a loss for words and unable to summon her resistance a second time, Jessy waited almost eagerly for the kiss she knew was only seconds away.

"You have nothing to say this time?" Dillon asked quietly. "No slap in the face? No cold, cutting words? Could it be, Jessy, that perhaps, just perhaps, you want me as much as I want you?"

"Perhaps." With great effort she drew back from the precipice he had brought her to and reached out shakily toward sanity. She was in a car parked in the middle of a street, in a barrio in a strange town, and in a breathless clench with a man she hardly knew. She was obviously out of her mind.

Her heart thudded against her ribs. Her head whirled. Fighting to maintain her fragile grasp on reality, she flattened her palms against his chest and shoved. "I think I've lost my appetite. Why don't you just take me back to my hotel or else drop me at the nearest cabstand?"

"Jessy." Her name sounded like a curse wrung from him against his will. His arms tightened around her. "No."

"No?" She could feel her will crumbling while she kept up her steady pressure against his chest, fighting herself more than him and trying to ignore the hard muscles that flexed beneath her hands. "Listen, mister," she said with far more strength than she felt, "if you expect me to make love to you right here and right now, then I suggest that you just get a grip on your libido, and do it real fast."

Light as a whisper, his fingertip traced the outline of her lips. "For a year I listened to Stephen try to forget you," Dillon said softly. "For a year I wondered why he tortured himself over you."

"Is that what you want? To experience firsthand what Stephen saw in me?" The idea turned her cold.

"No," he said instantly, then more slowly, "Yes." He dropped his hand from her face and loosened the grip that held her so close. "I have to admit, it did cross my mind, but no, that's not what I want, not now."

"Don't you think all of this is happening a little too fast?" She motioned to the car, the street and the world walking by outside, as much to remind herself as him.

Dillon smiled and reluctantly released her. "Yes, I do. How about you?"

Feeling as if she'd just had a narrow escape, and still hungry in spite of it, Jessy said, "I think maybe we should just go get something to eat and pretend the last few minutes never happened."

"That's going to be very hard to do. But I'll try." He turned in his seat to restart the engine. "Normally I'm not so bold with women," he said quietly. "This seems to be my day for apologies."

"Well, I must say, it certainly hasn't been dull." She took a deep breath and tried to calm her racing heart.

"Well, hell."

"What now?" She glanced over and found him holding his unfastened seat belt in his hand and scowling at the reddish brown smears on the front of his shirt.

"Why didn't somebody tell me this thing had blood on it?"

"That's blood?" She recoiled and felt her stomach lurch.

"Yeah." The scowl lightened, replaced by a chuckle and a quick smile. "Birthin' babies is messy work. Can you reach that shirt in the back seat?"

Jessy twisted around and saw a second black knit shirt, identical to the one he was wearing, neatly folded on the seat behind him. Stretching through the gap between the bucket seats, she retrieved the shirt and turned back toward Dillon just in time to watch him grip the tail of the shirt he was wearing and peel it up the length of his torso and off over his head.

Muscles rippled beneath coppery skin. The faintly musky scent of cologne blended with another, faintly musky scent that was Dillon's alone. He pulled his clean shirt from Jessy's clenched hand and flashed her a smile. "Thanks." Then he repeated the process in reverse, again treating Jessy to a view of bronzed skin rippling over a lean rib cage, flexing muscles and a stomach flat and hard enough to bounce a coin on.

Pausing to smooth his fingers through his tousled hair, he fastened his seat belt and started the car in motion once again. "Do you have any idea where you want to eat?"

Jessy, who had posed beside hundreds of incredibly handsome, barely clad males over the years without a single instance of increased heartbeat, shook her head and turned her face toward the window. As she lowered it, a blessedly cool breath of air washed over her flaming cheeks and into the stifling interior of the car.

"Do you eat real food, or do you eat, uh, model stuff?" Dillon asked without taking his eyes from the road.

"Model stuff?" Torn between insult and amusement, Jessy swiveled her head the 180 degrees back toward him. "What exactly is model stuff?"

"You know, salads, fruits, yogurt."

"Oh, you mean healthy food? The kind of things that are good for you?"

Dillon cast a quick glance in her direction and almost smiled. "Well, that wasn't *exactly* what I meant, but yeah, I guess so."

"I suppose you could say I eat mostly model stuff. I enjoy a good steamed fish occasionally."

"Yum."

Jessy laughed. "So, what do you eat?"

"This is Texas, ma'am. I eat chili, Tex-Mex and beefsteak a lot."

"And when you're not busy clogging your arteries, what do you eat?"

"Oh, I think I pretty much stick to pure artery cloggers."

"You're not going to tell me you keep a body like yours by eating food like that?" As soon as the words were out, Jessy knew she had made a mistake.

Dillon's slow, sly smile left no doubt. "Why, I wasn't sure you'd been watching."

"It was purely accidental, I promise you."

"You know, you're very different from the way I always imagined you."

"Different how?" she asked, willing to talk about almost anything if it would keep him away from the more dangerous subjects he seemed to prefer. "You mean the way I look?"

"Oh, no, I always knew how you looked."

"You did? How?"

"Jessica, you're a model. Your picture is everywhere."

"Jessy. Call me Jessy. No one ever calls me Jessica. And how did you know it was me? Did Stephen show you my picture?"

"Not exactly, but he had this French·fashion magazine he kept looking at. And the girl on the cover was in all the other magazines he bought. Which, by the way, were magazines no normal man should have been buying. So I finally asked him if the girl he was in love with was a model. Of course, I already knew the answer, and by this time I had become almost as fascinated by you as he was."

At his last words, the tingles in her stomach returned. Rather than dwell on the effect he had on her, Jessy hurried back into the conversation. "So you knew who I was as soon as you walked into the clinic?"

"Yep."

"Is that why you kept giving me those dirty looks?"

"It was like finding a black widow spider perched on my doorstep."

"Well, I'll say one thing for you. You certainly know how to dish those compliments." Jessy's hand tightened on the door handle, and she thought if they hadn't been speeding through heavy traffic she just might have opened the door and jumped.

Hot and cold didn't even begin to describe this man's attitude. Incendiary and arctic came a lot closer. She didn't know if he was just naturally rude or if he was one of those infuriatingly honest people who could turn a casual conversation into one long slap in the face.

"Sorry."

"Oh, don't apologize on my account. I'm starting to build a tolerance level. But I am curious. Are you always this insulting to women you barely know?"

"Not at all," he said, hardly fazed by her angry sarcasm. "I'm normally considered very charming. But then, I don't feel that I barely know you. I feel like I've known you a very long time. And there's a lot stored up inside. Besides, I'm not all wrong. You *did* come back for Stephen."

"But I didn't know he was married. A mutual friend told me he was a doctor, and where he was working. I was in the area, so—"

"So you decided to stop by and see if he still had the hots for you," Dillon finished for her.

"Look, Stephen is a wonderful man," Jessy said, reining in her temper. "My sister's married, happily, to someone else, and if Stephen was single there'd be no reason why I shouldn't still be interested in him, now would there?"

"So, you really loved him, huh?"

"Yes, I really did." Amazingly, the words didn't even hurt anymore. There was nothing left but a vague sadness.

"Do you still?"

She shook her head and whispered, "No. No, I don't. Not the way you mean, anyway. As soon as I met Lita, I gave up any thoughts I still had of Stephen."

"But you still waited for him." Dillon's voice was accusing, as if he still hoped to trip her up in cross-examination.

"I wanted to see him. Stephen was a friend first, for a lot of years, before I felt any more for him. I care about him, and I guess I always will."

"I hope that's all it is."

"Why? Regardless of how I feel, you don't think I'd try to break up his marriage to Lita, do you?"

"You broke up his engagement to your own sister."

Twisting in her seat to confront him, Jessy demanded, "Is that what Stephen told you? That I broke up their engagement?"

"He wasn't making a lot of sense at the time," Dillon answered coolly, unimpressed by her indignation.

"Well, let me tell you something." Angry, almost shouting, her hands firmly planted on her hips even though she was sitting, Jessy suddenly realized that the car had stopped. No speeding traffic hemmed them in. The coast was clear. "No, on second thought, I'm not going to tell you anything." She wrenched her seat belt open. "I don't owe you any explanations."

With that she opened the car door and got out with more speed than grace, slamming the door shut behind her as she stalked away. Blindly twisting her way through rows of parked cars, she slowed once she had put some distance behind her and checked her surroundings. She was in a parking lot, and beyond that was a busy city street.

Turning to see what was behind the parking lot, she saw a one-story building with a green-and-white awning in front and between her and the building she saw Dillon, bearing down on her like a thunderstorm rolling over the plains.

Jessy's first instinct was to run, but after a half step she caught herself and stopped. She could never get away. Dillon was a lot taller and faster, and from all appearances a whole lot madder.

## Chapter Three

"Where are we?" Jessy demanded when Dillon practically skidded to a halt in front of her.

"At the Golden Cow. Now would you like to get back in the car and continue this discussion rationally, or do you want to stand out here and make even more of a scene than we have already?"

"I want to stand out here," she said coolly. "I simply love creating scenes. Or did Stephen leave that part out?"

"Jessy, please." He glanced at the traffic passing by on the street, obviously uncomfortable.

"Oh, Dillon, relax. It's not like an argument between the two of us is going to make the evening news."

"You might be surprised."

"I doubt it," she answered, having absolutely no intention of getting back into the car with him. "I'm not exactly Christie Brinkley, and you're, what, a paramedic?"

"A paramedic?" Distracted enough to stop checking over his shoulder at every new sound, Dillon looked as if he might laugh. "You really haven't the foggiest notion who I am, do you?"

"Well, I guess not. Why? Are you supposed to be somebody important?"

"Some people might think so." He seemed about to say more. Then he threw up his arms and rolled his eyes in self-disgust. "Oh, good grief. Now you've got me trying to impress you." Without another word he turned and walked back toward his car.

"No, wait," Jessy called out and started after him. "Who are you?"

"It doesn't matter," Dillon answered over his shoulder and kept on walking.

"Well, maybe it doesn't, but you've got me curious." She trailed after him, trying to match him stride for stride and losing a little ground with each step. "Who are you? The fire chief? Police chief? Who?"

"I'm a lawyer."

"Wow." Jessy stopped walking. "I'm impressed *now*."

"And I'm in the Texas legislature," Dillon said without slowing or turning. "I'm a state senator."

"You're a—" Jessy took a step toward him and stopped again "—state senator," she whispered while the wheels turned in her mind, the cogs slipped into place and realization dawned like a cold chill. "You're Dillon *Ruiz*."

At the car Dillon stopped, turned and bowed. "At your service, ma'am." When he straightened again, his piercing gaze searched hers. "I should have known you wouldn't approve. Not everything you hear is true, you know."

"Oh, really? What a novel concept."

Dillon smiled without much warmth. "Touché. Could we discuss this further over lunch?"

Jessy walked toward him slowly. "My instincts say run, but my stomach says stay." She stopped with better than a yard separating them. "Anyway, running's never been my style."

"I hear this place has great fish."

"Oh, you brought me where I can order model stuff. How sweet."

He groaned and rolled his eyes again. "One slip of the tongue and you're going to beat me to death with it forever, aren't you?"

"I don't think so. I don't imagine we're going to know each other that long." With that she flashed a carefree smile and walked past him toward the restaurant.

Dillon caught up with her halfway across the parking lot. His hand rested lightly on the small of her back the remainder of the way inside and across the open, homey interior to their table.

The waitress who brought the menu called Dillon by his first name, giggling at everything he said. Jessy pointedly ignored them both while she studied the menu and struggled with a brief but powerful urge to sink her teeth into a greasy cheeseburger and fries. Finally she closed the menu, pushed it away and ordered a plain salad, no dressing, and a bran muffin with herb tea. Dillon made a gagging sound and ordered a greasy cheeseburger and fries. The waitress left still giggling.

"You seem to have made a conquest." She almost hated to keep sniping at him, but it seemed to be the only way to keep up her guard around him. One teasing smile from those sensual lips, one soulful gaze from his black velvet eyes, and she was as warm and malleable as well-worked modeling clay.

"I come here a lot when I'm in town," he said, not really answering her remark.

Relaxing despite her efforts to remain on edge, Jessy gave in once more to the curiosity Dillon aroused in her. "Is San Miguel your home when the legislature isn't in session?"

"I have a home here," Dillon said with a nod. He leaned well back in his chair. His fingers idly twisted a spoon atop the cloth napkin opened on the table. "I share it with my mother, Lita and Stephen and their two sons."

"Sounds a little crowded."

"I guess you'll get to see firsthand tonight."

"Oh, I'd almost forgotten that," Jessy said with a frown. Suddenly the prospect of a family dinner with Lita and Stephen seemed more daunting than ever. "I didn't realize—"

"That you were going to meet the *whole* family?"

"Yes."

"They don't bite," Dillon said with the warm smile that Jessy had so much trouble resisting. "And my mother's a fabulous cook. But you'll insult her if you don't eat more than you're having here."

"I'm not really so sure this is a good idea. An old friend of Stephen's coming home to meet his wife's mother. Something about that just doesn't sound right."

The waitress plunked down a dry salad in front of Jessy and a tall bottle of ketchup in front of Dillon, then whirled and was gone again.

"There *is* something just a little kinky about it, isn't there?" Dillon agreed helpfully.

"Don't start on me again," Jessy warned.

His smile broadened, but he said nothing as the waitress returned with a tray and began to unload the bulk of their meal. When she had gone, Dillon leaned forward and stared into Jessy's eyes across the table. "Do you have any idea how beautiful you are when your eyes are snapping like that?" he asked softly. "They turn almost completely cinnamon, with tiny gold flecks scattered all through them. What color do you call that?"

"Hazel."

"Hazel," he repeated and leaned back again. "In your pictures, they always look green."

"It's the lighting."

"I like them better in person. I like watching them change."

Jessy squeezed a lemon wedge over her salad and speared a healthy bite of greenery. "If you keep it up, Mr. Ruiz, you're going to make me blush."

"Surely you're used to compliments by now."

"I stopped listening to them a long time ago. I was starting to feel too much like a prize heifer."

He laughed and lifted his burger in both hands. "No, you really aren't what I expected at all."

Jessy broke her muffin in half and took a sip of tea. "You keep saying that. I'd ask what you meant, but I'm not really sure I want to hear."

The muscles in his jaws flexed steadily while Dillon stared at her and worked his way through the first half of his burger. Then he set it down and wiped his mouth. "I think I always expected you to be a slick femme fatale. You know, someone as cool and glossy as a magazine page. Someone who could take a decent guy like Stephen and turn him inside out against his will."

"I think you have me confused with Mata Hari."

"Not anymore. I haven't quite figured out who you are, but I'm beginning to see that I was wrong."

"You seem to have devoted a good deal of thought to me, or am I flattering myself?"

"No." He shook his head and lifted his burger again. "No, you were a frequent topic of conversation for a while."

"Lucky me. It would have been nice if somebody had tossed a little of that conversation my way. He never even said goodbye."

Looking back over the years she had spent hoping that Stephen would return and make her dreams come true, all she felt now was foolish. She had wasted her twenties holding on to a fantasy.

"I told him to call you, at least to say aloud all the things he had bottled up, but—" Dillon sighed, finding it hard to choose the right words. "He couldn't deal with his feelings for you. He didn't know if he really loved you, or if it was just lust, and I don't think he wanted to find out."

"Did he think he was the only person feeling guilty? Rebecca was my sister, after all." For years Jessy had barely been able to look Rebecca in the eye for fear she would guess the truth.

Dillon shook his head slowly. "Guilt, shame, fear. He was riddled with it all, and he still couldn't get you out of his mind. No matter how wrong it was, he wanted you, anyway, and that was what he couldn't forgive himself for."

To know that Stephen had suffered as much as she had only made Jessy feel worse, and all for one kiss that should never have happened. "At least he's happy now," she said quietly. "He's with the person who was right for him, and so is Rebecca."

"And you?"

"Me?" Slowly she lifted her gaze from the salad in front of her to Dillon. "I don't know what I am."

"He wasn't the man for you, you know." His dark eyes studied her as he spoke. "Stephen was afraid of the passion you made him feel. You would never have been satisfied with that. In time you would have either left him or stayed with him and been miserable."

"You seem very sure of that."

"I am, but I'm not sure you believe me yet."

"It really doesn't matter anymore, does it? I do think I should just go on back to Austin, though. I don't think this dinner tonight is such a good idea."

"No." He reached across the table and laid his hand over hers. "I want you to go. I want you to be sure, beyond any doubt, that it's really over."

"Why?" He'd barely touched her, and yet she felt consumed by him.

"Maybe because I want you for myself."

"Oh, Dillon." Her voice was barely more than a whisper filled with regret and frustration. She could feel his hand tightening on hers, and she pulled away, as exasperated with herself and her own weakness as she was with him and his manipulation. "Sometimes you make me feel like a bone being fought over by two dogs. I don't know what game you're playing, but I don't want to be the target."

She laid her napkin on the table and pushed her chair back. "I'd like to go now."

"On one condition," he answered without moving. "Promise me you'll still be here tonight."

Jessy closed her eyes and groaned inside. "All right," she said finally, "but only because I promised Lita."

Dillon tossed down his napkin and put a stack of bills on top of it. Then he stood and took Jessy by the arm. "Fair enough. And I'm still picking you up."

If he hadn't made her promise not to leave, she might have had time to pack and make a speedy escape before a deceptively soft sundown set the stage for an evening she dreaded. The prospect of catching up on old times with Stephen and getting to know Lita better no longer seemed so cozy under the matriarchal eye of Mama Ruiz and the disconcerting mood swings of Dillon.

But after a much-needed nap, Jessy barely had time to shower and change before he reappeared, as promised, to whisk her off to the family dinner she wished she had never agreed to attend. The neighborhood they drove to was nothing like the one where they had met. The houses were bigger, and the streets quieter. Lush trees grew along the block and across the broad lawns. The atmosphere smelled of money.and comfort.

When Dillon turned his humble car into a private driveway that curved under overhanging trees and past a manicured lawn to end in a circular driveway in front of a Spanish-style house that many would call a mansion, Jessy couldn't contain herself a second longer. "*This* is your house?"

"Yes." His tone straddled the fence between defensive and challenging.

"You dress off the rack, drive this car and you live in *this* house?"

"There was a time in my law career when I actually made money."

"You must have. And lots of it."

Without answering, Dillon got out and came around to open her car door. As Jessy put her hand in his and alighted, she shook her head in wonder. "But somehow this just doesn't seem like the kind of house you would want."

Instead of stepping aside to lead her into the house, Dillon pulled her closer and shoved the car door closed with a practiced flick of his hand. His eyes caught hers in the half-light and held for a long, riveting moment.

"You see a lot with those beautiful eyes of yours, Jessy."

"You mean you *don't* like this house?"

He lifted her hand and grazed the back of her wrist with his lips, then he released her and stepped away. "Maybe later tonight I'll tell you the long story of my sad youth."

"What's that got to do with this house?"

"The house is for my mother." His hand rested lightly on her waist as he guided her across the courtyard toward the entry. "And whatever opinion you may form of her tonight, she deserved this and more. Everything that Lita and I have, everything that we are, we owe to our mother and the sacrifices she has made."

"Whatever opinion I may form of her?" Jessy repeated. "You're not making me feel any better about this evening with warnings like that."

He paused again and smiled. "My mother is a woman with a strong will. In some ways, you remind me a lot of her. I hope the two of you like each other."

"I only hope she doesn't know as much about my history with Stephen as you and Lita seem to."

"I don't think she knows anything. And, by the way, you have nothing to fear from me. Stephen and I had a long talk this evening, and I'm not worried about the two of you anymore."

"You *what?*" She wheeled on him just as the front door opened and caught them in a broad beam of light.

"Dillon? Is that you?" a female voice called out in an accent closer to a cultured Texas drawl than the strong

Spanish lilt Jessy had expected. "What took you so long? The boys are getting hungry."

"I want to talk to you later," Jessy said for Dillon's ears alone.

"I have every intention of it." He smiled. "I even look forward to it, but for now, hungry children are waiting."

"Don't let her kid you." Lita appeared in the doorway like a benevolent ray of sunshine. "Stephen and I just got home. We wouldn't have eaten a minute sooner if you'd gotten here an hour ago."

Lita came forward to take Jessy's hands and guide her into the entry hall, where Jessy's image of a plump, cherry-cheeked Spanish mother with salt-and-pepper hair pulled tightly back in a bun was dashed upon the callous rocks of reality.

"My mother, Florence Ruiz," Lita said simply. "Mother, this is Jessica Carder. Jessy and Stephen grew up together."

"How do you do, ma'am?" Jessy extended her hand to the tall, slender woman with the pale cheeks and crystal blue eyes whose soft blond curls framed her still-lovely face. She looked like a blond Lita, and Jessy knew instantly that Dillon must look like his father, an ebony-eyed Aztec from the heart of Mexico who had forever changed the life of a blue-eyed Texas beauty.

"Jessica," Florence Ruiz said softly. The barest hint of a smile warmed her face as she briefly touched Jessy's hand. "And how long have you known my daughter?"

"I just met her today."

"And my son?"

"I just met him today."

"Hmm." Florence's smile widened without parting her lips and her bluebonnet eyes turned glacial. "And yet the two of you already seem so—" She paused, dragging out the moment. "Inseparable."

"Jessy, I'd like you to meet my sons," Lita said, shoving two squirming bundles of energy into the suddenly tense circle of adults. "Steve and Nicholas. Say hello to the nice lady, boys."

"Hi!" came a chorus in unison.

"Well, hello there." Jessy held out her hand to the elder and then to the smaller of the two. "How are you two this evening? I heard a rumor that you're getting pretty hungry."

"We sure are."

With that, everyone but Florence heaved a huge sigh of relief and turned toward the dining room, where Jessy found herself facing a stunning array of food. For someone who was used to a salad or a bagel with a cup of herb tea as a meal, just the sight of the table in front of her was overwhelming. And the thought of an evening-long inquisition at the hands of Florence Ruiz was more than overwhelming.

But Jessy's worst fears never came to pass. Between Lita and Dillon the dinner conversation was kept firmly in hand, focusing first on the boys' school day, which was discussed with enthusiasm. Then for Florence's benefit Stephen recounted with high praise Dillon's assistance in the childbirth earlier in the day. As the meal progressed, Jessy's image of Florence as a forbidding matriarch mellowed considerably.

After dinner Lita took the boys up to bed while Dillon lingered to help his mother clear the table. Left pointedly alone, Stephen led Jessy to the terrace where they could reminisce in privacy.

After an awkward pause that was followed by a flurry of how-have-you-beens, Stephen said, "I was a little surprised to see you this morning."

"I'll bet." Unable to decide which she felt more, embarrassment or amusement, Jessy released a short, uncomfortable laugh. "When Linda told me where I could find you, she didn't bother to tell me you were married."

"Then you didn't know?"

"No. I don't think I'd have shown up on your doorstep if I had."

"You handled it well."

"*Lita* handled it well. I just followed her lead." Jessy began to feel like an animal caught in a trap with no way out. She had come to San Miguel to declare her continuing love to a man who had kissed her once and then vanished.

"I love her very much."

"I know that." Jessy expected a stab of pain, but it didn't come. Instead she felt silly to have wasted ten years of her life on a teenage fixation.

"I was wrong to have left the way I did, without saying goodbye, never calling to explain. That wasn't fair to you, but at the time it was the only way I could deal with the way I was feeling."

"Oh, I think you probably made the right choice. I can be pretty headstrong, you know. I'm sure I would have fought you every inch of the way."

"It wouldn't have been much of a fight. I think I would have caved in instantly."

"Wouldn't we have been a pair?"

"Quite a pair."

"This is so silly. I feel like crying."

"Oh, Jess," he whispered as he wrapped a comforting arm around her shoulders and pulled her closer to him. "You always reminded me of a wild bird, soaring free and happy, unfettered by the cares that seemed to keep me so close to earth. Surely you must have fallen in and out of love a dozen times since I left."

"Oh, sure. At least a dozen." She lifted her head and smiled up at him while tears brimmed in her eyes. Yesterday she would have given anything for this moment, and today she felt nothing but the gentle tug of old friendship, and regret for the years that had been lost to her.

Stephen hooked his finger under her chin and lifted her head still higher as he frowned into her eyes. "You have, haven't you?"

Too ashamed to speak, Jessy silently shook her head.

"Jessy, why?" Stephen whispered.

"Excuse me for interrupting this cozy little scene," Dillon said quietly from the shadows behind them, "but Mother and Lita are finishing up in the kitchen."

Stephen barely moved, continuing to block the light from Jessy with his body. "We'll be along in a minute."

Instead of retreating, Dillon moved closer. "Look, Stephen, I know that what I'm seeing isn't what it looks like. But you've got a wife, two children and a mother-in-law inside this house, any one of whom could come through that door at any minute. And none of them would understand that this scene isn't what it looks like."

Stephen's arm slid away from Jessy, and he turned. "I thought we had hashed all this out earlier today."

"We did. And I never believed for a minute that you could spend time alone with Jessy without some of your old feelings for her returning. But I don't give a damn about that right now. I just don't want Lita to see anything you're going to have to spend the rest of your life making up for."

"But—"

"It's okay, Stephen." Jessy touched his arm to halt his protest. "I'm fine. You go on in now. I'll be along in a minute."

"Excuse me," Lita's cheerful voice sang out as she appeared in the doorway. "Am I interrupting anything?"

"Stephen was just going back in," Dillon said.

"So soon?" Lita swept past her brother and kissed Stephen lightly on the cheek. "The boys asked if you would come up to kiss them good-night before they fell asleep."

"Okay, sweetheart." Stephen returned her peck on the cheek and glanced toward Jessy one last time. "See you back inside?"

"Sure." Jessy waved him on. "Run along."

With Stephen dispatched, Lita turned to Dillon. "Why don't you go keep Mom occupied while Jessy and I spend a few minutes alone?"

As sweet as Lita's tone was, she was issuing an order and Dillon and Jessy both recognized the fact. He looked from his sister to Jessy, clearly ready to stand his ground with the slightest encouragement. Touched by his automatic defense of her, Jessy shook her head and watched him reluctantly walk away. She was tired of being made to feel like the other woman. She wanted Lita to know without any doubt that there was no competition between them where Stephen was concerned.

"I think he was hoping for some time alone with you himself," Lita said when Dillon was safely out of earshot. She flipped a switch on the wall and the garden at the foot of the stairs was flooded with light. "The roses are still in bloom. Would you like a tour?"

Not fooled for a minute by Lita's innocent words, Jessy found herself smiling in response. She knew she would be burning with a dozen unanswered questions if she were in Lita's shoes. Jessy moved to Lita's side, and they descended the staircase together.

"Who does the gardening?" Jessy asked, content to let Lita set the pace of the conversation.

"Mother. I don't know what we'd do without her. She keeps the house and grounds immaculate, cooks the meals and watches the boys when Stephen and I aren't here, which is too much of the time lately. But, at least, knowing that she's with them, I don't feel so guilty."

"It's a beautiful home."

"We have Dillon to thank for that. Did he tell you that he owns it and the rest of us just live here on his charity?"

"I don't believe that's quite what he said, *or* how he feels."

"I know, but it's the truth. He bought this house for Mother, and when Stephen and I started the clinic the next year, Dillon insisted that we move in here so that we wouldn't have to worry about keeping a roof over our heads."

"You all seem happy here together."

"Oh, we are. But Dillon's spending less and less of his time here. When he marries, I don't think he'll bring his wife here to live."

"I don't think your mother's going to be very happy about that." During dinner Florence had made no secret of her desire for Dillon to settle down with the right girl and produce another brood of grandchildren for her to watch over. The gleam in the older woman's eye had told Jessy clearly that she was not Florence's idea of the right girl.

"No. No, she won't be, at all. But Dillon has always been his own man. Even Mother realizes that no one is ever going to change that. But that's not what I brought you down here to talk about." Lita settled onto a stone bench at the edge of the path and patted the seat next to her.

The moment had come. Jessy sat next to Lita and turned to look into eyes almost as dark as Dillon's. "Was there something you wanted to talk to me about?"

"Oh, I just wanted to see how you were doing and how your day went. I hope Dillon was his charming self and not his abrasive self. He has a real talent for both."

Jessy had the feeling that Lita would eventually get to the real reason for their talk and saw no need to rush her. "He showed me a little of both. I think he's worried about you."

"I think he's more worried about himself. You know, Dillon was the one who first told me about you."

"Really?" Jessy wasn't sure she wanted to hear what had been said. "When?"

"The first year he roomed with Stephen. He wanted to introduce the two of us, but Stephen refused. Dillon told me about you so that I would understand why Stephen was avoiding women. Eventually I did meet him, and later, when I was an intern and he was a resident at the same hospital, we started dating."

"Well, you know, Lita, anything Dillon said was strictly his own point of view."

"He said you were the most beautiful woman he'd ever seen, but he wouldn't show me any pictures of you. He also said that you and Stephen would never have been happy together because you needed a stronger man, one who could handle you.''

''Handle me?'' Jessy interrupted indignantly.

''His words, not mine, and remember he was a lot younger then. But I could tell he was thinking of himself when he described the kind of man you needed. Of course, I'm sure he'd want to kill me if he knew I was repeating any of this.''

''Why are you?'' She hadn't forgotten the way Lita had insisted Dillon be the one to get Jessy back to her hotel.

''Because if it weren't for Dillon, Stephen and I might never have gotten together. And I'd like to return the favor.''

''What do you mean?''

''Well, when I see you and Dillon together, I just get this feeling that the two of you would be—''

''What?'' Horrified at what Lita was intimating, Jessy rose to her feet, sputtering. ''Dillon? And me? We don't even like each other.''

''Maybe you're just fighting it,'' Lita suggested gently.

''Fighting's the right word for it,'' Jessy insisted. ''That's all we seem to do.''

''Fighting what?'' From the nearby shadows of the garden Dillon's smooth baritone floated to them like a ghost through the night.

Casting a pleading glance toward Lita, Jessy turned and watched him step into the pool of light that cast its soft glow around the bench where Lita still sat.

''I know I heard my name. Has my sister been making suggestions?''

''Maybe just one or two,'' Lita said in a very small voice.

He shook his head and advanced toward her in long, steady strides. ''Between you and Mother—'' he pulled Lita to her feet ''—I end up feeling like a wishbone most of the time.'' Dillon guided her ahead of him and gave her a gentle pat on the backside. "Now scoot, little sister. I want to talk to Jessy alone for a minute."

"I really should be going back in. Your mother's going to think I'm terribly rude," Jessy protested as she watched Lita disappear without a backward glance.

"I've already made your excuses to Mother. I explained that you hadn't planned to stay after dinner. Your things are already in the car, and she's not expecting us back inside."

"But Stephen—"

"Stephen and I made plans for the four of us to have dinner in town tomorrow night."

"The four of us?"

"The four of us."

Jessy cast about in her blank mind for something to say. She and Dillon had become a couple. Stephen and Lita. Dillon and Jessy. *The four of us*. She tried to dislike the thought.

"If you're ready to go, there's someplace I'd like to stop on the way back to your hotel, if you don't mind." Dillon tucked her hand in the crook of his elbow and turned her toward another branch of the garden path.

She stared into his midnight eyes and was swept away by what she saw there. "No," she whispered, "I don't mind. Not at all."

## Chapter Four

The lone guitar's sad, sweet music rode just above the low hum of Spanish inside the dimly lit cantina. Jessy sat across from Dillon at a table just big enough for two.

"I hope you like it here." His fingers slid up the length of the bottle of Mexican beer in front of him. "It's one of my favorite places."

When his hand slid down again, the backs of his fingers brushed Jessy's in passing. The first time it had happened, she'd jumped. This time she merely lifted her margarita glass, licked a section of the salt crystals from the rim and took a healthy swallow. Her fingers barely missed his when she set her drink down again.

Bathed in a rosy mist of light and lulled by the rhythms of the music, she found it more difficult with each passing moment to ignore her body's natural sway toward Dillon. If she leaned just a little farther to the right, and tilted her head the slightest bit— With a jerk she collected her wandering thoughts and sternly set her mind back on track.

"I feel like I'm in another country here." Jessy stared at her drink, unwilling to let her gaze meet his for fear she would be lost again.

"Is that good?"

"I like it." Moved by an instinct that was stronger than reason, she lifted her head and looked into his eyes, drawn to him just as she had been in the garden, as irresistibly as if she were the ocean and he the moon.

"I'm glad." He smiled gently. "I'm afraid the rest of this night hasn't been much fun for you."

"I don't regret a minute of it. I finally got a chance to talk to Stephen, and now I can close that chapter of my life. And I'll always be happy that I met Lita."

"Just Lita? There's no one else you'd include in that?"

"Oh, Dillon." Thrown off guard, Jessy tried to look away, to hide the truth that she knew shouted from her eyes, but Dillon caught her chin with his hand and turned her face back to him.

"Jessy, I don't know what you want from me," he said softly. "Tell me, please. Do you want honesty? Or do you want games? Do you want me to pretend that there's nothing happening between us? That I don't want you?"

"I barely know you."

"Jessy." He took her hand between his and looked into her eyes, then stopped and refocused on her hand. "Your fingers are like ice. Are you cold?"

Her teeth clenched to keep them from chattering, Jessy nodded in short, quick jerks. Nerves had stolen every bit of warmth from her body. She felt like a teenager caught between the solid, unyielding walls of passion and conscience. She wanted Dillon—of course she did. What woman with red blood running through her veins wouldn't? But not now, not tonight, and not this way.

Dillon rubbed her hands between his. Then he ran his hands up her arms, chafing and stroking her skin as he went, but Jessy's shivers only worsened.

"You're not helping," she said, giving in to chills that ran over her shoulders and down her back.

"My jacket . . ." He moved his chair back from the table and prepared to take off his jacket.

"No. Movement." Jessy stood, afraid to have his arms lowering his jacket around her shoulders, afraid of what would come next. "Let's dance." She had danced with lots of men. There was nothing to fear in a dance.

Already on his feet, Dillon wrapped his arm around her shoulders and pulled her against his side. "That sounds like a plan to me." He led her onto the dance floor and turned to face her. Opening his sport coat, he guided her arms inside and around his waist, tucking her body tightly against his chest while he spread the sides of his jacket around her and held it in place with his arms across her back.

With Dillon wrapped like a cocoon around her, the music, as if on cue, became another slow, sweet dirge. Jessy felt the heat of his body pressed against her, tantalizing her with memories of rippling muscles and bronzed skin pulled taut over a washboard stomach and the all-too-male scent of him filling the close confines of the car.

Moving against her to the sensuous rhythms of the guitar, Dillon whispered, "Jessy?"

She lifted her head from the cushion of his chest and answered, "Yes?"

"Tell me you're not in love with him."

She knew who Dillon was talking about, and for once she didn't feel like arguing. "I'm not in love with him."

"Look at me."

Jessy tilted her head, lifting her face to his until their lips were inches apart and she was lost in the fierce blaze of desire burning in his eyes.

"I've wanted you for so many years. Since the first night Stephen told me about the child-woman called Jessy who had set him on fire with the kind of lust no gentleman should feel. I knew then that what Stephen was so afraid of, I would give anything to have."

"Dillon."

"Shh." He laid his finger across her lips to still her words. "I'm not asking you for anything. Not tonight, and maybe not ever. You deserve to be more than a fantasy, and I don't know that I can give you that."

"Why are you telling me this?"

"I don't know. When I saw you this morning, I swore I'd have you in my bed tonight, whatever it took. Now I can't do that."

His words called to mind all the stories she had heard about Dillon Ruiz, and Jessy stiffened in his arms, resentful of the power he had to arouse her. "Am I supposed to be flattered by that? I've heard about you, you know."

"I thought maybe you had. You seemed more cautious after you realized who I was. Is what you've heard *that* bad?"

"No woman wants to be just another notch on a bed-post."

"I'm no angel, Jessy. And when I was younger I imagine that a lot of what you heard about me was true. But I've never purposely hurt or misled any woman. And I don't intend to start with you."

"Thanks a lot." She slipped her arms from around his waist and stepped back. "Were you planning to give *me* a say in this? Or were you going to make all the decisions for both of us?"

"I put that badly. I'm sorry."

"I'd just like to go back to my hotel now, if you don't mind."

Cherry-wood flames lit the mahogany eyes that glared down at her. Lines of battle were drawn in the stern warrior's visage, and Jessy had a sudden mental flash of Dillon, dressed in a breechcloth, a lance driven into the dirt beside his moccasined feet. He would be a wild, untamed lover, one who could send reason fleeing and set oceans crashing and make a woman forget why she had ever resisted him in the first place.

Cotton mouthed, with her heart pounding in her ears, Jessy pulled her thoughts back from the erotic swirl of images that fogged her mind. Running her tongue over her dry lips, she straightened her back. "Did Aztecs wear breech-cloths?"

"What?"

"They didn't, did they?"

"I don't know." The storm clouds of frustrated passion were gone from his face, replaced by puzzlement. "I don't think so, but I really don't know."

"They might have, though."

"Why?"

"You're part Indian, aren't you?"

Dillon laughed suddenly as he unraveled the path of her thoughts. "My father never said, but it's possible. A lot of Mexicans have Indian blood intermingled. Aztecs, Mayan, Yaquí, even some of the tribes from this side of the border roamed down into Mexico."

"You look like your father, don't you?"

"Yes." A sudden gleam of something close to tenderness lit his eyes. "Will you come with me one more place before I take you back to your hotel?"

"Where?"

Still tender, but determined, he shook his head. "Just come with me."

"Why do I find myself trusting you when everything in me says that I shouldn't?"

"I would never hurt you, Jessy. Ever."

She would have sworn the same thing to her sister, Rebecca, at one time, but with the best intentions in the world Jessy had blundered badly. She knew now that some things couldn't be promised. Life was too unpredictable and human beings too fallible. But she went with him, anyway, and when they arrived, she was glad.

Dillon pulled the car to a halt on the gravel shoulder of a two-lane road beyond the outskirts of town. No other cars were around. Only the rustle of the wind and chirping of insects in the brush disturbed the silence. Without a word he took Jessy's hand and led her from the car to the crest of a hill overlooking a gradually sloping valley.

Dry tufts of brush dotted the long, shallow hillside. An occasional stunted tree cast a black silhouette against the moonlit sky, and a ribbon of silver wound a broad, flat path through the belly of the valley.

"The Rio Grande," Dillon said quietly. "My father swam across just a few miles from here. On a black night, in a rainstorm."

"He was—"

"An illegal. A wetback."

"And your mother?"

"Her father is Harlan Siddons."

Jessy knew the name. Harlan Siddons was one of the wealthiest men in Texas. The Siddons family had already made a vast fortune in cattle before oil was found on their land during the Texas oil boom years.

"How in the world—" Jessy stopped.

"Did she meet my father?" Dillon finished. "The first time she saw him he was a day laborer on their ranch. The next time she saw him he was driving a cab in Houston and she was his passenger. Her date got out at their destination, and she stayed."

"Just like that?" She smiled, trying to imagine Florence as a young girl romantic enough to take such a chance.

"Just like that. She and my father were never apart from that night."

"What did her father think?"

"He disowned her."

Jessy was shocked. "For falling in love?"

"For getting pregnant by a peasant with brown skin who was only using her to become a citizen."

The cold anger in Dillon's eyes was painful to see, but the thought of a father who could do such a thing to his daughter was even worse. "Is that really what he said?"

"I cleaned up the language a little."

"How awful for your poor mother. But she married your father, anyway?" Jessy began to see why Dillon admired his mother so.

"Yes."

"And then she had you?"

"No. She lost the baby she was carrying when she married, and another one after that. I was the third, and then she lost another one. Lita was the fifth."

"That must have been very hard." Compared to the story he was telling, her words seemed too pale. She could only imagine what Dillon's childhood must have been like, and marvel that he could have become what he was today.

"Worse than you could know," he agreed quietly.

He pulled her into his arms, with her back to his chest, and his words a soft caress in her ear. "I've never seen two people who loved each other more than my parents did. Our home was rich in the things money couldn't buy, but it was tainted by sadness, too. My father, Trujillo, was a proud man, and he never forgot what my mother gave up for him. He worked himself too hard and died too young trying to give her back what she had lost, and in the end he cost her the one thing she wanted most—the man she loved."

Jessy tipped her head back against his chest and stared up at the glittering sky, bright with the light of a million stars. "But surely her father changed his mind once he saw how wrong he was?"

"No." Dillon's voice hardened. "I never met my grandfather until I was in law school and he finally decided that maybe I wasn't just a worthless half-breed, after all. I wanted to spit in his face. But my mother was so happy, and she had sacrificed so much in her life, that for her I swallowed my pride and accepted my grandfather's benevolence until I couldn't take it anymore."

"And then?"

"I quit the big, prestigious firm he'd gotten me into and opened my own office working mainly as a public defender. I'd studied law to help people like my father—decent, hardworking people who come here in search of something better and instead find a life of poverty and struggle that's no better than what they had before."

"Why did you leave that to go into politics?"

"Because I thought I could do more long-term good for a greater number of people."

Jessy smiled, remembering that this was the Dillon the public knew. "You really are a crusader, aren't you?" Somehow he managed to keep his romantic prowess out of the spotlight, although it was well-known and much talked about by the women of Austin.

"I know what poverty can do." The timbre of his voice lowered, and he brushed his cheek against the soft texture of her hair. "I've seen it crush the spirit out of people before they ever have a chance to live," he said quietly. "My father worked night and day until he dropped dead at forty-five. My mother was ten years younger than him and left with two small children to raise alone. She was pregnant for the sixth time when my father died. She lost that baby, too. When she recovered, she went to work, night and day, to see that Lita and I would have a chance in life. And we made it. I worked my way through college and law school as a paramedic, and it took me years longer because of it. But now that we've made it we can't forget the ones who are still there, the Emilios who deserve a chance, too."

Jessy stared at the river in the distance, the river of promise and hope, a river that led to a treacherous and disappointing reality for so many. She had never felt closer to the complex and compelling man beside her, and she had never felt farther away. Dillon had shown her a piece of his soul, and in doing so he had reminded her how far apart their two worlds were.

"What's wrong, Jessy?" He brushed aside the swirl of brown-and-gold hair that blew across her face and turned her around to look into the soft hazel of her eyes. "Did I say something to upset you?"

"No." She shook her head gently. She didn't want to look at him, but she couldn't help herself. Her eyes sought his again and again and each time the knot in her stomach twisted tighter.

"*Something* is wrong," he insisted.

"This morning when I got out of the taxi in front of the clinic, I felt out of place. Here with you tonight, I feel even more out of place." She stepped back from the loose embrace of his arms.

"I see," Dillon said simply as the lines of his face slowly turned to stone.

"I'm not so sure you do. My life has been easy, Dillon. When I was fourteen I had clear skin and legs like a giraffe. That's all it took for me to become a model. Am I making any sense?"

The taut muscles along Dillon's jaw flexed. "Not really."

"Your life has been a struggle. Even now, when you don't have to struggle anymore, you still do, so that others can have better lives. Your mother gave up everything, and she had a lot, to be with the man she loved. Stephen and Lita could be making a lot of money, but that's not what matters to them."

"So what's your point?"

"I've never given up anything." She couldn't look at him anymore. She started to turn away, but he caught her arm and held her. "I've never struggled for anything," Jessy said, staring at the ground. "Life just came to me and I took it and, until today, I never felt guilty."

"And now you're feeling guilty?"

"Yes."

"I didn't bring you here for that, Jessy." Once again his voice was tender as he gathered her into his embrace and pulled her closer to him. "Everyone has pain in their lives. Rich or poor, the rain falls on us all. Why, I'll bet when you were a little girl in pigtails—" he caught a lock of her hair and twirled it around his finger "—you thought you had it rough plenty of times."

Jessy smiled and unconsciously leaned her head against his hand. "I guess I can remember feeling unfortunate once or twice."

"If you'd feel better about things, I may have an idea for a little something you can do while you're here."

"What?"

He shook his head. "You'll have to wait and see."

"Can't you give me a hint?"

"No." Dillon smiled and his hand cupped her cheek. "You'll just have to wait."

"Now I'm going to have trouble sleeping."

His fingertips wove through her hair, guiding her closer. "It'll be dawn before you know it, and I don't think either one of us is going to get much sleep tonight."

"You realize that for a model, this kind of thing is strictly taboo."

"For a politician it's not exactly recommended."

"I thought that was how you got your reputation," she said, as much to remind herself as to needle him.

"Are we back to that again? Maybe you heard those stories around Austin, but you never saw them in print. My reputation is built on my defense of the underprivileged, not my bedroom exploits. I'm no predator, Jessy, regardless of what you may have heard."

"I could believe that so much easier if you hadn't tried to seduce me almost as soon as you met me."

Dillon smiled. "Maybe I was just trying to take your mind off Stephen. Did I succeed?"

"Admirably."

"I want to kiss you so much I hurt. But I'm trying to prove you can trust me. How am I doing?"

"The jury's still out."

"For a femme fatale, you certainly play hard to get."

"I'm no femme fatale, Dillon, regardless of what you may have heard."

"Oh, yes, you are." His lips brushed hers. "You most certainly are." The tip of his tongue slowly stroked the crest of her lower lip. "Ah, Jessy," he breathed out with a sigh. His hands grasped her shoulders and held her while he stepped back. "I think I'd better take you home now. You're far too tempting for this hour of the night."

When the shrill intrusion of the phone woke Jessy from a deep and dreamless sleep, she opened one eye and snaked her way from under the covers toward the bedside table. A bright shaft of sunlight sliced through a gap in the heavy curtains and pierced the center of the room.

Rolling onto her back with the receiver in her hand and the telephone silenced, Jessy smiled with the sure knowledge that Dillon would be on the other end of the line, and though he was miles away he still simmered like a fever in her blood.

"Good morning," she crooned. With a warm rush, memories of the evening before came back to her.

"For another ten minutes," a cool, feminine voice replied.

Jessy struggled onto her elbow and frowned at the lemon yellow wedge of sunlight bisecting her room. "What?"

"I hope I didn't wake you. I thought maybe we could have lunch together."

"Uh." Jessy dragged her fingers through her thick mane of tangled hair. "What room were you calling?"

"This is Jessica Carder, isn't it?"

"Yes." Awake, hoarse and grumpy, Jessy swung her legs over the side of the bed and sat up, cradling her head in her hands. The clock next to the phone said it was five minutes till twelve. She had gotten more sleep than she felt like. "Who is this?"

"This is Florence Siddons Ruiz. I'm calling from the lobby."

"The lobby?" Jessy stood and turned toward the mirror over the dresser. The sight that greeted her wasn't reassuring. "Of *my* hotel?"

"If you don't feel like eating," Florence coaxed, "just let me buy you a cup of coffee. I feel very badly about last night, and I'd really like to get to know you better. Please?" she finished sweetly.

"Well." Jessy checked her reflection once again and waved her arm hopelessly. "I'm really not dressed."

"Oh, come now, dear. You don't have to worry about dressing up for me. I'm no one you need to impress, and besides, I'm sure you look lovely just as you are. I'll see you in the restaurant, then. In about ten minutes?"

Before Jessy could answer, the phone went dead. "Yeah, sure, great," she said to the empty air and replaced the receiver in its cradle. With no time to debate, she headed into the bathroom to wash up, then slipped into a pair of fashionably tattered and faded jeans and pulled on a bulky, oatmeal-colored sweater with push-up sleeves and a big, boat neckline that had a tendency to slide off one shoulder or the other with regularity.

The outfit was comfortable and casual, and the minute Jessy walked into the restaurant she knew she had made a mistake. With her clean-scrubbed face devoid of makeup and her hair hardly tamed by the quick swipe of a brush, she was no match for the formidable and sophisticated woman who rose to greet her.

This Florence Ruiz was nothing like the attractive but cozy mother hen of the night before. A tailored suit had replaced the simple dress. The blond curls were swept back into a sleek chignon. Money, breeding and a will of iron glittered without apology in the cool blue eyes.

"You look very different today," Florence said as Jessy took the seat across the table. "Younger and more innocent. I'm glad you could join me."

"I'm glad you asked me." For something to do, Jessy unfolded her napkin and spread it across her lap. "You're looking very nice today."

"Thank you." Florence smiled, but her eyes remained like ice chips. Wasting no more time on amenities, she asked, "Has Dillon told you much about himself?"

"A little."

"About his ambitions?"

"Only that he wants to help people."

Florence's laugh was short. "Yes, of course. And I suppose you view yourself as the perfect helpmate in his crusade."

"I don't—"

"Don't bother to deny it, dear. It was obvious every time you looked at him last night. And unfortunately, he seems quite taken with you, as well. However, there are a few things you should know."

Primed to tell Florence that as tempting as her son was, she had every intention of bidding him adieu and not looking back, Jessy said, "Look, you're wasting—"

"Stop!" Florence's hand went up. "I didn't come here to argue with you," she snapped. "My son has a potential that is limitless. Do you think the state senate is as far as he's going to go? Of course not. With my father's backing, Dillon could be governor in a few years. And after that, Capitol Hill, maybe even the presidency. And he wants it." She hissed the words with all the warmth of a coiled snake. "Oh, yes, Dillon is hungry for it. Do you think he's stupid enough to risk all that on someone like you?"

"Someone like me?" Jessy's back went poker stiff and she practically vibrated with anger. She hadn't pursued Dillon. He had pursued her. "Your son—"

"My son is engaged. To a woman beyond reproach," Florence said coldly. "A woman from a family the equal of a Siddons. And you—" She wagged a long, bony finger in the direction of the thunderstruck Jessy. "A woman who spends the night with a man she's just met, a woman who makes a living flaunting her body. You are a scandal waiting to happen, and you could ruin Dillon's career in the blink of an eye. Wouldn't the press have a field day with you?'' she finished bitterly.

Then, in hardly more than seconds, while Jessy struggled to catch her breath and debated whether or not to dump a water glass over Florence's head before leaving, the twisted expression on Florence's face softened and her smile returned, warm and genuine, and Jessy listened dumbstruck for the second time as Florence leaned closer and whispered, ''I know that for Dillon's sake you'll want to keep this little conversation just between the two of us.''

''Listen, lady.'' Jessy clenched the arms of her chair with white-knuckled fury and hurtled through her vocabulary for something besides four-letter words to express her current thoughts. *Nobody* but *nobody* talked to Jessica Carder the way this self-righteous witch just had.

At that moment strong fingers closed over Jessy's shoulder and squeezed a greeting. Tilting back her head in surprise, she found Dillon smiling down at her and in spite of her anger, her heart gave a leap of joy. Before she could turn he leaned over her and closed her open mouth with a long, slow kiss that left no doubt in anyone's mind how glad he was to see her.

''Did you get any sleep?'' he asked when he lifted his lips from hers just far enough to speak.

''A little.''

''That was more than I got.'' He kissed her again, briefly but thoroughly. ''Do you think you could excuse us for just a minute? I wanted to say something to my mother in private.''

''Sure.'' Dillon held her chair as Jessy rose, glad for a moment to collect herself in private.

''The powder room's that way.'' Dillon pointed across the room, then caught her hand as she began to walk away.

When Jessy turned he said, "Don't go too far. This won't take very long."

His eyes, dark and mysterious only yesterday, were lustrous and filled with a thousand unspoken promises. Jessy heard them all as his fingers slowly slipped through hers while she turned and started toward the powder room. With a racing heart and a head so light her ears were ringing, she practically floated across the floor, certain that if she wasn't falling in love she must be coming down with the flu. She was halfway across the room before she remembered that Dillon was engaged to marry another woman.

## Chapter Five

Dillon settled into the chair Jessy had vacated. "Mother."

"What a surprise, dear. I wasn't expecting to see you here."

"I'll just bet you weren't."

"I hope you're not still in a bad mood."

"Why should I be in a bad mood? You started off my day by telling me how to live my life, and after I thought we had settled everything, I find you here."

"I just wanted to get to know Jessy a little better, since you seem so determined to be seen with her."

"Is that what's bothering you, Mother? The fact that someone might see me with her?"

"What you do is news, Dillon. Photographers are everywhere. What if this little episode gets back to Melissa Harkin?"

"Melissa Harkin? Why should I care what she thinks?"

"Oh, Dillon, you're impossible. Melissa is everything you need in a woman. Her family has money and influence. She'd be the perfect—"

"Political wife," Dillon said, tiredly repeating a refrain he knew by heart. "I don't love Melissa, Mother. She's a lovely woman but I'm not going to marry anyone I don't love."

"Take it from someone who knows, Dillon. Love is seriously overrated."

He caught his mother's hand in his and held it tightly. "You don't mean that. You wouldn't give up a minute of the time you had with Dad for all the luxury in the world."

"You're so much like him. Sometimes when I look at you, it just breaks my heart. All I want is for you to be happy, Dillon. That's all I want."

"And I will be. You just have to let *me* decide what makes me happy."

"But she's a tramp, and she can ruin you."

Like a red tide, anger swept through him, and Dillon didn't even know why. He had thought the same thing himself about Jessy only yesterday. "Mother, I love you deeply and I owe you more than I can ever repay, but I won't allow you to talk like that about Jessy."

"Oh, my God." Florence clasped her hand to her heart. "It's worse than I thought. I knew it when you brought her home last night."

"Lita invited her."

"I may be getting older, but I'm not blind *or* stupid. You wouldn't let anyone else be alone with that girl for more than two minutes, and when you got tired of other people getting in your way, you took her with you and left. And you didn't come home until dawn."

"This isn't getting us anywhere. Jessy's going to be back any time now, and when she gets here I think it might be better if you weren't."

"Oh, I'll go," Florence said, rising, "but if I were you, I wouldn't waste my time waiting for Jessy. I saw her leave quite some time ago."

"Leave?" Dillon sent his chair scooting as he clambered to his feet. "Why didn't you say something?"

"It wasn't any of my business," she answered with a regal shrug of her shoulder. "I do hope it wasn't anything I said."

"Mother," he said through clenched teeth, "for somebody who's so damn nice most of the time, you can be such a witch when you want to be. Which way did she go?"

Steely eyed, Florence returned his glare for only a moment before she relented and heaved a sigh of submission. "Toward her room."

"Go home, Mom." Dillon touched her face gently. "And let me handle this my own way, okay?"

"Be careful. This girl could be dangerous for you."

"I suppose it would be asking too much for you to tell me what you said to her."

"Everything I said was designed to drive her away. I really don't know which part worked."

"Oh, man." Dillon closed his eyes and counted to ten. Then he left his mother in the lobby and headed up to Jessy's room, reminding himself the whole way that if his mother wasn't such a strong-willed, determined woman, he wouldn't be where he was now, but the thought carried more threat than reassurance at the moment.


Jessy flinched at the hard rap on her hotel door, then returned to her packing.

"Jessy?" Dillon called through the door. "I know you're in there."

She glared at the door, both thrilled and angered that Dillon had come after her. "Go away."

"Jessy, I'm sorry for anything my mother said. She— There's— Would you please open the door?"

She closed the suitcase and locked it. "I have nothing to say to you."

"I can understand why you're angry with my mother, but why are you taking it out on me?"

"Why don't you just give it some thought?"

"I'd rather talk to you about it. Could you open the door?"

"Look, I'm sorry I ever met you. My plane leaves in two hours, and I would appreciate it if you would just go away."

"No. You can talk to me now or you can talk to me in Austin. But I'm damn well not going to just go away. Now open this door."

He rattled the door menacingly, and Jessy looked at the phone beside the bed for moral support. "Don't force me to call hotel security."

"Jessy, what's this all about? What did I do?"

"What did you do?" Tired of arguing, she charged across the room and flung open the door to shout again in his face. "What did you *do?*"

"Yes." Taking advantage of the small opening given to him, Dillon slipped into the room and shut the door behind him. With his back against the door he asked quietly, "What did I do?"

"Well, for starters you neglected the small matter of your engagement." Jessy whirled and stalked back to the center of the room with Dillon close behind her.

"My engagement?" he repeated, bewildered. "What engagement?"

"Oh, come off it, Dillon. A man as smart as you are should be able to play dumb a little better than this." She stopped abruptly and turned to face him, then took a quick step backward when she found Dillon almost close enough to rub noses with her.

"This is something my mother told you, right?" When Jessy's only answer was a glower, Dillon continued, "I'm supposed to be engaged to somebody?" Finally, with a look of dawning realization, he said, "Oh, no, it's Melissa Harkin, isn't it? Mother told you I was engaged to Melissa Harkin."

"No."

"Good grief, you mean there's someone *else* she's trying to marry me to?"

"Your mother didn't bother with names."

"Oh. Well, she was talking about Melissa." Dillon sat on the foot of the bed and looked up at Jessy with frown. "And I'm not going to marry her, no matter how much my mother and grandfather would like for me to."

"Is she one of *the* Harkins?"

"Who else? Money, power and social acceptance all in one cute little brunette package."

"How convenient. Maybe you *should* marry her."

"Is that what you'd like, Jessy?" With a sweep of his arm Dillon shoved her suitcase aside while he reached up to catch Jessy's wrist with his other hand and pulled her onto the bed beside him. "Hmm?" He slipped his arms around her waist and drew her closer. "Is that what you'd really like?"

She refused to look at him. "It doesn't matter one way or the other to me."

"Doesn't it? Is that why you left the restaurant and came up here to start packing? Because it doesn't matter to you?"

"I just don't like being lied to," she snapped, giving in and looking into his eyes in spite of her efforts to resist.

"I'm sorry, Jessy. I would have stopped her if I'd known what she was planning, but I had no idea she'd do something like this."

"She seems to be under the impression that—" Jessy stumbled to a halt, groping for the right words.

"We're lovers," Dillon said, supplying the words she didn't want to say.

"Yes."

"The qualities that make Mother so special can also make her very hard to live with at times. She wouldn't tell me any of the things she said to you."

"I'd rather not repeat them, either."

"I'm sorry I brought this down on you."

She shrugged. "Parents are just people, too."

"That sounds like the voice of experience speaking." When Jessy smiled, Dillon caught her hand in his. "Come with me. There's something I want you to see."

"But my plane," she protested, knowing that if he persisted she would give in. She had never been easily swayed. She had never been indecisive. And yet, with a smile or a look this man could talk her into almost anything.

"There'll be another flight, Jessy, and this place is very special to me. You'd be the first person I've taken there."

"I don't know." She shouldn't. She should run like hell and not look back, but she knew that she would go with him, anyway. There would always be another plane, but there would never be another moment like this one. And there would never be another Dillon.

"Nobody else even knows it exists," he said, helping her to her feet as he rose.

"Should I change?"

"No. You're perfect just the way you are."

Nearly an hour later, Dillon's car rocked slowly down a dirt road in the middle of nowhere. Jessy braced her hand against the dashboard as they lurched across a cluster of potholes. Only a few minutes earlier they had driven between the posts of a rickety gate where an illegibly faded sign dangled from a rusted chain.

"Are you sure you didn't make a wrong turn back there somewhere?" she asked. In the distance an unpainted shack squatted between two tall trees. With each second that the car drew closer, she wished more fervently that they were lost.

"Nope. We're almost there."

Jessy followed his gaze and found herself looking once again at the shack. "That's where we're going?"

"Looks pretty disreputable, doesn't it?"

"Yes."

"I bought this acreage several years ago when I was hoping to start a youth ranch and rehab center."

She turned her head to gaze all around her at a vista of sagebrush and scrub oak, with a few scattered palmettos. She hated to think of what lurked unseen. "I guess it'd be a good place for something like that. There wouldn't be much for anyone to get into around here."

"I still plan to use some of the land for a center, but for right now I need this place too much for myself."

"*This* place?"

Dillon laughed. "Yes, *this* place, my oasis of sanity, miles from civilization, where the only sounds are my own voice and the gentle rustlings of nature."

At the thought of what creatures might be causing those gentle rustlings, Jessy suppressed a shudder. "How have you managed to keep this place a secret?"

"It's not that unusual for me to disappear for a day or two at a time. My family stopped questioning me long ago, and my friends know better than to ask."

"I can imagine."

"I assure you, my reputation is exaggerated," Dillon answered with a smile. "Although not even my staff will believe me when I say that."

"I'm afraid I have to agree with your staff. The name 'Hit-and-Run' Ruiz must have come from somewhere."

"Oh, you've heard that one, have you? Well, it's your choice," he said, still smiling. "But I intend to convince you that you're wrong."

Knowing that she shouldn't encourage him, Jessy nevertheless found herself smiling along with him. He was an almost irresistible temptation with a reputed track record that should make any sane woman turn tail and run. From her own reaction to him, she knew he was dangerously

seductive, and yet some small voice inside her urged her to
open her heart to this man.

"Well, here we are." Dillon turned off the ignition. "It'll
be a little chilly inside, but once I get the stove going the
place warms up fast."

While he came around the car to open her door, Jessy got
her first good view of the rustic cottage. Traces of blue
paint clung to the bare gray exterior, and through windowpanes that were relatively free of grime she saw the grace-
ful sweep of ruffled curtains. In spite of the obvious signs
of neglect, she could sense a certain faded charm that still
lingered in the cool green shadows beneath the old sentinel
trees.

"I have to warn you," Dillon said as he led her to the
door, "there's no telephone or television, and the only
music I have is from an old phonograph."

"Is there indoor plumbing?"

"There is that. There's even electricity and a backup
generator."

"All the modern conveniences."

When he unlocked the front door and reached in to turn
on the overhead light, she took a fortifying breath and
stepped inside, anticipating the worst. What she found was
compact and simple, but tidy.

"It's not so bad," she said with obvious surprise.

A black potbellied stove dominated the main room. Ar-
ranged in a U around three sides of the stove were two
couches and two chairs. Oxblood leather covered the big
solid chunks of furniture that seemed to shout, "Male, living alone." As a concession to warmth, a collection of
knitted and quilted throws draped the backs of each piece.

"The kitchen's through there." Dillon pointed to a
doorway on the right side of the room. "And there's a
bathroom behind the kitchen."

Jessy looked around for another doorway, but didn't see
one. Across the room from the entry door, full-length curtains were tied back to reveal a shallow alcove where an old

record player stood on a small table. On the left wall of the living room a staircase climbed steeply to a loft.

"What's up there?" she asked, nodding toward the loft whose open railing overlooked the main room.

"Another bathroom. And the bedroom. Want to see it?"

"No, thank you," she said quickly. "Is this all there is?"

"This is the whole shootin' match. You can check out the kitchen if you want, while I build a fire in the stove."

With nothing better to do, Jessy wandered into the kitchen and Dillon exited through the front door. She heard him when he returned—the clang of the stove door opening, the thud of the wood against the hollow metal inside—while she opened the door of the well-stocked refrigerator. The expiration date on the open gallon of milk was more than a week ahead, which told her that Dillon had either made a recent trip out to the cottage with supplies or he really did spend a lot of his time here.

In the bathroom she found a claw-foot tub and vintage fixtures. Again, the room was clean and well stocked, with signs of frequent usage. Coming back into the kitchen, she noticed an African violet in full bloom on the pine harvest table. The pink iridescent blossoms sparkled in the bright natural light that flowed through the bare windows, bringing the Spartan kitchen to life.

"Are you hungry?" Dillon called from the next room. "There's a pretty tasty beef stew in the refrigerator. Or there's a chicken we could bake." He appeared in the doorway. "If you think that would be healthier. There are some fresh vegetables in the crisper. And I've got potatoes in the potato bin."

Jessy stopped beside the table. "You spend a *lot* of your time here, don't you?"

He nodded slowly. "More and more."

"And nobody knows about this place? Not even your family?"

"Especially not my family." Dillon advanced a few steps into the kitchen to lean against the counter, facing Jessy.

"You heard my mother last night. She wants me to marry and produce more grandchildren for her to take care of."

"You could just say no," Jessy suggested.

"That's just it. I *want* a wife and children. But I want the woman who bears my children to be the one who takes care of them. And I'm not going to bring my family into a home dominated by my mother."

"I'm sure your wife will appreciate that."

Dillon's dark eyes caught hers and held with an intensity that made his words for Jessy, and Jessy alone. "I hope so."

In the space of a second the air around her became suffocatingly hot. She ran her hand around the back of her neck and lifted her heavy veil of hair from her shoulders. She had to be imagining his meaning. He couldn't have just intimated that he wanted her to be the mother of his children. And if he had, he couldn't have been serious.

Comforted by her thoughts, she went to the refrigerator and stood in the open door, grateful for the cool air while she gazed at the contents without seeing them. "Stew would be fine."

"Are you sure?"

"Yes."

Dillon joined her, standing just behind her while he peered over her shoulder. "There are some pickled beets there, if you like them." The tip of his finger trailed down the length of her shoulder where her sweater had slipped to reveal bare skin. "I like this sweater. It seems to have a mind of its own."

"Not unlike you." She stepped to the side, away from the hand that was closing over her arm. Then she turned and brushed past him in a hasty exit, leaving Dillon standing alone in front of the open refrigerator.

Jessy stopped when she reached the table. From a safe distance she watched him carry the container of beef stew to the stove. After he put the stew on to heat over a low fire, he turned and asked quietly, "Did I offend you just then? When I touched you?"

"No, you didn't offend me."

"I haven't made any secret of the fact that I'm attracted to you, Jessy."

"No, you haven't." She braced her hands against the table behind her. For a woman who made her living striking artful poses, she felt incredibly awkward at the moment.

"Do you have any idea how beautiful you are right now? How seductive you look just standing there?"

Never one to cower, Jessy tossed her head and sent her hair flying over her shoulder. "Did you bring me here to seduce me?"

"I want to make love to you very much. I told you that. But I won't lay a hand on you until you want it."

"I have to be in Austin by Sunday evening."

"That gives us three days."

"Less than forty-eight hours," Jessy corrected with a shake of her head. "That's not enough time to start a good friendship, much less an affair."

"We have to start somewhere, Jessy."

"I've—" She stopped herself just as she was about to confess that she had never been with a man—any man. Instead, she squared her shoulders and lifted her chin to a defiant height. "No. I won't be a one-night stand for any man. Not even you."

Before she could betray her own resolve, she pushed away from the table and left him standing alone in the kitchen. Instinct took her across the living room to the front door, where escape and safety lay just beyond. While her pounding heart urged her to hurry and her clumsy fingers struggled with the unfamiliar lock, Dillon caught up with her before she could open the door.

"Jessy, no." His voice was a sultry caress in her ear as he pulled her against him, her back to his chest.

"Let me go."

"I'm sorry. I shouldn't have started it." Wrapping his arms around her waist, he promised, "I won't bring the subject up again."

"You don't understand."

"Yes, I do." He brushed his cheek against her hair. His lips grazed her temple with each whispered word. "I didn't bring you here to seduce you, Jessy." He held her still against him until she gradually stopped fighting him. "I wanted to be with you, and I had to keep you from leaving town. But all I wanted was for us to talk, believe it or not."

"Talk?"

"Uh-huh." He nodded gently, his head resting against the side of hers. "But you kick up such a ruckus with my hormones that I always seem to end up doing things I never intended." He loosened his hold on her waist and turned her to face him. "If I promise to treat you like a nun, will you come back into the kitchen and have dinner with me?"

"A nun?" She couldn't help smiling at the thought, and Dillon smiled with her.

"I have a very good imagination."

At that, Jessy laughed. "This I've got to see."

The sun was low in the western sky when they finished the filling meal of beef stew, pickled beets and buttered corn bread. The accompanying conversation was carefully casual and yet told Jessy more about the private Dillon than anything she had seen or heard before. Their discussion ranged from politics to poverty and finally to family expectations, a subject Jessy knew well. Her whole life she and her twin had fought comparisons that cast them both in roles they didn't want to fill.

"My mother meant well," Jessy said a little sadly, continuing their dinner conversation as they cleaned away the remnants of the meal, shuffling dishes from the table to the sink and relegating what little was left to the refrigerator.

"Mothers usually do, but that doesn't stop the damage a careless remark can make."

"She didn't know I was outside the window, or that I could overhear what she was saying."

"Have you ever talked to her about it?" Dillon filled the sink with hot water and billowing suds.

Jessy scraped the plates clean and slipped them into the sink. "Once, a few years ago. She doesn't remember anything about it, but she admits she might have said it because when we were little, Rebecca *was* the good one, and I *was* the rambunctious one. Then she just patted me on the cheek and smiled. She never understood what I was trying to say."

"Surely at the time you were too young to know what a word like rambunctious meant."

"I was four, and no, I didn't know what it meant, but it sounded too big and scary to mean anything good. Do you want to wash or rinse?"

"Lady's choice."

"I'll rinse, then." She moved around him to the other sink. "You know, until that day I'd always thought I was a good little girl. At least, I'd always tried to be. After that, I became a lot more defiant. I pushed the limits more."

"I'll bet you were a terror."

"Well, yes," Jessy admitted with a laugh. "I guess I really was." As if it was yesterday, she remembered the day she finally asked her older brother, Houston, what the word *rambunctious* meant. After a few aborted explanations he pointed to their new puppy, happy, heedless and clumsy as it chased its tail in the backyard. While they watched, the lanky pup careened into a flowerpot, knocking it over and trampling the remains before taking off after a butterfly.

She had liked the new image of herself. "After I learned what rambunctious really meant, I realized it was a pretty good description. In time, I was even grateful that I wasn't the one my parents expected so much of. Poor Rebecca. I got the freedom, and she got the responsibility."

"Is that how she felt about it?"

"At times. But then, you can't fight nature, and Rebecca really was a kind and gentle person. She always gave too much of herself and it left her vulnerable, so I had to watch out for her because she wouldn't watch out for herself. She mothered the world, and I mothered her."

Unable to say any more, she ended with a whisper as she thought of the time she hadn't been there to protect Rebecca.

Guilt twisted like a knife in Jessy's heart, and she turned her head away to hide the tears that gathered without warning. She should have been there. She should have been the one it happened to. No one would have been shocked if she had turned up pregnant without any explanation. It would have been just one more of Jessy's outrageous escapades, only a little worse than usual.

But then, she would never have turned up pregnant. Not from rape, not from anything, because unlike Rebecca, Jessy could never have gotten pregnant.

The guilt melted away again, replaced by grief, and for one endless, frozen moment she stood there with her back to Dillon lost in her own private hell. Pain compounded pain, stabbing deep into her heart where the truth she'd never spoken, and rarely thought, lay hidden. She would give anything—*anything*—for the hope that she could someday bear a child.

Just one small baby she could call her own. Just one eternal gift created with the man she loved. But that one, small thing she wanted most was the one thing she would never have.

## Chapter Six

"Jessy?" Dillon touched her shoulder. "Are you all right?"

"Just great." With years of practice behind her, Jessy blinked away her tears and turned to greet Dillon with a smile that had been honed through cold, wind and rain. Adept at smiling while her tired, aching muscles screamed for relief, she could smile just as well while her heart silently broke.

"Are we through here?" she asked.

Dillon took the dish she held in her hand and set it in the drainer. "We sure are. Why don't you find a comfortable spot on the couch while I put on some music?"

"That sounds good to me."

Hesitant to meet his discerning gaze head-on, she glanced at him cautiously through a veil of lashes. She had already said things to Dillon that she hadn't revealed to another soul except Rebecca, and at times Jessy had found herself dangerously tempted to confess the few secrets she still kept.

Dillon slipped his arm around her waist in a protective and casually possessive gesture. With each step they took from the kitchen to the living room, his thigh brushed hers in a subtle reminder that however innocent he had promised to be, he was still and forever a man, and he wasn't about to let either one of them forget it.

At the end of the couch he took his arm away and walked on. Jessy sank gratefully into the soft, well-worn leather of the sofa while Dillon continued into the shadowed alcove. Resisting the urge to watch him, she busied herself with arranging a knitted afghan over her legs, hearing only muffled bumps and thumps from behind the half-drawn curtain until the scratchy strains of Western swing floated into the room with dusty vigor.

As the nostalgic roadhouse music mingled with the warmth of the potbellied stove, and the sound of Dillon's footsteps signaling his return, Jessy couldn't fight the temptation any longer. She rose up to peer over the back of the couch at his approach. "Who is that?"

"Bob Wills and the Texas Playboys."

He walked around behind the couch and slid into the corner beside her. "When I bought this place, I found that old Victrola phonograph and a crate of albums under a painter's tarp in the alcove."

Before Jessy could move away he slid his hand between the back of the couch and her rib cage, then wrapped his arm around her waist and guided her back against his chest while he continued his story. "It was a real treasure trove. There was everything from Muddy Waters to Perry Como in that old box. That was when I decided to not make too many changes too fast around here. I didn't want to lose the flavor of the place."

Too content to be cautious, Jessy relaxed within the solid wall of his embrace. "And the rest of this?" Her hand twirled to include the furnishings around them.

"Secondhand stores and castoffs. These couches came from the offices of a retired friend. And a lot of these—" he plucked at the afghan that spilled over Jessy and onto him as he snuggled closer "—were gifts from women who wanted to impress me with their domestic skills."

"You don't sound very impressed."

"I hate to seem ungrateful, but afghans just aren't what I'm looking for in a woman. When I choose a mate it won't be because she won a county bake-off with her apple pie."

Jessy held her breath, afraid to encourage the stirring of excitement his words caused. In her experience, men were limited to two types—those who were attracted to Rebecca, the perfect Earth Mother and apple pie baker, and those who wanted Jessy just for the way she looked. Men never seemed to care that she had qualities to offer beyond that, qualities like loyalty, generosity and a heart yearning for love. No one seemed to want those things from her.

"What *are* you looking for, Dillon?" she asked finally after saying a silent prayer that he would be different, and not like all the others she had met and rejected.

"That's not easy to put into words." He rested his cheek against her hair.

"Try."

"You may not like what you hear. What I want is very selfish."

His reluctance only made her more determined. She turned her head slightly and felt the soft brush of his lips against her temple. "How selfish?" she asked with a voice that was suddenly breathless.

"Very selfish. The way that keeping this cottage for myself is selfish."

"That doesn't make any sense. Everyone wants a home. There's nothing selfish about that."

"No." He held her closer as he shook his head slowly. "I bought this to share with others, and instead, I kept it for myself. Just for me. For *my* needs. For *my* enjoyment."

"I think you're blowing this out of proportion. It's only a house. Everyone's allowed to have one."

"And what if I want the same thing from a woman?"

"What do you mean? A secret woman?" For the first time, Jessy felt her stomach tighten. Just as he had predicted, she wasn't sure she liked what she was hearing. "One you can keep all to yourself and go to when you need her, the way you do this place?"

"Yes." His voice was like velvet as his fingers lightly stroked the base of her ribs. "A woman who can turn out the lights and make me forget that the rest of the world exists, at least for a little while."

While her body responded with a will of its own to his enticingly sensual touch, her mind stubbornly resisted. "What you're describing sounds more like a mistress to me," she said with a coldness at odds with the mingled fires of desire and anger that burned inside her. "The perfect woman for a man who's already married to his career."

"No, I want more than that, Jessy." His whispered words brushed her cheek with a soft gust of air. "I want a life like other men have. I want a real, normal life, with a good woman waiting for me when I come home at night and babies to bounce on my knee."

*Babies.* The word twisted in her heart like a knife, and Jessy tasted the all-too-familiar bitterness of sorrow rising in her throat.

"I don't know, Dillon," she said with quiet resignation. Mistress or wife, it no longer mattered. She wouldn't or couldn't be either. "This job sounds tailor-made for an apple pie bake-off winner. You might want to reconsider some of these women you've already rejected." Her fingers plucked idly at the afghan as she struggled to keep her voice level.

"Jessy." Dillon brushed aside the hair that had fallen to hide her face. "You haven't been listening. I don't recall that cooking was a requirement."

"Somebody's going to have to feed all those kids."

"First things first. A lot of other needs are going to have to be satisfied before there *are* any children."

His words should have been a balm to her aching heart, but she couldn't let herself rejoice. There were some things she could never have. She had accepted that fact long ago, and wishing otherwise would only leave her with a broken heart in the end.

"I'm sure you'll find the right woman some day, Dillon."

"Do you think so?"

"Yes."

"But what if the woman I want doesn't want me?"

"I wouldn't worry about that if I were you." She couldn't imagine any woman not wanting him. He wasn't an easy man to resist, no matter how good the reasons were.

"That's nice to hear." His fingers wove their way through her hair, pulling it away from her face. "I love to watch your eyes change from brown to a soft golden hazel. Is it your mood or the lighting that does it?"

She longed to turn away, to shake her hair loose and let it fall between his watching eyes and her vulnerable emotions once again. "Both, I think."

"And these freckles." His fingertip traced a path from her cheek across the bridge of her nose to the other cheek. "With all the pictures I've seen of you over the years, I never realized you had freckles."

"Makeup. They cover them," she stammered while his fingertip continued down her cheek to the corner of her mouth. "With makeup."

"You're not wearing any today, are you?"

"Wearing any what?" While a flash of anxiety cleared the steam cloud fogging her mind, Jessy did a quick mental inventory of all essential garments.

"Makeup." He stroked the curve of her lower lip. "You're not wearing any."

"I don't think so. I was a little rushed this morning." The thought of Florence was almost enough to dampen the trail of fires Dillon set with each fleeting caress. Almost, but not quite.

"I like it." He ran the pad of his thumb over the tips of her eyelashes, long and dark, without any embellishment. "You're a beautiful woman, Jessy."

"I didn't have much to do with it."

He shook his head, rejecting her answer. "No. Even in the dark you'd still be beautiful." With the back of his hand he brushed the smooth skin of her cheek. "You'd still be soft and warm and sweet smelling. You'd still be the kind of woman who can make a man ache just being near her."

"Dillon." Her voice carried a warning that her traitorous heart could never back up. She wanted him so badly she could hardly breathe.

"I won't try anything. I promised, and I don't intend to go back on my word."

He drew away from her, then lifted his arms high overhead and stretched. "Man, I'm beat," he said, relaxing against the arm of the couch with one arm draped lightly across her shoulders. "How about you? Are you tired?" The back of his thumb lightly stroked the side of her neck. "Neither one of us got much sleep last night."

"A little, I guess." She was a lot more aroused than she was sleepy, but she wasn't about to admit it.

"It's a long drive back into town, and we don't need to be there for a while." He took his arm from her shoulder and brushed his hand down the back of her hair. When he reached the end he wound a lock around his finger. "Would you consider doing me a favor?"

Only then did he look away from her hair and raise his eyes to hers with a sincerity that was hard to resist, but it wasn't enough to quiet her suspicions. "What?"

"Well, I'd like to take a nap before we go back. There's a bed in the loft. It's old and it squeaks, but it's pretty comfortable. And I was wondering—"

"Oh, sure," Jessy interrupted, eager in her relief. "You go ahead and lie down. I'll just curl up here on the sofa."

Dillon's grin was wide with genuine amusement as he shook his head slowly. "No, that's not what I was going to ask."

Her suspicions back in an instant, she frowned. "What?"

His rich, deep voice was almost soothing as he asked, "If I promise to do nothing but sleep, would you lie down beside me? Just to keep me company?"

Torn by her need to distance herself from him and her temptation to agree, Jessy pulled away and then snapped back around to face him. "Look, if this is a come-on, it's not very subtle," she said, summoning all the indignation she could find.

"It's not a come-on. I just don't want to sleep alone."

She tried to imagine being curled up next to him in bed while she drifted peacefully off to sleep. The image left her feeling anything but peaceful. "Just sleep?"

"Well, I *do* like to cuddle. It helps me relax," he said with a disarming grin. "But that's all. I won't try to seduce you. That won't upset you, will it?"

"Upset me? If you *don't* try to seduce me?"

He shrugged. "It's just that every time I get near some women they automatically assume I'm going to jump their bones, and then they get all upset when I don't try. You're not like that, are you?"

Though his expression was solemn, a teasing gleam shone in his dark eyes, and Jessy began to relax. Once again she had been cajoled into agreement despite her efforts to resist, but try as she might, she couldn't be angry about it. If anything, Dillon had always been honest with her, sometimes far too honest with her, and she saw no reason to doubt him now.

While her head said run, her heart said stay. This evening he had given her a glimpse into the weary man behind the fiery facade of the crusader, a man who sometimes yearned for a more normal life, if only for a few hours. At least for tonight, for the few hours left to them, she could give him the one small thing he asked for.

"Okay," Jessy agreed finally. "But one wrong move and I'm out of here."

"Yes, ma'am."

With a smile to match the gleam in his eye, he took her hand in his and led her up the stairs to the loft where the double bed that awaited looked far too small to contain them both. Jessy instinctively slowed, and Dillon tightened his grip on her hand, giving it a gentle squeeze.

"Which side do you want?" he asked.

Her startled gaze swung from the bed to him. "What?"

"Which side do you usually sleep on?"

Jessy tried to think, but all she could focus on was that she had never shared a bed with a man before, not even innocently. She always slept alone. "The middle?"

"Aha, a bed hog. But that's okay. I'll take the right side, and you can have the middle. It'll just make it that much easier to cuddle."

A full arm's length from him, Jessy came to a dead halt. "You know, I'm really not feeling very sleepy right now. Why don't I wait downstairs while you—"

"What are you really afraid of, Jessy?" Dillon gently pulled her a step closer. "Is it me? Or is it yourself?"

She stiffened her backbone and jerked her hand from his. "I'm not *afraid* of anything. I'm just not all that comfortable curling up to sleep with a man I barely know."

"You were perfectly comfortable curled up with me on the couch. What's so different up here?" His voice was soothingly soft.

"That was a couch. Not a bed."

Dillon grinned. "You've never made love on a couch? Not even once?"

"It may startle you to learn—" Jessy bit off her words before she blurted out the fact that she had never made love anywhere.

"Startle me to learn what?" His teasing grin widened. Moving closer again, Dillon twirled a lock of her hair around his index finger. "What were you going to say, Jessy? Startle me," he coaxed.

"Nothing." She raked her fingers through her hair and walked to the foot of the bed, putting needed distance between them. "I guess I'm more tired than I thought. Can we just lie down now and get this over with?"

"Sure." Dillon lifted a quilt from a rack and carried it with him to the bed. While Jessy curled into a fetal tuck on the far side of the bed, he spread the quilt over her and lay down beside her, being careful to keep the quilt between them.

After several minutes of silence he said quietly, "Jessy?"

"Yes?" came her hushed reply after another long pause.

"I didn't mean to upset you. I guess it's just the attorney in me. I can't seem to pass up a good debate even when I should." He rolled toward her. His hand rested lightly on the quilt that covered her shoulder. "Or maybe it's because I want to know more about you, and the only time you tell me anything is when I make you angry enough to forget caution."

Jessy wanted to cry out for him to stop, please. It was hard enough for her to resist him when he pounded at her defenses like a battering ram. But when he was sweet, sincere and gentle, she couldn't help wondering what it would be like to open her arms and welcome him in, to discover that one night of heaven she had waited a lifetime for.

"Jessy?" He rose up on his elbow and leaned over her to brush aside the hair that fell across her face.

His scent curled under the edge of the quilt and hung there, tantalizing her with every breath she drew. Like a casket of spice hidden deep in the musky stillness of an autumn wood, the fragrance was strongly male and uniquely Dillon.

"Jessica?" he whispered.

Heeding a will that wouldn't be denied, Jessy turned and found his eyes, dark and luminous as a midnight pool, waiting for her. The bold, sensuous lines of his face were serious, all teasing gone. His parted lips hovered inches above hers, and Jessy felt her pulse surge with a naked desire to know the secrets Dillon could unlock.

"Were you asleep?" he asked.

Afraid to trust her voice, Jessy shook her head.

"You're not still angry, are you?"

Again she shook her head.

"Good." He smiled softly and brushed his fingertips over her cheek. "I sure do like those freckles. Your skin, your hair, your eyes." His hand traced a path across her temple, from the corner of her eye to her hair. "You're all in shades of honey and toast and cinnamon, with a little ripe peach thrown in."

Abruptly he withdrew his hand. "I guess we'd better get some rest. I don't want you getting sick because I wouldn't let you get any sleep."

Without speaking, Jessy rolled back onto her side and jammed her clenched fists between her knees, exerting all her self-control to keep from grabbing his hand and pulling him back to her. She ached from wanting him, from wanting the wonder and ecstasy that she could only imagine but that she knew he could show her.

She'd never meant this to happen. She'd never meant to care, not this way, and not this much. Even while restless whispers of desire rose inside her, taunting her with what could never be, a stab of pain slashed through her, cutting across her lower abdomen from pelvic bone to pelvic bone.

Every other month the cycle of pain returned as a vigilant reminder that only half of her reproductive system worked, and that half none too well. Jessy caught her breath in a soft gasp and curled into the cramp until it passed. Severe but brief, the ache was nothing compared to the one in her heart, the one that taunted her with the certain knowledge that she could never conceive, never feel the joy of a child growing inside her, and never share that gift of life with a man she loved.

Beside her, Dillon stirred and moved closer in his sleep. Needing the comfort of his presence, Jessy edged toward the center of the bed until she felt his knee press the back of her thigh. His hand brushed her waist and came to rest against the small of her back. Content with the moment, she smiled and drifted into a cushiony world of half sleep where it was enough to be near him, enough to have almost loved him.

She could never be the woman Dillon wanted. She could never live in the shadows or bear his children. She could never please his mother or give of herself like his sister. She could never be more than a passing fancy to Dillon, and she could never allow herself to be that for any man, not even a man who could offer her all she'd ever wanted, even if only for a little while.

In a few days she would be gone, and her memories of him would be nothing more than a pleasant dream filled with promises of what might have been if only fate had been a little kinder. With that, Jessy sighed and snuggled closer while Dillon's arm slid over her waist and pulled her into the curve of his body.

When she opened her eyes again, the room was in shadows. The white ceiling above the bed glowed with the reflected light from a living room lamp, and throughout the loft eerie splashes of illumination alternated with pockets of gloom.

Dillon pressed his face to her neck and breathed a softly heated gust of air over her skin. "Mmm, you feel so good to wake up next to." He nuzzled his way past her curtain of hair and pressed his lips to the tender juncture of her shoulder and neck.

Flushed skin, a pounding heart and throbbing loins told Jessy instantly why she had awakened. Dreams of a hand gently caressing her breast suddenly seemed all too real, as did the obvious arousal of the body that was pressed tightly against hers.

She tried desperately to summon her resistance. Giving in to this moment of passion would only make it harder in the end when she'd have no choice but to walk away and never look back. There was no future with Dillon. They were wrong for each other and no amount of wishing could change that. She would never be his mistress, and he would never make her his wife.

"Jessy," Dillon whispered as his mouth found hers in a kiss that lifted her beyond reason and into a realm where only the most basic of human needs survived.

And once there, she needed him as surely as she needed air to breathe. In a way she had never needed another man, she needed him. Driven by instinct, she clung to Dillon without shame while she pressed the length of her body against his and returned his kiss with a fervor that only left her wanting more.

Spurred by the passion of her response, Dillon answered her need with an equally powerful one of his own. Emitting a deeply guttural growl, he stripped away the quilt that separated them and shoved it to the foot of the bed. In an almost unbroken motion he rose over her, sliding his hand under her hips to lift her free of the bed while he tugged up the hem of her sweater with his other hand.

Startled at first by his actions, Jessy tried to protest, but resistance wouldn't come. She wanted him to touch her. She wanted him to see her—all of her—and most of all, she wanted him to need her with the same dizzying desperation that she felt for him.

"Dillon." His name was torn from her lips as he released her and rose higher.

Grabbing the hem of his T-shirt in both hands, he peeled it over his head in one smooth, savage motion and tossed it aside without ever taking his eyes from Jessy. Sweat glistened like a fine dew over the deep bronze of his chest as he spread her blue-jeaned legs apart and knelt in the valley of her thighs, slowly lowering his weight onto her.

Jessy's pent-up breath released in a long, slow moan while spiraling shafts of pleasure-pain radiated outward from where his body pressed against hers.

Holding the bulk of his weight above her, Dillon moved his hips in slow undulations against her, watching a fever of need build in her until her breathing came in quick gasps and her soft groans begged for release. Then he slowed, gradually pulling away until he eased himself back onto his knees and slowly guided her sweater up over her ribs until the filmy lace of her bra revealed the rapid rise and fall of her full breasts.

"Jessy, sit up," he ordered in a soft voice that was as ragged as her breathing.

Helping her rise far enough to guide the sweater off over her head, he reached behind her and unhooked the bra, tossing it onto the floor beside the growing pile of discarded clothing. Only then did he take a long, simmering look at the lush treasures he had revealed.

With closed eyes Dillon whispered softly in Spanish before he lifted his gaze once again to her waiting eyes. "Jessy, I'm on fire." He took her hand and laid it over his pounding heart. "I wasn't supposed to do this. I promised you I wouldn't."

With his other hand he reached out to stroke her breast with his fingertips, tracing its curve from the valley to the crest, encircling the pouting edge of the areola, drawing the flat of his palm over the hardened peak. At the sound of Jessy's soft moan, he cupped the base of her breast in his hand and lifted the firm, generous mound, gently testing its weight.

"I want you, Jessy. I want you so badly I can hardly breathe." Releasing her breast, he took the hand he still held against his heart and moved it lower. With her hand held in his own, he pressed the flat of her palm to the hard ridge that strained against the front of his blue jeans.

Not knowing what was expected of her in the first instant of contact, Jessy resisted, pulling against the pressure of his hand until the ridge jerked against her palm and Dillon closed his eyes and groaned. Fascinated by the life she felt beneath the denim, she cupped her hand over the contours of the ridge and stroked gently. Almost immediately she was rewarded by an answering throb from the other side of the fabric, and in the next instant Dillon caught her wrist and pulled her hand away.

"No," he gasped. "My fault. Bad idea." With a huge sigh he collapsed onto his side next to her and laid his hand over the soft, bare skin of her midriff. His head rested on the pillow beside hers. His face was inches away, and his midnight eyes stared into hers without blinking as he draped his leg over hers and nestled his still-flagrant arousal against her hip.

Like a yo-yo, Jessy could feel herself going first in one direction and then in the other. Her whole body ached for him, for the release he could offer, for the mysteries he could reveal, for the pleasure he had only begun to give her. But she was scared of the very emotions he aroused so forcefully. Once she had seen the mysteries, once she had felt the pleasure, how would she be able to turn and walk away? How would she be able to give up what she had never found with any other man?

"I can see the fear in your eyes," Dillon said softly. "And I don't know why it's there."

"It's nothing you've done."

"You'd make love to me tonight if I asked, wouldn't you?"

Lying beside him, still throbbing with the desire he had set free inside her, Jessy felt the bitter tears of frustration burning in her throat. "Yes." With one touch he could destroy her resolve and make her glad that he had done it.

He drew a finger across her cheek to her mouth. "And I'd feel like a bastard for doing it. Ah, Jessy." He pushed himself upright and off the bed. "I don't understand what you do to me, but you certainly do it. I think I'm going to take a cold shower. You want to join me?"

She held a sheet protectively over her torso. "I think I'll let you go alone."

"You're probably right. I don't think there'd be enough cold water in the world if either one of us was wearing any less." At the door to the bathroom he paused and turned halfway around. "Jessy?"

"Yes."

He stared at her with a look that held more than a little pain. Then he shook his head. "Nothing." He went inside and closed the door.

Moments later the sound of a shower brought Jessy to her feet. Gathering up her clothes, she fled the loft and dressed in the safety of the living room, afraid to be anywhere near him until he was finished, and they were ready to leave.

The drive back into town was long and silent. Dillon switched the radio from station to station, changing each time a love song came on, until he finally found some classical music to fill the conversational void for the last half of the trip.

When they finally reached the hotel, Dillon pulled up to the front and stopped. Jessy reached for the door handle, only too glad to escape before Dillon could say the dreaded words, "It was nice meeting you. Have a good trip back to Austin." Because after the pain of the past few hours she had no doubt that he would never want to see her again.

"Wait," he said instead, grabbing her by the wrist before she could bolt away.

She froze, afraid to turn and face him.

"I'll go in with you." He opened his door and started to get out.

"You really don't have to," Jessy protested. She wasn't sure she could take a long, silent walk through the lobby and a long, silent ride up in the elevator on the way to her room.

"I want to."

He got out without giving her a chance to reply, leaving Jessy with the choice of waiting graciously or making a run for it. She might have run if she'd been certain Dillon wouldn't chase her down and overtake her in the lobby.

When he arrived at her car door, she extended her hand for him to help her out and walked quietly beside him into the hotel. Throughout the long, quiet walk across the lobby, his hand rested on the small of her back, and the side of his body brushed against hers, while the warm, special scent of him reminded her of how much she would miss him tomorrow.

At the elevator Jessy tried once again to end the slow torture of their goodbye. "I'm sure I'll be fine now. You don't have to go any farther."

"I'd like to see you to your door." With the piercing gaze of a hawk who'd spotted prey just out of reach, Dillon gazed down at her. "I won't apologize for what happened at the cabin, Jessy, but I will promise that I won't touch you again if you don't want me to."

The elevator door opened and they stepped aside to let a middle-aged couple and their two children out. When the elevator was clear, Dillon guided Jessy on with a gentle nudge at the small of her back.

She turned to face him as he stepped in behind her. "Dillon, I'm not—"

Another couple came dashing from the side and made it into the elevator, laughing and out of breath, just as the doors slid closed.

Jessy moved closer to Dillon and said under her breath, "Upset with you."

"You're not?"

"No," she said, still whispering as she pushed the button for her floor. "I thought you were."

"Upset isn't the word I'd use." Dillon tightened his arm around her waist, holding her close enough to lean his head against hers and murmur into her ear. "Frustrated. Miserable. And a few others I'll leave to your imagination. But not upset." He leaned even closer and said very softly, "I thought I'd blown it with you."

"Why?" Jessy whispered back.

"The look in your eyes. It was—"

The elevator stopped and the door opened. Jessy glanced up and saw that they had reached her floor. "This is it."

She almost hated to leave the cozy clench with Dillon and the safety of knowing that with others around, it could go no further. He had promised not to touch her again unless she wanted him to, but every time he got near her they both ended up wanting him to do more and more.

He walked her to her door. His hand still rested on the small of her back, a gentlemanly act that seemed like so much more, but the sense of intimacy had evaporated when they left the elevator. He never finished his sentence, and she didn't ask.

Jessy found her key and fumbled with the lock until Dillon steadied her hand and together, his hand curled around hers, they opened the door.

He held her hand in his and laid the key in her open palm. "Do you mind if I come in for just a minute? I wanted to talk to you about tomorrow."

"Sure." She led the way, laying her purse and key on the dresser and going to the far side of the room to draw the draperies and stare out at the lights of the town.

On the carpet of the room, Dillon's footsteps were all but silent. She felt him behind her and a little to the side, staring out at his own piece of the night.

"Have you decided yet when you're leaving?" he asked quietly.

"I have a flight out tomorrow afternoon."

"I have a little something planned for tomorrow morning. Do you think you'll be able to go?"

Jessy turned her head and looked at him across her shoulder. "What is it?"

"It's a surprise." At the wary expression that crossed her face, he laughed. "It's not another cabin, I promise. But it is someplace that's very important to me, and I think you might like it, too."

"This sounds very mysterious."

"It's a public place," he offered. "No touching."

Resisting the temptation to try guessing their destination, Jessy smiled. "Okay, I'll go. I haven't got anything else to do, and who knows, I might even have a nice time."

With a smile of his own, Dillon brushed her hair back over her shoulder. "Good. Now what about tonight? I can cancel it if you want."

"Tonight?"

"Dinner. With Lita and Stephen."

"Oh." Jessy groaned and turned to lean face first against the wall. "I forgot all about it." With her forehead pressed to the wall, her voice bounced back at her as she spoke. "What are we supposed to do?"

"They're supposed to meet us downstairs in the lobby in about thirty minutes, but it's not too late for me to catch them if you'd prefer to call room service and go to bed early."

His voice sounded surprisingly noncommittal, which left Jessy in even more of a quandary. "I don't know. I'd hate to spoil their evening."

"I don't think it'd spoil their evening. They'd probably just go out without us and have a perfectly good time."

Dillon took Jessy's hand and led her away from the wall and over to the bed, where he turned her around and sat her down, then sat beside her, still holding her hand. "They might even have a better time without us. It's been a while since they've been out alone."

"You don't want to go, do you?" She'd have been hurt, except that his feelings so closely echoed her own.

The past two days had been long and intense. She'd been with Dillon almost constantly, and the strain was beginning to show. At the moment she wanted only one of two things—either to be alone to rest and gather her tattered emotions back into a tidy bundle or to throw herself into Dillon's arms and make mad, passionate, no-turning-back love, because nothing else was going to give her any peace.

"It's not that I don't want to go," Dillon said. As he spoke he turned her hand over and drew his finger slowly up the inside of her arm to where her sweater stopped him just below the crook of her elbow. "It's that I'm not in any shape to be good company tonight. I can't get my mind off—" he lifted his hand to brush his knuckle gently against the base of her chin "—what almost happened tonight. And I imagine you can't, either."

Not trusting her voice, Jessy shook her head.

"See? There's that look again." He drew his hand away from her face. "You want to, but you're afraid. I don't know why you're scared, Jessy, but as long as I see fear in your eyes I won't go any further. And for tonight, my beauty," he said with his voice dropping to a whisper, "I just can't be around you anymore and not touch you."

As he rose, he took her hand in his and lifted it to his lips. "I'll give you a wake-up call in the morning," he said as he released her hand and walked out, closing the door behind him softly.

## Chapter Seven

"Well, what do you think?" The sweep of Dillon's arm indicated a large adobe building inside a tall adobe wall.

"It looks like an old Spanish mission," Jessy said from their vantage point on the sidewalk outside. Inside the walls she could hear laughter and the sounds of children at play. "What is it? A day-care center?"

"Close. It's a community center. Senior citizens watch the children on the playground, and inside professional volunteers teach classes on the weekend."

"Classes in what?"

"You'll see." He took her hand and led her to the iron-work gate that swung open into a bare dirt courtyard where the pounding of children's feet had trampled any hope of vegetation.

Jessy stopped to study the simple elegance of the building, with its smooth, rounded lines and many arched windows. Up two steps from the courtyard, a large terrace of hand-hewn granite led to the entrance. "Old places like this always make me feel like I've stepped into a fairy tale. What was this originally?''

"A hacienda. It was here before the town was. After a few generations the original family sold it, and the next one passed it down until they couldn't afford it anymore. Someone finally picked it up for back taxes and donated it as a center.''

Jessy gazed up at him with a knowing smile. "Did *someone* live in it first, or did you give this one up without a fight?''

Dillon laughed. "No, I never stayed in this one. It was too big to appeal to me personally.''

"How many other places have you bought and donated?''

"A few. But they were all small, like the building the clinic's in.''

"No wonder you keep getting reelected.''

"My reelection is based on my record and nothing else,'' he said, the teasing light gone from his eyes. "All the rest is done through a foundation I set up, and as far as anyone else knows, I'm just a board member, nothing more.''

"I didn't mean to touch a nerve. I just assumed that in such a small community everyone must know. I can't imagine your mother keeping a secret like that.''

"Neither could I. That's why I've never told her. Of the family, only Stephen knows.''

"But why?'' Belatedly realizing how shocked she sounded, Jessy added, "I mean, most people would want everyone to know.''

"You've never met my grandfather, have you?''

From the bitterness that twisted Dillon's face, Jessy knew he meant Harlan Siddons. "No.''

"He uses his wealth to buy power and his power to buy fear. And he wields it all like a weapon to control everything that comes near him.''

"I thought you had reconciled with him.''

"Oh, I have. But you don't take a snake to your bosom without remembering that he still has fangs. I never want to be like my grandfather in any way. Even philanthropy has power, and I never want to be tempted by that power."

Touched by the struggle and isolation that was still so much a part of Dillon's everyday life, Jessy reached out to him instinctively and rested a comforting hand on the hard muscles of his forearm. "Nothing in your life has ever been simple, has it?"

"No." Her touch brought a soft smile to his face and, placing his hand over the one that rested on his arm, he led her toward the front door. "Not simple, and not easy. But the crucible creates the strongest metal. I had to learn how to survive, and now I can help others learn those same lessons."

He turned to face her, his shoulder leaning against the heavy wooden door as his voice grew reflective. "I wouldn't trade the life I've had, Jessy, but I do want more." His thumb stroked the soft flesh of her lower lip. "Much more."

Heat seared through to her core, reducing to ash all the hours she had spent strengthening her will to resist him. With her resolve scattered like cinders in the wind, Jessy knew that she couldn't go on fooling herself. She wanted him so badly she could taste it, and she would know no peace until she was his, if only for a night.

"Dillon." She looked into his midnight eyes and felt the impact like a blow, pushing the breath out of her. "Dillon," she whispered. Her hand rested on his chest, the chest of gleaming bronze and corded muscles that had brushed against her bare skin only the night before.

Without warning the door Dillon leaned against gave way and he staggered backward into the opening. A strong hand reached out of the shadows to catch him.

"Dillon! I was wondering where you were, man," a masculine voice said in a strong Texas drawl. "The game's about to start." A long, low wolf whistle followed as a tall, lanky man with a shock of bright red hair stepped into the doorway for a closer look at Jessy. "Excuse my enthusiasm, ma'am, but Dillon doesn't usually bring us quite such lovely volunteers."

Jessy cast a questioning glance toward Dillon, waiting for him to explain that they were just passing through. He answered her with a reassuring smile and turned to the other man.

Clapping him on the shoulder, Dillon said, "Father Timothy, I'd like you to meet Jessica Carder, known as Jessy to her friends."

With a broad smile the unlikely priest stepped forward and extended his hand. "Jessy."

"Father." As she pumped the man's hand, her questioning gaze went once again in search of Dillon, but to no avail.

"I run the Saturday-morning basketball games here," Father Timothy said, forcing Jessy to return her wandering attention to him. "And Dillon, here, is our best point guard. We can't start the game without him when he's in town."

"If I know Tim," Dillon said with a teasing smile that lingered on Jessy, "he was on his way to find me."

"Actually, I was on my way to find Emilio and send him after you."

Remembering the little boy she had met Thursday, Jessy brightened. "Is Emilio here?"

"Somewhere." Father Timothy turned to Dillon. "Well, are you ready to play?"

"I'll be along in a minute. I have to get Jessy settled first."

"Fair enough." The priest dipped a bow toward Jessy. "It's a pleasure to have you with us, Jessy. I hope you'll be back again real soon. You sure brighten up the place." With that he turned and hurried back down the long hallway and through another door.

"Is he a real priest?"

"As real as they come."

"Well, correct me if I'm wrong, but that seemed an awful lot like flirting to me."

Dillon chuckled and took Jessy's hand to guide her through the doorway while he closed it behind her. "Timothy does have quite a way with the ladies. From five to eighty-five, he flirts with them all, but with the really pretty ones he's especially sincere."

Still holding her hand, Dillon began to amble slowly down the long hallway. "The way Tim puts it, he is and always will be true to his vows, but he's still a man and he still knows a woman when he sees one."

"I guess that takes a special kind of dedication," she said quietly, reminded once again how out of place she was among these people to whom sacrifice was a way of life.

"We're blessed to have him here," Dillon agreed, "and we try very hard to do what we can to help."

With a teasing grin she shook off the somberness that had settled over her momentarily. "Like being his point guard every Saturday morning?"

"When the legislature isn't in session, and every weekend I can get away when it is."

"And what am I supposed to do while you're playing basketball?" she asked, only half teasing. "Sit in the stands and cheer?"

"Not exactly."

They turned a corner and started down another corridor. In the distance Jessy could hear laughter, but not the laughter of children. This was older, with more of an edge, not quite adult, but—

A flushed, motherly face peeped out of a doorway and lit up with recognition. A plump body followed immediately, hands clasped in obvious joy. "Oh, Dillon, I can't thank you enough. And you must be Jessy." The eloquent hands unclasped and reached out in greeting. "My dear, I can't tell you how happy we are to have you helping us today. The girls are just ecstatic."

"Girls?" Jessy gazed at the woman in wide-eyed surprise. "Helping?" She whipped her head around to Dillon. Her eyes narrowed and her voice lowered. "What is this?"

"The deportment class. You know. Makeup, grooming, learning how to walk with a book on your head." Undaunted, he gazed straight into her eyes and said, "Mrs. Dawson was thrilled to have a real model agree to come and speak to her class."

"Agree?" Jessy turned back to Mrs. Dawson and, smiling through clenched teeth, asked sweetly, "Could Dillon and I have just one moment alone?"

The older woman nodded quickly. "Oh, yes, of course. Just come right on in when you're ready."

When Mrs. Dawson was safely out of earshot, Jessy whirled on Dillon. "Are you out of your mind?" Her whispered words came out in an angry sputter. "How could you do this to me?"

"Do what? Inside that room is a group of girls who could benefit from what you know. Maybe something you say today could give just *one* of them a reason not to get pregnant before she's seventeen."

"And what if I don't know what to say?"

"Jessy." His fingers tightened and loosened on her shoulder in a slow, soothing massage. "All you have to do is answer their questions. They'll do all the work." He rested his hands on both of her shoulders, still massaging gently as he worked out her tension and willed her to relax. "Once you see them, you'll understand. *Anything* you have to offer them is more than they have right now."

"How long?"

"An hour." Before she could protest he said, "The time will fly, I promise. They're great kids." He brushed his thumb over her chin. "You'll enjoy yourself."

"You should have told me," she said, refusing to be so easily placated.

"I was going to," he said in a voice as soothing as his touch. "We just got off onto something else, and then after Timothy arrived it was too late. The class was already starting, and I figured the best way was just to toss you into it."

"Thanks a lot." Taking a deep breath, she squared her shoulders and resigned herself to her fate.

"I knew you could handle it."

"Don't bother giving me a snow job now. It's too late. Go on." She shooed him away. "Go play basketball, and I'll go do my model stuff."

"You're never going to let me forget that, are you?"

"Probably not in this lifetime."

"Are you mad at me?" He moved a step closer, not ready to leave her yet.

"I should be."

"But are you?" he insisted.

"No." She shook her head, not smiling but no longer angry. "Not anymore."

"You could end up enjoying this, you know. You may like it so well, you'll want to come back."

"Is this how you get your volunteers? You just drag unsuspecting people in off the street, toss them into the pit and let them fight their way out?"

Dillon shrugged innocently. "If you warn 'em, they won't come."

"You *are* shameless."

"We'll discuss that later." He leaned closer and kissed her quickly, softly on the lips. "Good luck," he whispered as he drew away.

"Don't leave me here too long." She hated to see him go. Once she walked through the classroom door she had no idea what she was going to do, but she knew it wouldn't take long to exhaust the sum total of her knowledge.

"I won't desert you, Jessy. And thank you. I should have told you, and I know what I'm asking you to do isn't fair, but I know you'll be wonderful."

"You know a lot more than I do, then." She took a deep breath and let it out slowly. "Well, I'm not accomplishing anything out here. Have a good game." With that she turned and walked through the doorway of the classroom.

Inside, she stopped to scan the faces that turned toward her. The group was more varied than she had expected. In shades from deepest brown to alabaster, the girls reflected a melting pot of coloring. Eyes from ebony to azure gazed up at her—some with hope, some with challenge, some with open defiance. And it was the defiance that made Jessy feel at home.

"Good morning." She greeted them with a smile that was genuine. "In case you're not too sure why I'm here, I have to confess that I'm not too sure, either. But what little I know, I'm more than willing to share with you."

The response ranged from clapping hands and broad smiles to rolling eyes and index fingers slowly twirling in a parody of joy. For the first time since agreeing to do this, it occurred to Jessy that not every girl was necessarily there by choice. She wondered how many of these young ladies were here by court order as a condition of their probation. The idea should have been daunting, but it wasn't.

"I realize that for most of you the idea of becoming a model seems about as likely as, oh, I don't know, taking a walk on the moon, maybe." She paused and was greeted with laughs, nods, sneers and, from the most resistant, snorts that sounded like agreement. She regarded this as progress.

"But what shouldn't seem like a bad idea to anyone is learning how to make the most of what you've got." Again Jessy paused for a response, and again she got it. Every face was turned in her direction, and even the most hostile of the girls seemed to be listening.

"For better or worse, in our society, the way a woman looks is going to affect the way a lot of people relate to her," she continued, knowing that she could lose her audience at any moment. "The same is true of men, but to a lesser degree. That's just the way people are." She shrugged and swept the room with her gaze.

"Now, what I'm here to tell you is this—you don't have to be born with a beautiful face, or a gorgeous body, or a lot of money in order to look nice. I can teach every one of you—" Jessy pointed to the girl seated closest and saw her face light up "—how to turn heads when you walk down a street."

Jessy's pointing finger moved on, including everyone in her promise. "I can teach every one of you how to stand tall and walk proud, how to take what you have and make the most of it, and how to walk out of here today feeling better about yourselves than you did when you walked in."

As a body, they leaned toward her eagerly, upturned faces wreathed with smiles. Whispers of "yes," "okay" and "all right" rustled through the room in a chorus of assent, and then one lone voice of disgruntlement called out.

"That's easy for you to say. Look at you." A dark-skinned girl, overweight, with two-toned hair and perm-frizzed ends rose up to challenge Jessy and her promises. "Look at me. You gonna stand up there and talk to me until I turn beautiful?"

"What's your name?" Jessy asked, quickly scanning the girl's appearance for positive points.

"Loretta." The girl shifted her weight to the other foot, planted a hand on her rounded hip and jutted her jaw defiantly.

Jessy remembered her as one of the most hostile in the beginning. "Well, Loretta, I'm not here to create any Cinderellas. I'm Jessy, by the way, in case Mrs. Dawson didn't tell you. And nobody's perfect, Loretta. The way people look their best is by emphasizing their strongest points and minimizing their weakest points."

The girl continued to stand, and Jessy moved closer, comparing their sizes as she neared. "You and I seem to be about the same height, which for a model is not really all that tall. But when I was fourteen and this same height, I was very tall, and I was *very* skinny. I've seen sticks with better figures.''

There was laughter in the background and Loretta stood a little taller, because even if she was overweight she had a figure that was round in all the right places.

''But that was okay,'' Jessy continued, ''because when I started modeling, flat was the look they wanted. Then a few years later when my career was really starting to take off, so did my figure. By the time I was nineteen I was still skinny, but all the other models were taller than I was, and I had curves that nobody wanted in their clothes. For years after that, the only work I could get was modeling swimsuits and lingerie. Then curves came back in, and now I'm hot again.''

Hands outstretched to emphasize her slim and very shapely body, Jessy did a slow pirouette. As she came back around to face them, she dropped her hands and became serious. ''But I'm also twenty-nine. So I'll never be a top model. It's too late. Am I making my point here?''

She paused and looked at the expressions that showed a little enlightenment and a lot of confusion. ''To you, Loretta, my life has been easy because I'm pretty.'' Jessy looked at the girl to single her out. ''To the modeling world, I haven't always had the right look at the right time. But I've always worked, and I've made good money, because there are plenty of jobs for models who aren't perfect, who are short, or overweight, or past fifty. Now am I making my point? Loretta?''

''Yeah,'' Loretta said, slouching back into her chair with a satisfied grin. ''I may get to walk on the moon.''

As laughter rang out, Jessy joined in. Retracing her steps to the front of the room, she turned and held up her hand. Over the fading commotion she called out, ''I think it's time we all learned how to walk tall. And I think Loretta's just the person to start us off, don't you?''

More laughter and resounding agreement answered her. Still grinning, with arms outstretched in submission, Loretta rose from her seat and walked toward Jessy.

"Okay, make me beautiful," the girl said, no longer sounding quite so sure it couldn't happen.

"I think we just might do that." Jessy smiled, already envisioning Loretta's tall frame held elegantly upright, her dark, attractive eyes highlighted in subtle earth tones, and a bright scarf framing a face that really did have very nice bone structure.

When Dillon arrived to take her away, Jessy realized with dismay that she had worked her way through only half the room. Loretta and Mrs. Dawson had taken over the posture training while Jessy moved on to makeup, but still there were girls she had spent hardly any time with. The lovely Oriental girl named Dotty, who had hung shyly in the background all morning, looked sad enough to cry when it seemed that Jessy would have to go.

"Oh, Dillon, please, could I have just a little while longer?" Jessy touched his arm and gazed with pleading into his eyes.

"It's been two and a half hours already, Jessy. I've checked on you three times, but Mrs. Dawson kept shooing me away. Are you sure you want to stay longer?"

"One more hour. I promise, just one more hour, and I'll be through. Oh, Dillon, I've never done anything like this before." She laughed softly, a little overcome by her own enthusiasm. "It's fun. And they really seem to be learning something from me."

"I can probably find something to do around here for another hour, if you're sure you want to."

"I'm sure." She let go of his arm and stepped back. "And thank you."

"Oh, you're entirely welcome." With a nod to Mrs. Dawson, he turned and left.

When Jessy faced the group again, all the girls were staring at the doorway where Dillon had last stood.

"Is that your boyfriend?" Loretta asked, putting their collective thoughts into words.

"Well, uh, we're friends."

"Uh-huh," Loretta said, while her tone made it clear she thought there was much more to it than that. "Well, honey, you're one lucky woman, that's all I've got to say. Ain't that right, girls?"

Agreement, sighs, whistles and mutterings descriptive enough to make Jessy blush were earnestly offered. "Yes, well, thank you. I think we'd better get back to work now. I've only got an hour left."

Dotty came forward immediately, and Jessy was grateful to have something else to think about besides the fact that when it came to sex, she was the novice in this group. There was only so much she could do in a few hours, but for the first time she realized how serious Dillon had been about the danger of pregnancy with these girls.

While she offered them advice on blusher, hairstyles and accessories, their everyday lives included the reality of alcohol, drugs and unprotected sex. After she taught them to walk with straight backs and squared shoulders, they had to worry about dodging danger every day in their streets.

"Pamela and I," Dotty said softly while she turned and motioned forward another girl, "have job interviews next week." Pamela arrived to stand beside her and nodded her agreement. "We both type really well," Dotty continued, "but we're worried about looking right for a big office. Can you help us?"

"We really need these jobs," Pamela said. Behind her thick glasses her eyes were intense with determination.

"We're going to get an apartment together, away from here," Dotty added.

"Okay." Jessy smiled, already visualizing the changes she would make. "Let's work on makeup while we talk about clothes."

By the time Dillon returned an hour later, Jessy was putting the finishing touches on a circle of six girls who had gathered to learn the basics of dressing for effect. Pamela's eyes no longer disappeared behind her glasses. Her thin lips no longer seemed stern and humorless. Dotty's delicate beauty blossomed. Clarice's teased pouf of blond curls no longer overpowered her small, heart-shaped face. Rosita's flamboyant makeup no longer hid her own naturally exotic beauty.

Still wishing she could stay longer, Jessy waved goodbye finally with the satisfaction of seeing even a small amount of real change in the short time she had spent. "I'll be back as soon as I can," she promised when she turned in the doorway for one final look.

"Yeah, sure. That's what they all say," Loretta answered with a touch of her old sullenness.

"Well, I mean it. I promise. And in the meantime, you work on what I taught you. And, Dotty, when you and Pamela get those jobs, you leave word where I can find you, because I want to see how you're doing when I come back."

"You can't take them with you," Dillon said softly from behind her.

"I know." Lifting her hand in one last goodbye, Jessy stepped backward into the hallway, then turned and walked swiftly away. If she let herself, she would stay there all day, trying to do just a little more, trying to change things she couldn't change.

At the end of the corridor Dillon caught her by the arm and brought her flight to a halt. "Jessy, wait." Taking her by the shoulders, he turned her to face him. "I'm sorry."

"For what?" She stared at his shirtfront through eyes that burned with tears, and she felt like an idiot for wanting to cry. The world was full of people in need, and she'd never wanted to cry before.

"For being a jerk. I didn't take your feelings into consideration before I shoved you into this." He put his hand under her chin and nudged her head up until she had to either look at him or turn away.

Reluctantly she looked at him. "I don't know why I'm so upset. Maybe it's because I can remember how I felt when I was their age."

"I can, too. That's why I like to come down here. But there's only so much people like us can do, Jessy. These kids still have to make their own choices." He smoothed his thumb across the teardrops gathered in her lashes. "And we have to let them. But I'm proud of you for caring."

"It's no big deal." She shrugged and blinked back the tears that still threatened. "All I did was show them how to put on blusher."

Dillon tilted her chin a few degrees higher and nuzzled the tip of her upturned nose with his. "Yeah. Right," he murmured in a velvety soft rumble. "You try to hide it, but that marshmallow heart of yours is starting to show."

Suddenly breathless, Jessy whispered, "I don't know what you're talking about."

"I'm crazy about you. You know that, don't you? I didn't set out to be, but I am. And you just keep making it worse, because the one thing I never expected was that you'd turn out to be so damned sweet."

With his last words his lips brushed hers, gently, then grew harder and more insistent while his hands flattened against her back and pulled her solidly against him. The tip of his tongue passed between her parted lips, spreading them wider and drawing her deeper into his kiss. His hands moved slowly down her back and over the curve of her hips, drawing her high against the hard-muscled leg that slipped between her thighs.

Flames shot through her, and Jessy jerked her head back with a gasp. Dillon's lips followed, raking hers with an almost mindless hunger as he whispered, "God, Jessy, you set me on fire."

His arm locked around her waist, holding her body entwined with his while he cupped the back of her head with his hand and caressed her mouth with his kiss, plunging deeper and deeper into that soft, moist cavern that promised delights untasted and passion unbound.

Lost in the thunder and lightning firestorm that Dillon's embrace unleashed on them both, Jessy saw and heard nothing but the incandescent riot of her own emotions until a voice, young and female, called out from no more than a foot away.

"All right!"

Immediately, a second voice followed, and then a third.

"Way to hang."

"Go to it, Jessy."

Dillon broke off the kiss to bury Jessy's head against his shoulder. His body subtly shifted to hide hers.

"I *knew* they was more than friends."

A fourth voice that sounded suspiciously like Loretta's was followed by a fifth, sixth, and on, while the tramping of feet and jostling of bodies flowed like a endless parade past where Dillon and Jessy stood frozen in time.

"Yeah, I'd like some man to look at me the way he looked at her."

"Hell, I'd like *that* man to look at me the way he looked at her."

"I'd like any man to look at me, period."

"I heard *that,* girlfriend."

"Girls, please," the voice of Mrs. Dawson urged. "Show that you've learned *something* in these classes and move along quietly."

"Yes, ma'am."

"Too late for that now. Did you see the way he was wrapped around her?"

"Shh."

Eventually the muttering voices and shuffling feet faded and the torture of waiting ended. Her face aflame with mortification, Jessy slowly lifted her head from Dillon's shoulder and gazed up into his eyes, expecting kindred embarrassment.

Instead, he grinned. "Aren't kids cute?"

"Cute?"

"That sure takes me back to my high school days. I got caught necking so many times. Actually, I got caught doing a lot worse than that."

"Well, I didn't."

"Oh, come on, Jessy, you're not really upset, are you?"

"Of course I'm upset. I can't even remember exactly what we were doing, but I can just imagine how it must have looked."

"Pretty hot. But, sweetheart, I'm Latino." He laughed, trying to tease her out of her mood. "It's expected."

"I'm sorry," she said, stiffening, "but I'm just not as easygoing about these things as you apparently are."

"Easygoing about what things, Jessy? It was a kiss." Dillon was no longer laughing. "A kiss embarrasses you, but stripping down to the sheerest little piece of lingerie imaginable and having your picture spread across the nation doesn't?"

"I don't know what you think you're seeing in those pictures," Jessy shot back hotly. "But I guarantee you, it's all an illusion. And no, it doesn't embarrass me. I don't reveal any more than the average woman on the average beach in America, and I'm *not* ashamed of what I do."

"Oh, no? Well, you sound a little defensive to me."

"Oh, yeah? Well let me tell you something, mister. I don't have to defend myself to you or to anyone, and if you don't like what I do—"

"Ahem. Excuse me," Father Timothy said cautiously, and Jessy and Dillon both turned to him with sparks still flashing in their eyes.

"Yes?" Though he struggled to control it, Dillon's tone was more clipped than usual.

"Uh, there's a slight problem." Timothy pointed toward the back of the building. "If you could—"

"I'll be right there," Dillon said, looking back at Jessy.

"And I'll wait out front," Jessy said. Breaking eye contact with Dillon, she pushed her way between the men. "I need some fresh air."

"Just a minute," Dillon said.

The request came out as an order and Jessy knew it was meant for her, but she kept on going. Whatever he had to say, she didn't want to hear it, not until she'd had time to calm down.

Sanctimony was something she had encountered before, but it wasn't something she had expected from Dillon, not from a man with his reputation with women and not from a man with his supposed social enlightenment. He hadn't said much, but he had said enough, and she didn't want to hear the rest.

She had had her fill of men who had seen a picture of her rising from the surf in a wet bikini and thought they had seen the real her. She had had enough of men who lusted after her portrait in a black lace nightgown and assumed she would be easy prey. And she had had all she wanted of men who prejudged her morals, or lack of morals, based on fashion layouts in magazines.

She had put up with it at cocktail parties and airports and photo shoots and restaurants around the world, but she didn't have to put up with it here. Not now, and not with Dillon, not with the man who already had far too big a piece of her heart.

With her temper leading the way, Jessy burst through the front door of the center and into the bright sunshine of the courtyard. Blinking against the blinding light, she heard the sound of crying. Only a few feet away, on the hard stone of the terrace, a tiny girl sat huddled in tears, her little body quaking with each shuddering breath she drew.

## Chapter Eight

As Jessy started toward the little girl, a boy came racing up the steps of the terrace and dropped to his knees beside the toddler. Talking earnestly, he tried to gather her to him, but she struggled, pounding him with her little fists as her cries grew louder.

"What are you doing?" Jessy demanded, prepared to pull the boy away if she had to. When he lifted his stricken face to her, she recognized him immediately.

"Help her, please," Emilio begged. "She won't let me."

"What's wrong with her?" Jessy crouched down on the other side of the girl.

"I don't know. I only left her alone for a minute, and she wandered away."

At the sound of a woman's voice the little girl, who couldn't have been more than two or three years old, lifted her head, and Jessy found herself gazing into the tear-streaked face of a tiny angel with thick black curls and huge dark eyes. Sniffling while her lower lip trembled enough to break the hardest heart, the little girl lifted her chubby arms to Jessy, who reached without thinking to gather her up.

While Jessy rocked to and fro, the child rested her head on Jessy's shoulder and cried long, bitter tears. Emilio rose to his feet and stayed close, worriedly following every move that was made with the girl.

"What's her name?" Jessy asked, as much to include Emilio as to learn the child's name.

"Angelina."

"She was with you?"

He nodded vigorously and reached out to touch the girl almost unconsciously. "I was watching her, but she's very quick. I only looked away for a minute."

Jessy freed a hand to brush the hair from Emilio's worried brow. "She probably just fell down. I'm sure she's not really hurt."

"Maybe." He sounded uncertain.

"She sounds more angry than in pain to me."

"Angelina?" He touched the edge of a scrape on the girl's knee where bare, reddened skin showed fresh amid the coating of dust from the playground.

The toddler twisted away from him and snuggled closer to Jessy, but the tears slowed to a sniffle. Without looking, Angelina reached out a hand and touched Emilio's shoulder. The silent touch said a lot, as did the relieved smile it brought to the little boy's face.

"Do you know her well?" Jessy asked.

"She's my sister." He took the chubby hand in his and held it with pride. "I take care of her."

"I didn't know you had a sister, Emilio." As Jessy spoke, Angelina lifted her head and touched Jessy's cheek with her other hand while her big brown eyes gazed up with something close to love. "Well, hi there, sweetheart," Jessy said with a soft chuckle. "Are you feeling better now?"

The little girl slowly nodded. Without speaking, she wrapped her arms around Jessy's neck and tucked her head under Jessy's chin.

"She misses our mother," Emilio said quietly. The eyes that watched his sister were very sad.

"You have your grandmother, don't you?"

"She's very old. We're too much for her. We make her sick a lot, I think."

"What? What do you mean?"

"Well, look who you've found." Dillon's voice from the doorway turned the conversation in a new direction. "I see you've met the light of Emilio's life."

At Dillon's approach, Angelina's arms tightened around Jessy's neck. "Angelina," he said softly, "you remember me, don't you? You and Emilio and I all went to get ice cream together, remember?"

At the words "ice cream" the little girl's head turned toward Dillon, though she continued to cling tightly to Jessy. Hardly realizing she was doing it, Jessy wrapped her arms protectively around the small body, giving the child the silent support she needed to be brave.

"Are you still scared of me?" Dillon asked quietly.

Without lifting her head from Jessy's shoulder, Angelina shook her head, then lifted a chubby hand and waggled her fingers in a silent greeting.

Dillon laughed. "Hello, little one." Looking past her to Emilio, he asked, "Do you two need a ride home?"

Emilio shook his head. "We can walk. It isn't far."

"How about some ice cream money? It's not too close to dinnertime, is it?"

The boy smiled and shook his head. He quickly pocketed the bills Dillon handed him and mumbled, "Don't want to be flashing the cash." Then he touched Angelina's arm. "Angeline, come on. We've got to go. It's getting late."

The little girl lifted her head and fixed sad eyes on Jessy, who felt a similar wrenching in her own heart. The tiny body felt good against hers. It felt wrong to let her go, to send her back into the world alone except for one little boy who already carried too much weight on his slim shoulders.

Reluctantly Jessy set Angelina down and watched her walk away with her hand in Emilio's.

"They'll be all right," Dillon said as if he could read her mind.

"Are you trying to reassure me or yourself?"

"Both of us. Every time I send that kid back out on his own, it gets harder."

"Why don't you do something about it?"

"The world's full of kids like Emilio and Angelina. I'm doing all I can."

"I'm not talking about the rest of them. I'm talking about those two." Hand in hand, Emilio and Angelina crossed the street and disappeared from view. "I've only met him twice, and each time, something about him almost breaks my heart."

"I know." Dillon seemed about to say more, but he only repeated, "I know." After a long silence, while they stood side by side, lost in their own thoughts, he asked, "Are you ready to go?"

"Yes. I guess I'm more tired than I thought. Maybe I just need to rest for a while."

"How about grabbing a bite to eat? I'm starving."

Once he mentioned it Jessy realized that she *was* hungry. She hadn't had a thing to eat since breakfast. "Well, maybe a salad."

Dillon chuckled softly and brushed an errant strand of hair away from her face. "You and your salads."

"At least I'm a cheap date." Still not ready to call a truce in the cold war between them, Jessy turned away and walked ahead of him to the car.

He joined her there, and as they drove away, Dillon said, "I owe you an apology. Two apologies, actually. You were right about the kiss. I went too far, and the time and place were all wrong. But I had to give my hormones time to calm down before I could admit it, even to myself."

"Was that one apology, or two?" Jessy asked coolly.

"One. The second is that I was way out of line with that crack I made inside. The one about your pictures. And you had every right to tell me off."

"I know." Just the thought of it made her angry all over again. "Am I supposed to thank you now?"

Refusing to take offense, Dillon smiled again. "You can be tough when you work at it, can't you?"

"I wasn't trying to be amusing."

"I know, and I didn't mean to get you stirred up all over again. It's just—" With a shake of his head, he broke off and shrugged.

When he didn't finish, Jessy's anger quickly lost ground to her ever-present curiosity. Adding to the confusion was the tiny voice of reason that urged her to drop the subject, cut her losses and run as far away from Dillon as she could get.

"It's just what?" she asked, finally bowing to the curiosity that always seemed to overpower her better judgment.

"It's just that I find almost everything you do right now to be utterly charming." Without taking his eyes from the road, he curled his fingers around her wrist and gently stroked his thumb over the back of her hand. "I've enjoyed these last few days with you, Jessy," he said with feeling that was as genuine as it was disconcerting. "Even when we argue, I've felt more alive than I have in a long time. So forgive me if I smile at the wrong times. I'm just happy."

"I—I don't know what to say." The voice urging her to run was screaming in her ear, but the pounding of her heart was louder still.

"You don't have to say anything." He continued to massage the back of her hand as he drove. "What time is your flight?"

"A little after five. I still have to go back to the hotel and finish packing." The voice of reason had dropped to a whimper, while her heart thundered like the hooves of a runaway horse.

"Could you stay one more night?"

"Oh, Dillon." If she agreed, she was lost. She couldn't take another night like last night, and neither could he.

"One night, Jessy. Just one night."

There were a lot of things she could have said, and maybe should have said. That they had known each other only two days. That they would probably never see each other again. Or even that she simply didn't do this kind of thing, all of which were true, but instead she said only, "Yes."

Dillon let out the breath he had been holding and slipped his arm around her shoulders, pulling her closer to him. He held her there, his cheek brushing her hair, as he pulled into a fast food take-out lane and surprisingly ordered salads for both of them, then headed the car east out of town, toward the cabin.

Behind them a huge yellow sun sank in an empty blue sky. Along the horizon, delicate brush strokes of orange and pink painted the sky. Gradually spreading higher, they darkened to swirls of tangerine and rose while the yellow sun grew larger still and turned to crimson before slowly sinking beneath a rose-red sky.

There was only a narrow strip of pink below a lavender sky by the time Dillon stopped the car in front of the cabin. A twilight haze softened the air that was already cooling for the night as Jessy put her hand in his and walked toward the cabin door.

She felt that she should say something, but she didn't know what. *Be gentle?* Maybe she should warn him that this would be her first time, or maybe she should call the whole thing off. If she gave her heart to Dillon tonight, would she have the courage to leave him in the morning? Would she have any choice?

"You're quiet." Dillon unlocked the front door and pushed it open but made no move to enter. "Are you having second thoughts?"

*It's now or never, Jessy,* she warned herself. If she was going to back out, this was the moment. Once she walked through that door, Dillon would rightfully assume she had agreed to stay the night in every sense of the word.

"Are you?" she asked, forcing herself to meet his unwavering gaze.

"No." In his eyes dark fires flickered.

"None?" Caught by the whispers of her own reckless heart, Jessy told herself that she didn't love him. She couldn't love him.

"No."

At the certainty in his voice, a shiver of anticipation crept up through her, taking her breath with it. She no longer feared becoming one of the many. She no longer worried that Dillon would use her and cast her aside. She wanted him, and if heartbreak followed, then so be it.

For one night in Dillon's arms she would risk the heartbreak. Stepping through the doorway, Jessy walked into the cool darkness of the room that already seemed familiar. Like an old friend the silent cabin welcomed her. She would hate to leave it in the morning, knowing she would never return. But to linger would be even worse.

One night with Dillon would be a memory she could carry next to her heart for a lifetime. More than that would be more than she could bear to lose.

"Jessy." His lips brushed her hair as his hands caught her shoulders from behind and pressed her back against his chest. "I feel like I've waited a lifetime for you."

Jessy laid her hand over the one on her shoulder and tilted her head back to rest just beneath his chin. She closed her eyes and smiled at her private joke. "Funny, but I feel the same way."

"I'm as eager as a schoolboy." His voice was ragged as he stroked the backs of his fingers over her cheek and down the slender column of her neck. "Can you feel it? My hands are actually shaking."

She expelled her pent-up breath in a sigh and rolled her head from side to side on his shoulder. The riot inside her own body made it very hard for her to feel anything else. Desire coiled hot and hard in the pit of her stomach. And with each sensual stroke of Dillon's hands, each passion-coated whisper from his lips, lightning bolts of need slowly turned her legs to putty.

"I didn't want it to be like this." His hand flattened against her stomach, pressing her against him. His voice sounded frustrated, almost angry, then softened again to a croon. "I wanted to seduce you by inches," he whispered against her ear, "to show you a slow torture of pleasure that would leave you calling out my name in your dreams. I wanted to be the one man you'd never forget."

Jessy turned slowly in his arms and looked up at him in the moonlight that spilled through the open front door. "I don't think that'll be a problem." The husky rasp of her voice left no doubt that she meant it.

Dillon smiled softly. "You don't think so, huh?"

"I don't think so."

"I wish I could be that sure." His voice sounded almost sad. "I want this night to be special. I don't want to be just another lover you say goodbye to the next morning and never think about again."

"Is that important to you, Dillon?"

"Yes."

"Why?" She wanted to ask if he felt the same way about all his women, but for once she held her tongue, afraid she might not like the answer. Tonight Dillon belonged to her and only her. This night was hers, and nothing was going to ruin the memory for her.

"I've waited ten years for this night, Jessy." He raked his fingers through her hair and pulled her face closer to his. "I've made love to you a thousand times in my dreams."

His words frightened her. She wasn't the woman he imagined. The real Jessy could never live up to the one in his dreams, and if he didn't realize that now, he would soon. "I'm not a fantasy, Dillon," she reminded him gent-ly. "I'm a woman."

"I've wanted you for so long, I'm not sure I can tell the difference anymore."

"Is that all this is to you?" The fever in her blood cooled and suddenly she wasn't sure she could go on. "A trophy hunt?"

"No!" Urgently Dillon pulled her to him and brushed his lips over hers, lightly, hungrily. "But real or fantasy, you've eclipsed every woman in my life for ten years, Jessy. And there's only one way I'm ever going to be free of you."

"Free of me?" she repeated. Shocked and hurt, she stiffened against him and tried to pull away. "So tonight you're going to make love to the real me," she said with icy anger flowing through her veins. "And if you can pleasure me the way you've always dreamed of doing, then by some magic you'll be free of this hold I have on you? Is that right?" On fire with anger, she shoved harder against the embrace that held her captive.

"Yes," he said automatically, then reversed himself as he struggled to keep her in his arms. "No! Hell, Jessy, I don't know anymore."

"Well! I guess it's a good thing I'm such a heartless bitch!" she spat with eyes narrowed and heart racing. "Otherwise you might have to spare some thought as to how *I* might feel about all of this."

Furious, she wrenched herself free of his arms finally and, whirling away from him, stalked into the deep shad-ows at the back of the room.

"Jessy, damn it."

Not about to calm down before she had said what she wanted to say, Jessy paced in the semidarkness under the overhanging loft and practically shouted, "But since I just use men and then toss them away like discarded tissues, there's no reason you should feel bad about doing the same thing to me."

"That's not what I meant, and you know it!"

She heard him close behind her and moved again, calling over her shoulder, "One night of passion and a pat on the rump in parting? Is that the idea, Dillon?"

"*You're* the one who insists on leaving tomorrow. *You're* the one who's led me around by the nose for two days now."

She turned back toward the sound of his voice and demanded, "Do you mean you were seriously trying to seduce me that first day we met?"

In the dark, Dillon's hands closed over her arms and pulled her to him. "I've seriously thought of nothing else since I walked through that clinic door and saw you standing there."

"But you didn't even like me!"

"I wanted you so bad my teeth hurt just looking at you, but I was furious with you because I thought you were only there to seduce Stephen."

"Well, actually, I was," she admitted with a shrug that seemed to release all her anger like a balloon floating into the sky and out of sight.

Dillon let out his breath in a gust that was half laugh, half sigh. "Let's not start all that again, Jessy."

"Dillon?"

He nuzzled his chin against her hair as he wrapped his arms around her waist and pressed his body to hers. "Mmm?"

"I think we're talking entirely too much."

"Ah, baby, I'm so glad you agree." He lifted her into his arms and carried her up the staircase to the loft.

"What about the door?" Moonlight spilled into the room below through the door that stood open.

"We're at the ends of the earth. Who's going to bother us out here?" He lowered her onto the bed and rose over her, a shadowy outline against a pale glow.

"Coyotes?"

"Maybe I should close it." He leaned over her and kissed her lightly, then drew away only to return immediately in a kiss that was hard and hungry. His hand closed over her waist. His thumb traced the outline of a rib, then stole higher to brush the base of her breast.

When he broke off the kiss long enough to unfasten the large round button at the base of her deep V collar, Jessy drew in a ragged breath. "The door?"

"To hell with the door. So long as nothing comes up the stairs, they can *have* the first floor." He unbuckled the belt hampering his steady march down the buttons that fastened her shirtwaist. "They'll leave when the sun comes up, anyway." As he neared the final button at midthigh, Dillon's hand slowed.

Fear, eagerness and a feeling that defied description pounded at Jessy in equal measure. He would never be hers to keep. Their worlds were too far apart. Their needs were too different. But Dillon would be hers forever in a way that no other man could ever be. He would be her first, and the memories of this night would last a lifetime.

The last barrier gone, Dillon spread her dress apart like gift wrapping on a present. His knuckles brushed her thighs in passing. Cool air touched her bare skin while heat simmered along the path raked by his slow, hungry gaze from the sheer, golden silk of her bikini briefs over her torso to the matching gold-on-gold, silk-and-lace bra.

Jessy had seen hungry eyes on men before, and she had never enjoyed it. But these eyes, and this man, were different. The flames that burned in Dillon's gaze lit a fire in her soul.

"Tonight you're mine," he whispered. "Only mine." He slid his hand along her back and lifted her toward him while he peeled the dress away from her shoulders with his free hand.

Trembling, Jessy laid her forehead against his chest and slipped her arms from the sleeves. A scent that was distinctly his wrapped itself around her, reminding her once again of forests primeval and man at his most basic, a blend of purity and passion.

Scooping her into his arms, Dillon pulled the dress away and dropped it onto the floor. Still holding her, he drew the quilt aside and pulled back the sheet before he stretched Jessy full-length onto the billowy center of the feather bed.

The aroma of fresh linen and sunshine rose around her, blending with the moonlit mood of the night. Dillon stood over her, looking down with a fierceness more suited to conquering than to lovemaking, but the fear that had whispered through Jessy's heart was gone.

Whether he came to her as a lover or as a warrior, it made no difference. For tonight, she trusted Dillon with an instinct beyond logic or reason. For tonight, she was his, and he would lead the way.

Hardly realizing what she did, she held out her arms to him, and in the space of a heartbeat the warrior was gone. Fabric rustled against fabric as Dillon stretched out beside her. His fingertip traced the silk strap that arched over her shoulder.

"My golden girl," he said softly, "with the kaleidoscope eyes."

The words sounded familiar. She drew in a languid breath and smiled her pleasure at his touch. "Did you read that somewhere?"

His fingertip traced her collarbone to the hollow at the base of her throat, where her heartbeat fluttered against his finger. "That layout they did a few years ago, with you dressed all in golds and yellows. Where they did those close-ups on your eyes."

She looked up at him, so close, so overpoweringly male. "That photographer liked my eyes."

The backs of his fingers stroked the length of her neck. "*I* like your eyes."

Jessy arched her neck at his touch as shivers of pleasure eddied through her. She had never imagined that something so simple could feel so wonderful, could draw her like a magnet and hold her mesmerized.

"And I like yours," she said, lost in the gaze that spoke as eloquently as any words. "Dark as midnight, shining with the fire in your soul." Her fingertips slowly drew a line from his temple down his cheek as she spoke.

"You didn't read *that* anywhere," Dillon said, turning his face into her hand.

She smiled. "I made it up myself."

"I like it." He leaned over her and kissed first one eyelid and then the other, soft, feathery kisses that were warm and sweet and loving. "I like it a lot. It makes me feel very special."

"You are special."

"For tonight, maybe. But tomorrow you'll be gone and I'll be just another memory."

Again his words pricked painfully at her happiness. "Well, don't count the heel marks on your back just yet," she said, falling back on the mild sarcasm that had defended her tender feelings so well for so many years.

Dillon laughed. "You don't think I should?"

"No." She touched his cheek. "I don't think you should."

"Ah, Jessy, Jessy," he whispered. "I'm in pain."

He gathered her into his arms and laid his leg across the top of hers. Against her thigh she could feel the pressure of a rock-hard ridge that throbbed suddenly as Dillon breathed out with a groan.

"Are you all right?" she asked hesitantly.

"Am I all right?" He laughed again. "Oh, I'm dandy." He groaned again and rolled away from her to sit up on the side of the bed. "Just let me catch my breath here a minute."

She sat up behind him and touched his arm. "Is there anything I can do?"

He glanced at her over his shoulder with one eyebrow cocked at a wry angle. "That's very funny, Jessy." He patted her hand, then drew away. "Just don't touch me for a minute while I try to locate my self-control."

"Dillon, I think there's something I should tell you." As soon as the words were out, Jessy clapped a hand to her mouth, wishing she could call them back. The last thing in the world she wanted to confess right now was her lack of experience.

"What?" he asked without turning.

His elbows on his knees, he sat hunched over with his back to her. The white ceiling and walls seemed to glow with the reflected light of the moon, but the center of the room that commanded his attention was a pool of shadows.

Jessy took refuge against the mound of pillows at the head of the bed while she gathered her courage. "I might not be quite as experienced as you seem to think."

"You think not?" He turned toward her, with the moonlight at his back and his face all but hidden. His fingertip traced a line from her shoulder to her elbow, then along the inside of her arm to her wrist.

"I think not." She struggled to keep her voice level, but the effort was hard. Ripples of excitement started in the pit of her stomach and eddied outward. With the merest touch of his hand, she no longer cared what he thought. "But it doesn't matter. I don't want your self-control, Dillon. I want *you.*"

"Jessy, I don't want to rush this."

"I've never been a patient person, Dillon." She rose slowly toward him until her face was close enough to feel the heat of his breath. With the lightest touch of her finger she stroked the tensed ridge of muscle along his jaw. "I run at life, and when I catch it I hold on with both hands until I have what I want. I'm greedy and demanding. And I want you. Like I've never wanted another man, I want you."

"You make it very hard to say no."

"Then don't."

"I don't want to scare you."

"Why would you scare me?" Her heart pounded inside her chest with the deep, steady rhythm of a kettledrum, and his hesitation only made her more determined to end the waiting.

"Maybe I wouldn't. Maybe I'm worried about nothing."

He slid one golden strap off her shoulder until it dangled against her arm. Then he guided the second one off her other shoulder. Catching the lacy top of her bra in both hands, he folded the fabric down across her breasts until they tumbled free to lie heavy, soft and warm in his open palms.

Slowly lifting one creamy mound toward him as he lowered his head, Dillon flicked his tongue over the crest, then closed his mouth over the tip, suckling gently. Jessy's breath seeped out in a sigh that was more than half moan. Her hand glided over the muscles of his shoulder. At the back of his neck her fingers interwove with the thick curtain of his hair, and she urged him closer.

Lost in the wondrous feel of flesh on flesh, tender, succulent and maddening, she caught her breath and held it, willing the moment to last. In the pit of her stomach pleasure tumbled in a messy riot, spreading wider, higher and deeper with each second that her breast was held captive by Dillon's kiss.

His mouth lifted without warning, and Jessy's fingers tightened convulsively in his hair. "No."

Her voice was a soft moan that was silenced when his lips traced a lingering path down the rounded slope of her breast, into the deep valley between and slowly climbed to the peak on the other side. With the pad of his thumb he caressed the swollen tip he had just abandoned, still aching for his return.

Jessy leaned nearer and brushed her cheek against his hair, calling his name in a husky murmur while the chaos inside her grew wilder with each second that he touched her. Shivers of desire moved lower, coursing like electric currents across her belly and down her legs while a slow, steady throb tugged at her thoughts.

"Dillon," she whispered, impatient for more.

"Yes?" He lifted his head, brushing his chin over the moist peak that was still swollen and pink from his touch. "Are you ready?" His hand left her other breast and trailed down across her ribs and stomach to slide beneath the lacy edge of her bikini briefs. "So soon?"

His fingertips ruffled through the soft mound of curls he encountered. When Jessy gasped and stiffened, Dillon smiled. Once again brushing the tender tip of her breast with his chin, he murmured, "I guess so."

Before she could recover from the first jolt his touch had produced, he moved on. Swiftly, surely, his strong fingers located the valley secreted beneath the curls. Still not hesitating, he slipped within the waiting walls, and his barest touch set her heart to hammering with a fevered rush. Unconsciously Jessy twisted away from a pleasure almost too intense to endure.

Gasping for air in a shuddering intake of breath, she dug her nails into the bed and groaned as she pushed herself higher, away from sensations that were too strong and too quick.

"Jessy." Her name floated to her like a sigh on the wind, softly soothing for the instant of reprieve that was granted while Dillon rose over her and lifted her gently with one arm while the other peeled her briefs slowly over the fullness of her hips and down the long length of her legs.

The last whisper of silk brushed over her ankles and tickled across her feet, then was gone as Dillon's hands gently closed around the backs of her thighs, lifting her legs up and apart. Kneeling over her, he released the front clasp of her bra, straightened and tugged his own shirt off. He let it fall from his hand without a glance as he raked hot, hungry eyes from her breasts downward to the tenderest depths that lay open and unguarded before him.

Inside Jessy, the pulsing rhythms that had slowed to an almost sane pace began to accelerate. Each time he touched her, the feelings grew more intense. Each new sensation was so much more than she had imagined. Already Dillon had brought her to heights she never knew existed, and yet she knew he had only begun.

In him now she could sense the calm, the control he had been striving for, the same control she had long ago cast aside, trusting in Dillon to guide her safely through the waters that were so deep, so terrifying and so wildly wonderful that at times she longed to run away rather than endure the intense, torturous pleasure another instant.

The waiting ended with a suddenness that was dizzying as Dillon's kiss teased at the satiny softness at the base of Jessy's thigh. Hardly believing that such a simple touch could feel so dangerously wonderful, she gasped and surrendered what small grain of reason was left, while the delicious probing moved deeper, delving into the unexplored coves of her body that were as large a mystery to her as to him.

Sanity fled into a swirling, pulsating ecstasy that dipped and soared through an endless range of peaks and valleys before Jessy finally dropped out of the heavens to fall to earth as Dillon gathered her into his arms and held her tight against him.

His heart pounding in her ear while her cheek rested on the sweat-slick cushion of his chest, she realized that so far everything had been for her. The real lovemaking in its truest and most permanent sense had yet to begin, and already she knew that leaving him tomorrow would be the hardest thing she'd ever done in her life. But she knew, as well, that if she could have only one man in her lifetime, it would be Dillon.

Like a man emerging from a trance, he brushed his cheek over her hair and held her tighter. "You're so unbearably sweet," he said in a voice husky with desire. "Like a flower blossoming just for me." He pressed a kiss against her brow. "Are you always this responsive?"

"No."

"Ah, Jessy, I wish I could believe you." His hand stroked her arm while his lips sought hers. "But thank you for lying."

His crushing kiss drove all thought of argument from her mind. It didn't matter what he believed. All that mattered was that tonight she was his, and she would always be his in a way that nothing could ever change.

His hand left her arm to briefly caress her breast and then move lower to stroke the gentle rise of her stomach, the tender inner flesh of her thigh, and finally that hidden part of her that instantly rekindled a fiery need in them both.

Casting aside his hard-won patience, Dillon rolled away from her, unzipping his jeans as he rose from the bed and stripping them away in one smooth, unbroken movement. When he turned back, Jessy moaned softly at a sight that had never moved her to such emotion before.

Flagrantly aroused, Dillon returned to the bed beside her. Even as she reached toward him, his hand caught hers and guided her to him. Secret desires stirred. Promised pleasures beckoned. Images of a warrior lover sprang to life once again as a shiver of longing for the unknown swept over Jessy more powerfully than ever.

With a groan Dillon moved her hand away. When he rolled to the side she was treated to the sight of sleek, firmly muscled flanks with a natural tan. The muscles of his back flexed and rippled beneath caramel skin so silky smooth that it drew her hand with an irresistible urge.

Her fingers stroked the hollow of his spine as she heard the muffled sound of a drawer opening and closing beside the bed. Dillon turned back toward her, catching her hand as it slid over his ribs and lifting it to his lips. He pressed a kiss in the center of her palm, then lowered her hand and placed a flat disk of rubber in her open hand. Around the outside was a rim like the edge of a balloon and in the middle was a mini mountain peak.

Puzzled, she stared at the gift, then lifted round, wondering eyes to him as he slowly lowered his lips to hers in a deep, searching kiss. Opening and offering himself to her with a vulnerability that left her as shaken as the wildest flights of passion had, Dillon gently broke off from the kiss to guide her hand once again to the rigid staff that waited so impatiently.

Swimming in waters that were clearly out of her depth, Jessy let him set the pace and only hoped that she wouldn't give herself away as Dillon folded his fingers around hers and lowered her hand over and past the swollen glans that jerked at her touch. Releasing his breath in a long, shuddering sigh, he cupped her fingers around the hardened shaft beneath and smoothed her hand along with the unfolding rubber ring down the impressive length.

Almost faint with the knowledge of what was to come, Jessy lay limply against the pillows behind her when Dillon released her hand and raised himself over her. Having already experienced more than she had ever imagined, she gazed at the ensheathed appendage that hovered just above her and felt the first fluttering sense of power that was part of being a woman.

As much as she wanted him, he wanted her in equal measure. As badly as she ached for him, he ached for her, as well. And while her desire was a secret nurtured deep within her, his was a blatant proclamation that shouted his need for the world to see.

"Ah, Dillon." She released his name in a sigh that shimmered with banked passion. "Please." Desire so strong it was almost a pain swept through her. Any moment she might die of longing.

At the threshold he paused, and she pressed herself toward him. "Now," she urged.

"Slowly," he answered, soft as a whisper while he slipped inside as slowly as he promised.

Jessy could feel herself spreading to wrap around him, each second filled with pleasures deliciously new as he crept deeper with a patience that savored each instant. When he reached the unbroken barrier, pain sharp and unexpected sliced through her.

Against her will she gasped and Dillon stopped still as a statue. His eyes narrowed and the lines in his face grew hard and unforgiving. He pressed against the barrier again, and again Jessy's quick intake of breath was a signal of something gone wrong.

"It's impossible." His voice was stony.

"Please." She pressed harder. As much as it hurt to continue, to stop would hurt more. She had waited a lifetime for him, and she refused to wait one day more.

"No."

He tried to withdraw, but Jessy caught him, pulling him deeper with all her strength.

"I want you," she whispered.

"This is wrong." The cold stone of his expression turned to desperation, and again he tried to withdraw.

"I won't let you." She locked her legs behind his and held him imprisoned in a standoff. Each time he moved she tightened her hold, urging him deeper into the bittersweet ecstasy that held them both captive.

"God, Jessy, no," he gasped one last time, but she could see in his eyes that he wouldn't stop.

As much as he wished he could, Dillon wanted her with the same blind desire that drove her on, and with a final angry thrust, he gave in to the need that tormented them both. Jessy cried out in pain and triumph, and Dillon leaned closer, capturing her face between his hands.

"Damn you," he whispered as his mouth covered hers with unsated passion. He lay still within her, his body taut atop hers, while his kiss plundered with a savagery that left her breathless and aching for more.

When Jessy moved under him, urging him on, Dillon broke off his kiss. "You lied to me," he rasped, still holding her face in his hands.

"You never asked," she whispered. Her fingers stroked the quivering muscles of his back. Moving down over his flanks, her hands tightened and pulled him closer as she arched her body toward him.

"It shouldn't have been like this." Blindly he followed the urging of her hands. "I should have known." Thrusting deeper, he withdrew slowly, breathing in as he braced his hands to the side of her and rose higher. He thrust again, and his whole body trembled as he gasped her name and froze. But it was too late to stop.

The tremors that shook him went on and on, building until he gave in to them finally and, with an angry cry, plunged deeper still only to withdraw and return in a steady, relentless rhythm that grew faster with each thrust, carrying Jessy with him to a peak so high and wild she thought they must have reached the ends of the earth, a place where no man had gone before, a place that was theirs alone for an eternity.

She cried out as Dillon took her in his arms and held her and together they tumbled to earth in a long, soaring free-fall. And when they touched down, he rolled away.

Throwing his arm across his eyes, he whispered sadly, "Jessy, what have you done to me?"

## Chapter Nine

Still reeling from the emotional chaos set loose inside her, Jessy turned away and pulled the covers over her shoulder. She had never felt more alone in her life.

This was the moment when she should be telling Dillon how much she loved him while he held her in his arms and professed his undying devotion. Instead, her most cherished hopes and dreams had been fulfilled and then trampled in a matter of minutes.

"You're a virgin?" Dillon couldn't have sounded more dismayed if he'd just found out she was an international terrorist.

"I *was*." She tucked the quilt under her chin and stared at the wall with a sadness she couldn't let him see. "The last time I checked, it wasn't a crime."

"I don't know whether to laugh or cry."

"Neither do I." But she knew what she wanted to do. She wanted to hit him as hard as she could and then scream with frustration. This wasn't the way it was supposed to be.

"You should have told me." The bed squeaked loudly as he shoved himself upright and swung his legs over the side.

"Why?" Turning her head, she watched him over her shoulder. Light still poured in through the open doorway downstairs, and a night as cold as any winter came with it.

"Why?" Dillon whirled and glared at her. "Why? Because I'm the man making love to you, and I have a right to know. Did it ever occur to you that it might have made a difference to me?"

"I stopped telling men I was a virgin a long time ago. I didn't like the reactions I got."

"So you just let me go on thinking that you were..."

"A woman of experience?" Jessy supplied when he seemed lost for words. She turned toward him and rose up onto her elbow. "I thought that was why you wanted me, Dillon."

He leaned toward her and caught her by the shoulder, pulling her closer. "Maybe I did. Maybe I was wrong. But you still should have told me. I could have made it better for you, better for both of us. The first time should be special."

"It was—" She caught herself just before she told him the truth, that it was wonderful, that he was everything she'd ever hoped. It wasn't until he'd tossed her aside at the end that the moment was shattered. "It was just fine, thank you."

"All right, then," he said angrily while the hand on her arm tightened. "*I* had a right to know. I'm not some stud you hired for the night, you know. I've got feelings involved here, too."

"Do you?" she asked coldly.

Still stinging from the pain of his rejection, Jessy tried to pull away, but he wouldn't let her go. She could feel tension between them building to a battle pitch, but her feelings were too close to the surface and running out of control. She hadn't stopped to consider the emotional impact that making love to Dillon would have on her, and now it was too late.

All she wanted was to stay here with him, in his arms while her head rested on his shoulder, until the end of time. All she wanted was what she couldn't have, and there was nothing left inside her but anger and a sadness that dragged at her heart.

"Yes!" Dillon shouted, giving her arm a shake. "And they're some damned confused feelings at the moment, thanks to you. Just tell me why. Why now? Why me?"

Sadness won over anger as she gazed into his eyes, dark as night and burning with ancient fires. She longed to tell him that something about him touched her soul, that she was more than half in love with him even though she knew it was doomed and, most of all, that he ignited a need in her that was too strong to fight, and whatever this night cost her she would never be sorry.

Instead, she said, "You're a passionate man, Dillon. Everything you do, you do with all your heart. I wanted that kind of passion my first time, and I wanted a man with experience."

If her arm had been a hot poker, he couldn't have released her faster. Drawing away, he straightened until his face was cast in shadows. "Maybe I'm wrong," Dillon said coldly. "Maybe I *am* just a stud you hired for the night. What's my payoff, Jessy?"

"I think you made that perfectly clear," she answered, refusing to cower before his anger. "For you I'm nothing but a fantasy fulfillment. You wanted me as much as I wanted you, Dillon, and your reasons were just as questionable."

"Did you get what you wanted?"

"You were everything I'd hoped for."

"You know, Jessy," he said in a voice that was much softer as he leaned toward her once again. "If I believed half of what you were saying, I'd be one angry man."

The seduction in his tone was a potent antidote to her embattled emotions. "You don't believe me?" she challenged with a show of ire that was nothing more than a cover-up.

"Oh, I believe part of it. But I can't be the first man you've met who turned you on. So again I ask, why me?"

He paused while his coal black eyes searched hers for an answer. Defiantly Jessy returned his gaze, daring him to find the truth that was too frightening for her to confess— that she loved him. Unreasonably, foolishly, she had given herself to him out of love, and she would rather throw herself into an open fire than to admit it to him now.

The longer Dillon searched her eyes, the colder his gaze became until finally, as if he had found his answer and didn't like what he'd found, he recoiled. When he spoke again, the words were more embittered than ever.

"Is it because of Stephen?" He took her by the shoulder and shook her with each angry word. "Do you *want* him to find out about what happened between us tonight? To know that what he passed up all those years ago, you gave to me?"

Too surprised to sustain her anger, Jessy drew back and stared at Dillon as if he'd grown an extra head. "Stephen? I haven't thought about Stephen in days. Why can't you just forget about him?"

"Maybe it's because he's the reason you're here. And unless I miss my guess, he's the reason you were still a virgin. Because if you couldn't have Stephen, you didn't want anybody." Dillon drew her closer, until they were almost touching as he whispered, "Until you realized you could have his brother-in-law, and then what, Jessy?" He shook her again, as if he could make the admission come tumbling out. "Make sure Stephen finds out about it?"

Angry as Dillon was, Jessy could see the hurt he tried to hide, and she realized that she would have to tell him the truth, at least as much of it as she dared to reveal.

"Oh, Dillon, you don't know how wrong you are," she said quietly. "Stephen has nothing to do with this, with *us*. I chose you because there's something—" she searched for words before hurrying on "—something wild and un-tamed about you, something pagan." She touched his face. "I could see it in your eyes the day we met. I could feel it in your pride and your defiance. And I knew it would be there when—" her voice faltered, and she finished in a husky whisper "—when we made love."

The covers slid away and Dillon pulled her hard against him. She could feel the beating of his heart next to hers.

"Jessy." Her name was barely more than a strangled cry.

"I recognized it, because it's in me, too," she mur-mured as she pressed her lips to his fevered skin, wanting to finish before her courage failed her. "I've tried to tame that part of me my whole life, but it wouldn't go away. Now I know why. It was looking for you."

"Jessy." He rolled, pinning her beneath him as he kissed her hair, her eyes, her throat.

"I'm tired of talking, Dillon."

"Ah, Jessy." His lips grazed her breast. "You're like a fire in my blood. I can't get enough of you."

She caught his face between her hands. "Shh. Love me, darling," she whispered while her mouth hungrily sought his. "Just for tonight, love me like there's no tomorrow."

If the first time had been an awakening that stirred her to the depths of her soul, the next was a celebration of pas-sion lifted to the heavens and set free to soar. In Dillon she found her mate, her match, her fulfillment. In his arms there was no shame, no fear, no hesitation.

When dawn's first, silent light crept through the down-stairs and slowly climbed the narrow staircase to the loft, Jessy watched with eyes that had kept a vigil through the night. She rubbed her cheek against Dillon's bare shoul-der. Her breasts nuzzled his ribs. Her legs were entwined with his.

They had spent the night making love, and still she ached for him. They came from two different worlds that should never have met, but she didn't care. They were wrong for each other, and any hope for a future was doomed before it started, but she would give anything to hold back the dawn just a little longer.

When Dillon's arms tightened around her, Jessy realized that he was awake and had probably been awake, just like her.

"The night was too short," he said quietly.

"Yes." Sorrow burned in her throat, but she couldn't give in to it. She didn't want his sympathy. She didn't want false promises. She had made her bargain with herself and she would live by it.

"I wish I had more to offer you right now."

"I'm not asking for anything." She knew then that however he felt, he wouldn't say the words she was longing to hear, and all the feelings she had would stay locked inside her.

"I don't know when I'll see you again." His finger toyed with a lock of her hair. His hand stroked the soft skin of her arm while his words held her away. "I have commitments all through the holidays. It may be after the first of the year before I'm back in Austin for any length of time."

"I'm not there all that often myself. My assignments take me to a lot of other places." She ran her hand down the muscled contours of his chest and into the hollow at the center of his stomach, storing up memories for all the nights to come. "If I'm gone, my answering service takes my calls."

"So I can always get hold of you, one way or another."

"One way or another." Jessy withdrew her hand and steeled her heart for the parting that was inevitable.

"That's good, then. Maybe after the first of the year we can get together again." His voice didn't hold out much hope.

"Maybe." She pulled away and sprang from the bed to gather her scattered clothing. "But you'll have to catch me before the spring shows start."

"With schedules like ours, I guess it's amazing we could ever get together in the first place."

"Maybe it was just destiny." Her heart pounding inside her chest, Jessy turned away to hide the telltale trembling of her chin. She had never dreamed the fabled morning after could be excruciatingly awful.

Dillon followed her from the bed and caught her hand. "Then maybe destiny will smile on us again." He pulled her against him, pinning her clothes-laden arm behind her back and holding it there with his hand. "I'm going to miss you, Jessy Carder. I'm going to miss you like crazy."

Barely able to breathe through the pain tearing at her, Jessy lowered her gaze to his shoulder. "This isn't going to be easy for me, Dillon. Please don't make it any harder."

"There you go acting tough again," he said in the deep, silken tones that could melt her in seconds. "I bet if I scratched the surface I'd find that same sweet, soft marshmallow interior."

She stiffened, fighting the emotions he could set loose so easily. "Maybe. But that wouldn't do either one of us any good, would it? I still have to catch a plane this morning, and we still don't know when we'll see each other again."

"Do you want to see me again?"

The part of her that longed for miracles cried out, *yes, yes, yes.*

"I don't know," she said instead, reminding herself that clean cuts hurt less and healed faster. One night was the bargain she had made with herself. If she saw him again, the second parting would only be worse. "I really don't know." Still arguing with herself, and losing steadily, she added, "But I think I might."

"I think I might like that, too."

Though their parting at the cabin ended with a note of hope, the trip to the airport was largely silent, as if they had said their goodbyes and were afraid to disturb the still waters they had achieved.

Even Dillon's final kiss before she boarded the plane was distant and restrained, though his eyes, in the last glimpse she had of him, were burning with a fire as hot as any she had seen.

If their last moments together were a silent agony, the next two months for Jessy weren't much better. Thanksgiving was spent in Savannah with her brother Houston and his wife, Laura; Christmas in Dallas with her parents, her other two brothers and their families; and New Year's in quiet little Eden, Texas, with her very pregnant twin, Rebecca, and Rebecca's very happy husband, Cody.

Jessy stayed on the go steadily, throwing herself into her work with an enthusiasm she hadn't shown in years; baffling the people who knew and loved her with her sudden need for family togetherness; and doing everything in her power to forget the man who had waved goodbye to her at the airport in San Miguel and then disappeared from her life without a backward glance.

In early January on a sunny day in romantic San Antonio, Jessy finally stood still for too long, and her sorrow overtook her. She had found the man who was everything she had ever wanted, and she had let him go without a fight.

"Jessy, dearie, yoo-hoo."

Jessy looked up to find Bradley, the photographer on the shoot, waving to her.

"You're supposed to be happy, sweetheart," he called. "You want to try smiling for the camera?"

"Sorry, Brad." She shook herself, tossing her hair in the wind. Then she spread her arms wide and twirled.

When she came to a halt facing the camera, a brilliant smile lit her face. It was springtime. She was happy. She was in love. With each twist and turn of her body she enticed the camera, flirting with the unseen lover behind the lens, until finally Bradley released her. "That's great, Jessy. You can go change now."

Relieved to shed the phony happy face, Jessy turned away and started toward the empty shop that was their changing room for the day. Emotionally drained, she kept her eyes downcast, wrapped in her own private sadness, and almost tripped over the man in front of her before she saw him.

He reached out to steady her, his strong hands catching her by the shoulders and holding her even as she began to pull away. "I didn't mean to startle you."

The voice was one she would never forget. Too happy to be surprised, Jessy lifted her unbelieving gaze to Dillon's face.

"I hope I haven't come at a bad time," he said. "Your answering service told me where you'd be."

"Are you in San Antonio on business?"

"The only business I have here is you."

"Me?"

"I'm not going to lie to you, Jessy. I tried to forget you. I tried damned hard, but it just didn't work. How about you? Are you glad to see me?"

"Well, I was." She frowned, less than flattered by his statement. "Now I'm not so sure."

"One thing I'll never do is lie to you."

"Well, thanks, but do you have to be so brutally honest? I just can't imagine a politician who hasn't learned the art of sugarcoating."

"It was never an art I cared to know. Are you glad I'm here?"

"Yes."

"That makes me very happy." A slow smile accompanied his words. "Because I thought I was going to die if I had to go another day without seeing you."

His hand slid around her waist and tightened. In his eyes was the suppressed passion of a man about to ignite. His lips parted and Jessy could almost feel his kiss.

"You're a very difficult man," she whispered as she felt herself melt toward him.

"Jessy, dear, we need you." Flora, the editor in charge of the shoot, stood in the door of the store with a dress in her hand. She lifted the dress toward Jessy and shook it. "Please?"

With effort, Jessy stepped back from Dillon. "Duty calls."

"Mind if I stay around and watch until you're through?"

"You may get pretty bored."

"I don't think so." Reluctantly he released her hand, then watched until she disappeared inside.

"I don't believe I've seen him before," Flora said as she unzipped the back of Jessy's dress and handed her the next one. "Is he a model?"

"No."

"Well, he should be. He's gorgeous. Do you think he'd consider it?"

Jessy grinned. "You could always ask him."

"Hurry it up, Jessy," called a harried voice from the doorway. "Bradley's ready for you again."

Slipping into shoes to match the new dress, Jessy moved to the mirror and added the earrings and necklace laid out for her. Then she flew out of the store and across the brick walkway where Bradley waited impatiently.

"Sorry, Bradley, dear." Taking her place in front of the camera with a smile that was anything but apologetic, Jessy let her imagination take flight at the thought of Flora asking Dillon to pose. His possible reactions kept Jessy smiling with delight until Bradley dismissed her once again and she looked around to discover that Dillon was nowhere in sight. About to go in search of him, she was stopped by Flora.

"Hurry. I've got something brand-new I want you to try on next."

"Okay," Jessy answered absentmindedly while she craned her neck for a glimpse of Dillon amid the crowd gathered to watch. "I'll be there in just a minute."

"Oh, no, you don't." Flora caught Jessy by the arm and dragged her toward the changing room. "Bradley's setting up for the shot now. We've got to hurry."

"But—"

"No buts. This is something very special, and I don't want you to argue. Just trust me, dear. If this comes off, it'll be the showpiece of the layout."

Inside the shop Jessy looked hard at Flora and could almost see the canary feather at the corner of her contented-cat smile. The word *Dillon* flashed in Jessy's mind, but she pushed it aside. Flora was a fast talker, but no one could be fast enough to talk Dillon into something as frivolous as being an impromptu male model in a spring fashion layout. He didn't have that kind of vanity, and his career certainly didn't need that kind of attention, not when his reputation was based on his defense of the common man and the underprivileged.

All the while Jessy argued with herself, her makeup was being heightened for dramatic effect while her hair was being twirled, curled and poufed into a lion's mane of tawny gold and burnished brown. Looking into the mirror, even she had to admit she looked gorgeous, if slightly untamed.

The evening dress, when Flora presented it, was as striking as the look they had chosen for Jessy. Shimmering gold satin, it followed every curve, hollow and nuance of her body like a sensuous second skin.

"Are you sure about this, Flora?" Jessy stared into the mirror, almost embarrassed by the opulence that looked back at her.

"Jessy, dear." Flora frowned, about to say something. Then she patted Jessy's arm. "Oh, Jessy, dear. Just go with it, honey."

Taking a deep breath, Jessy put her own preference for modesty firmly behind her and turned to face the sunlight and the gawking onlookers in a dress that was meant for moonlight and a lover's eyes. Gasps and a smattering of applause arose from the spectators when she stepped out. Jessy acknowledged the crowd's greeting with a good-natured smile and a nod, but quickly returned her gaze to the ground in front of her.

Underneath the air of bravura she had cultivated since childhood was a basic shyness she had never overcome. At times like these, that shyness made her long to run and hide. She had never let herself give in to the fear that sometimes engulfed her, but it was always there, and some, Flora among them, had guessed Jessy's secret long ago, working with her as much as they could and seldom pushing her into the kind of public spotlight she was in at the moment.

"Jessy."

At the sound of Dillon's voice Jessy lifted her eyes in search of the man himself. She found him a few yards away, leaning against a tree, dressed in a tuxedo he hadn't been wearing earlier, his raven hair styled to rakish perfection. His smile beckoned with a secret that was theirs alone.

As she walked toward him the camera began to click, but she heard it only as an afterthought. When she was almost within reach, Dillon peeled away from the tree trunk with the grace of a jungle cat and held out his hand to her. At the touch of his fingertips, an electric current sizzled through Jessy, awakening memories that she had almost convinced herself were only her imagination.

Nothing could feel the way she remembered feeling with him. Nothing could be that wonderful.

His hand closed around hers and pulled her nearer. As his arm surrounded her waist, Jessy gazed into his ebony eyes with awe she didn't even try to hide.

"How did she talk you into it?" she asked.

"She agreed to let me work with you, and to give me a copy of the prints."

"Are you sure it's wise for you to be doing this?"

"Wise?" Dillon threw back his head and laughed as music swelled around them. "No." His voice dropped to a seductive whisper while his arm tightened possessively around her. "This isn't wise at all."

Ignoring everything but her, Dillon led Jessy to the open courtyard in front of the fountain. A reckless light burned in his eyes as he swept her with him into an exhilarating dance of gracefully swirling circles. "You're my fantasy, remember?" he asked softly. "And a man shouldn't take it lightly when his dreams come true."

More moved than she wanted to be by his words, Jessy smiled flirtatiously, playing more to him than to the camera that followed their every move. "*This* is a fantasy?"

"A prelude." His voice carried promises for her ears only. "The real fantasies will be fulfilled later tonight, unless you disagree."

At the thought of what his words meant, she closed her eyes and swayed toward him, her legs suddenly unsteady under her while images of passion played across her mind.

Dillon caught her against him and stopped the dance as he looked down at her with longing. "I'll take that as a yes."

His breath brushed her cheek in an intimate promise of things yet to come. Jessy's eyes opened again to gaze up at him in wonder. "I thought I'd never see you again," she said.

"I couldn't help myself. I'd have come looking for you sooner, but I was too busy to spare the time." Without loosening his hold he began to move again, a slow sway that followed the rhythm of the music and allowed him to feel the lush pressure of her body against his.

"That morning I left," Jessy said slowly, "when you said goodbye at the airport, you weren't planning to see me again, were you?"

"No." In case she tried to pull away, Dillon tightened his hold on her until he could say his piece. "From the beginning I had planned to sleep with you, get you out of my system and move on.''

''Why didn't you?'' She wanted to be angry, and she might have been if her own feelings hadn't been so similar.

''Because it was a stupid idea. You have to understand, Jessy, that for almost ten years I had compared every woman I met to this image I had of you, and you trounced them all. No one was as beautiful. No one was as exciting. No one was as seductive. I mean, look at you.''

Holding her hand, he stepped back and twirled her around, releasing her when she came to a stop facing him. From the cinnamon-and-gold streaks in her honey brown hair to her amber-and-gold eyes to her ripe lips to the body that could make the simplest dress sinful, she was a woman custom-made to drive the sanest man wild.

''What man in his right mind would walk away from a woman like you? I must have been crazy.''

''Maybe you were thinking the same thing I was.'' Jessy walked back into his arms and they resumed the slow dance that was nothing more than an excuse to touch. ''Run while you still can.''

''I don't want to run anymore. One night with you wasn't enough. I don't know what will be.'' He brushed his mouth over hers and whispered, ''Do you think we've done this long enough?''

Forgetting the camera totally, Jessy wrapped her arms around his shoulders and captured his lips in a kiss filled with two months of hunger and longing. Dillon's throaty growl echoed her feelings as he lifted her into the air and molded her body to his. Abandoning caution and restraint, they clung to each other for long passionate minutes while their kiss went from hot to molten, and finally, from lack of air, they parted reluctantly.

''I think that's a wrap,'' Jessy said breathlessly.

His arm around her, they turned and walked slowly to the storefront while Bradley followed, clicking away until the last possible moment. As the doors closed behind them, shutting out the public, Flora swooped in to separate them.

"Okay, let's get you out of those clothes." She pushed Dillon in one direction and Jessy in the other. "Then you're free to go."

Jessy stopped. "I'm through?"

"You're through," Flora said with a nod toward Dillon. "He drives a hard bargain. But it was worth it. If those pictures pack half the heat you two were giving off, they'll be sensational." She moved closer and put her hand on Jessy's arm. "You've been holding out on me, dear. This one looks serious. Be careful, little one. A man like this one could be a real heartbreaker."

"I know, Flora." Jessy patted the motherly hand that lay on her arm. "Believe me, I know."

Without opening her eyes, Jessy lay in the semidarkness and felt the breeze from the open balcony door graze across her skin. From the knees down, her legs entwined with Dillon's. Her arm draped across his torso. His arm lay over hers while his hand rested on her back, holding her close even in his sleep.

With each breath he took, she felt the sigh of air brush across her face and smiled at the thought that they had slept this way for most of the night. For the past month they had been nearly inseparable, spending every free hour of the day together, and sleeping wrapped in each other's arms at night. And the longer they were together, the more complete she felt.

Jessy stroked her hand over the muscle that ran the length of Dillon's back. Her fingertips brushed the hollow of his spine. She loved the warm, satiny feel of his skin against her palm. She loved the solid, muscled strength of him next to her in the quiet, waking moments of the day. Each morning was like a miracle that might never come again.

"I love it when you do that," Dillon said softly.

Jessy opened her eyes and saw him just inches away. "What?"

"Wake up smiling like that. Every morning when I open my eyes, you have a smile on your face." He traced the curve of her jaw, then retraced it toward her mouth. "It makes me feel good. Like maybe I had a little to do with putting it there."

"Maybe you did."

"Your eyes are a tawny color this morning." He brushed the gold-dusted tips of her dark eyelashes.

"That means I'm happy."

"They change colors with your moods?" His voice was still soft and sleepy.

She smiled. "Brown when I'm worried and taupe when I'm sad."

"And when you're angry?"

"Hmm? I'm not sure. Deep hazel, maybe?"

He nodded in agreement. "Like warm cinnamon, with gold flecks."

"And your eyes…" She touched the black, arching brow above one eye. "They can turn as dark as a starless night." Her finger trailed down his temple and across the high, prominent cheekbone that added so much to the pride and strength in his face.

Dillon growled deep in his throat as he caught her finger and brought it to his mouth. Drawing just the fingertip inside, he traced its circumference with his tongue and suckled gently. Jessy moaned and snuggled closer. Then, unable to endure the shivers of pleasure any longer, she withdrew her finger from the soft succulence of his kiss.

He smiled and tightened his arm around her. "I hate to get up. You feel so good." Sliding his leg higher between hers, he lowered his gaze to where her bare breasts were crushed against his chest.

"I'm free today," Jessy offered.

He closed his eyes with regret. "I'm not. I've got meetings scheduled all day, but I'll try to get home early."

"I'll have dinner ready."

"If it's another salad, could you at least make it a chef salad?"

Jessy laughed at his plaintive tone and snuggled closer. "We're having baked chicken with new potatoes, steamed broccoli and glazed carrots. And I'm not all that bad a cook when I have the time to do it."

"You'd better be careful. You're in danger of becoming too perfect."

"What happens then?"

Dillon ran his fingers through her hair and brushed his lips roughly over hers. "All kinds of things you never planned on."

"That sounds dangerous."

"For both of us. But it might be fun."

Lying there with her body molded to his, his lips nibbling at hers while he talked of a future she had never dared to dream of, Jessy stopped pretending to herself that she wasn't crazy in love with him—wildly, deliriously swept off her feet and aching with every fiber of her being to spend the rest of her life with him.

Only yesterday they had lingered in bed, talking and cuddling, until his kisses had grown serious and his hands had begun to roam. They had both been late for work and totally unrepentant. When Dillon's hand smoothed over the curve of her waist and began to climb the rounded swell of her hips, Jessy released another sigh, luxuriating in the feel of his hand on her skin and in the memory of how quickly such a small caress could escalate.

"You know," Dillon said softly, "I lie awake at night sometimes just to watch you sleep. I still can't believe I'm the one here with you."

In that moment she wanted desperately to tell him how she felt, to confess her love and her fears and to have him brush away her doubts with a wave of his hand while he told her that he loved her, as well. Her thoughts hovered at the tip of her tongue an instant too long, and the sudden, harsh ring of the telephone jarred her back to reality.

Automatically Jessy turned toward the bedside phone, but Dillon caught her hand.

"Don't answer."

"But it could be work."

"Let the machine get it. You can call them back later."

"All right." She rested her head on his shoulder while she listened to her recorded voice answering in the next room. Dillon's own messages stacked up on the answering machine in his apartment, which he checked once in the evening and once in the morning before going to his office. They both put their professional lives on the back burner during the few brief hours they had together each day.

"Jessy, this is Lillian." The muffled voice leaving a message carried into the bedroom from the living room. "Miss M's is putting out a new catalog, and they've requested you. Give me a call, and let me know if you're interested."

"Miss M's," Dillon said into the silence after the machine clicked off. "Isn't that..."

"Lingerie," Jessy said when he paused. Very sexy, very expensive lingerie. It had never been her favorite work, and with each year that passed it became less so—but it was the work that had helped pay the bills during the lean years when her healthy curves hadn't been so popular.

Dillon made a huffing sound deep in his throat and then grew silent, while his body stiffened and a frown gathered across his brow. Jessy could feel his mind moving farther and farther away from her until finally she broke the silence.

"Dillon? Is something wrong?"

"Are you going to take it?"

"I don't know." She didn't want to. She was getting tired of the whole business, especially of parading around in her underwear, but it was how she made her living.

"Do you need it? This one assignment, I mean. Do you need the money from it?"

"Not particularly. I've got lots of other offers coming in right now."

Dillon drew her against him. His cheek brushed her hair as he whispered, "Don't do it."

As pleased as she was surprised and totally mystified as to why, Jessy tilted her head back to stare up at him. "Do you really care?"

"Yes."

"Why?"

"Maybe jealousy isn't an emotion to be proud of," he said as his hand closed around her breast. Cupping the firm weight in his palm while his thumb stroked possessively over the crest, he continued, "And maybe it's just my machismo showing, but I don't want other men looking at you like that. Not while I'm the man sleeping with you."

Uncertain whether she felt flattered or hemmed in by his request, Jessy hesitated. "I don't know. Miss M's was asking for me when other people weren't."

"I'm not asking you to give up the way you make your living, Jessy. Just moderate it a little. If it upsets you that I feel this way, I'm sorry, but I can't help the way I am. I'm a possessive man when I care about something, and I care about you. A great deal."

Still not sure if she was making the right decision, Jessy ran her fingers through his hair. The thick black strands were like silk against her skin. She had never loved him more. "Oh, well, it would have taken me out of town, anyway."

He raked her lips with his. "I warned you that I could be a selfish man when it came to the things I wanted."

She tightened her grip on his hair and drew back far enough to look into his eyes. "Just remember to *ask* for the things you want, because I won't be ordered around. I wouldn't stand for it as a child, and I for damn sure won't stand for it now."

Dillon smiled. "My amber-eyed firebrand. Did I make you angry?"

"Almost."

"We both have a lot to get used to, Jessy. You have to get used to a man who takes command without asking permission. And I have to get used to caring for someone else more than I've ever cared before. I want to keep you all to myself, and I can't. Be patient with me."

"I think I can do that."

"I want to make love to you."

"You'll be late."

"I know, and my first appointment is with my grandfather."

Moved to surprise even through the haze of longing Dillon had aroused in her, Jessy frowned. "What does he want?"

"I don't know, but the only time I hear from him is when he's after something."

"Maybe you should go, then."

He brushed the tip of his nose against hers, obviously in no hurry. "Don't you think powerful men should learn patience just the same as other men?"

Jessy laughed. "I think you're as bad as I am about not wanting to jump through anyone else's hoop."

"I think I might be worse." With a sigh he lay back on his pillow and glared at the ceiling. "But yesterday my aide said if I was late one more time he was going to demand your phone number so he could call and roust me out of bed in the mornings."

She rolled over onto her stomach, shoulder to shoulder with Dillon, and propped herself up on her elbows. "Have you told him about me?"

"He knows there is someone, and he knows I'm breaking my pattern, but he doesn't know who you are. Yet."

"Pattern? What do you mean by pattern?"

He wrapped a lock of her hair around his finger, toying with it as he idly brushed his knuckle against the tender skin of her shoulder. "Casual. Short-term. Multiple."

"One-night stands?"

"No." He laughed softly. "That would mean I slept with them all, and I didn't. I just dated them."

"You slept with *some* of them."

"Well, of course, Jessy. I'm a man." He ran his finger down the curve of her throat. "As I'm sure you've noticed. I slept with a lot of them, but never for more than a week or two before I broke it off. And the women I've been seen with off and on for years, I've never slept with."

"Like Melissa Harkin?"

"No, I slept with Melissa. That's why I quit seeing her. I've never given any woman reason to believe there was a commitment where there was none."

His answer brought an unexpected stab of jealousy mingled with a sudden blossoming of hope. "And now you're breaking this pattern?" She almost held her breath, waiting for his answer.

"I've never spent the time with anyone else that I spend with you. I've never all but moved in with anyone before. I've never seen anyone else exclusively, in or out of bed. I've never forgotten appointments or come dragging in an hour late for anyone, *ever*. The list goes on, and everyone's beginning to notice. Pretty soon the world is going to find out about us, and they're going to come knocking on your door." He touched her cheek and brushed the pad of his thumb over the curve of her lips. "How are you going to feel about that, Jessy?"

Mesmerized by his litany, she realized that he had come closer to professing his love than she had ever hoped, and possibly closer than he ever would again, at least for a long time.

"I don't care who knows. Besides, we're just two people. What does the world care about us, anyway?"

"I hope you're right. And if you're not, I hope you can take the heat."

"How bad could it be?" she asked, confident that neither one of them had anything to hide.

Dillon closed his eyes and concentrated, then slowly reeled off the worst headline he could conjure. "Crusader legislator caught in love nest with pinup model."

The picture wasn't a flattering one, and it stirred old memories. Jessy sat straight up in bed as the image of a seductive, midday dance flashed through her mind. "Oh, Dillon! We forgot about San Antonio. Those pictures are going to be out in next month's issue."

He crossed his hands behind his head and shrugged. "So maybe that wasn't one of my better ideas. But they'll probably know before then, anyway. I heard there's a society columnist who's been snooping around."

"But why?"

"I'm in the public eye. I'm a bachelor. My grandfather's Harlan Siddons."

All the reasons made sense. She remembered vividly the write-ups she'd seen in the past, when Dillon Ruiz was just a name to her and nothing more. "Power, money, looks and a promising future," she quoted.

It had been enough to land Dillon on the Texas most-eligible-bachelor list for as many years as he had been in office. It was enough to keep him in the kind of inquisitive spotlight she had never had to endure.

"It's all just a bunch of crap, but it makes great copy."

"Not the looks part." She stretched out next to him, as content as a cat basking in the sun so long as she was with him. "You definitely have the looks."

Dillon looked down at her and smiled, but it faded quickly. "I hope you don't regret getting involved with me, Jessy. If I'd known the truth about you in the beginning, I would never have pursued you the way I did."

At his words, cold fear crept in around her heart, reminding her once again just how tenuous her bond with Dillon was. Any day now he could tire of her and disappear from her life the way he had with countless other women, pattern or no pattern.

"I don't know if I like the sound of that," she said with a breathlessness she couldn't control.

"I thought you were sophisticated. Experienced. The kind of woman I'd get enough of in a night or two." Dillon held her close. "The kind of woman who wouldn't be hurt by the kind of things people might end up saying. Don't forget, Jessy, I'm still the son of a wetback."

Underscoring his meaning, he took her arm and laid it over his, contrasting the creamy light tan of her skin with the deep, natural bronze of his own.

"It might mean nothing to you and me," he said, running his fingers through the tawny streaks of her hair, its shades of sunlight and honey as naturally differing as the colors of her eyes. "But there are still lots of people out there that it matters to. People like my grandfather. Maybe even some of the people in your own family."

"They wouldn't dare." She turned his arm over and leaned across him to kiss the inside of his wrist. Her bare breasts nuzzled against the hard muscles of his arm as she rose higher to stare into his eyes. "Don't ever think I'm weak, Dillon, because I'm not. I've been a fighter all my life. And I'll go toe-to-toe with the devil if he threatens someone I care about. Does that set your mind at ease?"

"Jessy." Dillon wrapped his arms around her and rolled until he was on top with his weight suspended over her. His voice was husky with more than passion as he said, "I guess I'll just have to give your phone number to my staff when I get there, because I am definitely going to be late again this morning."

## Chapter Ten

"Relax, sweetheart," Dillon crooned as he massaged the knotted tension in Jessy's shoulders. "It's just a dinner."

"It's not just a dinner. It's your grandfather." Feeling woefully inadequate, Jessy spared a moment from her frantic grating of the hard block of Parmesan to glance around her kitchen at the salad of Bibb lettuce, already prepared, and the cooked fettuccine awaiting its sauce. "Oh," she groaned, "I should have had this catered. I'm not even dressed yet."

Dillon nuzzled her neck. "It's just one more rich old man, Jessy. I know you must have dazzled plenty of them."

She put down the cheese and grater and turned to nestle in his arms for some much-needed reassurance. "None that mattered. And regardless of what you say, Dillon, he *does* matter. He matters to your mother, and he matters to your career."

"Not nearly as much as he wishes. And what influence he does have is based on lies." Dillon's voice grew tight and his body tensed as he talked. "The mighty Harlan Siddons doesn't exactly advertise the fact that he abandoned his daughter and her children to a life of poverty. Or that I was already in law school before he lifted a finger to help."

Jessy lifted her head to gaze up at him, shocked by the intensity of Dillon's resentment. "If your grandfather gets you this worked up, why did you invite him?"

"I didn't. He invited himself." Dillon threw back his head and sighed. "I didn't want to tell you everything."

"What?" An icy chill swept through the pit of her stomach. To give herself something to do, Jessy went back to grating the remainder of the cheese, but no amount of effort could stop her hands from shaking.

"He heard the rumors that there was a new woman in my life. He hired a private detective to find out who you were."

The icy chill gave way to a heat wave. Jessy slammed down the grater and whirled. "What?"

"He has pictures of us, and a bio on you."

"I'm busting my tail to cook fettuccine Alfredo from scratch for a jackass who's been spying on me?" she practically shouted. "I could have just made tuna salad and been out of this kitchen half an hour ago."

Dillon laughed and his own anger began to recede. "It's not too late to change, sweetheart. I love a good tuna fish sandwich."

"I'm very tempted," she said, mollified by Dillon's support. As her annoyance diminished, her curiosity increased. "So, if he already knows everything, why is he coming here?"

"He wants to meet you." Dillon caught her by the wrist and pulled her back into his arms. "You seem to have that effect on men."

"I'll bet he's expecting some slick seductress."

Dillon nuzzled her neck. "I wouldn't be at all surprised."

"Maybe I should go scrub off all my makeup and put my hair in a ponytail," she suggested, wanting to look as far from slick and seductive as possible.

"He'd probably think it was a very crafty attempt at innocence."

Jessy laughed as she realized how right Dillon was. "Maybe I should just get back to making this stupid sauce before he gets here. Why don't you go open the wine?"

"I'm really sorry about this," he said, unwilling to release her.

"It's not your fault."

"Yes, it is. This is my life, and the more I draw you into it, the more you get entangled in all the problems that come with it."

"I'm here because I want to be."

"I hope you don't change your mind." His hand cupped her cheek and guided her face toward him. "I don't want to lose you."

His lips parted and tenderly covered hers in a kiss that was slow, gentle and loving. His hand slid through her hair as his mouth grew harder and more demanding. His tongue slipped between her lips, delving, possessing and withdrawing only to plunge again, deeper.

Moaning softly, Jessy molded her body to his. Her arms stretched up to wrap around his neck, and the belt that held her robe pulled loose as the tip of her tongue circled his and began a passionate duel, thrusting with a tantalizing promise of all that awaited.

When the doorbell interrupted with a jarring, insistent chime, Dillon threw back his head and cursed while Jessy slumped against the island counter to support her trembling body.

Glancing down at the arousal that strained at the front of his trousers, he said, "I'll bet nobody can guess what we've been doing."

The gaping front of her robe left her heaving breasts half-exposed as Jessy drew in deep, ragged breaths and tried to slow her galloping heartbeat. "I sure hope the night doesn't go downhill from here."

"I just want to get it over with and get back to what's really important." He lifted her chin with his fingertip and pressed a soft kiss to her lips, then stepped away. "I'll go let him in and keep him busy while you change and finish the sauce."

Used to quick changes, Jessy dashed to the bedroom on legs that still shook and slipped into the white cotton blouse and floral jumpsuit she had laid out. Then she raced back to the kitchen to find Dillon stirring the simmering sauce while a distinguished, white-haired gentleman looked on.

Dillon greeted her with an apologetic smile. "I couldn't keep him out of the kitchen."

"That's okay." Jessy flashed a mischievous grin, one of many she could command at a moment's notice. "I'm willing to share the kitchen with anyone who'll help." She extended her hand, determined to be gracious no matter how badly she wished she could be alone with Dillon. "You must be Dillon's grandfather."

With a look of relief, Dillon said, "Jessica Carder, this is my grandfather, Harlan Siddons."

"Call me Jessy."

"And I hope you'll call me Harlan."

Jessy gazed up at the thick white hair, the kindly blue eyes, the gentle, affectionate smile and realized how truly dangerous this still-handsome man could be. And even then, it was hard not to like him, until she remembered that he had hired someone to spy on her private life.

"Dillon." She turned away from those piercing blue eyes to the hawklike black ones that were already waiting for her. "I'll finish the fettuccine if you'll take the salad, and your grandfather, into the dining room."

Dillon handed her the spoon he had been using to stir the sauce and dipped his head to place a quick kiss on her lips. "I'll see you in a few minutes." His voice dropped to a sensual intimacy. "Do you want me to pour you a glass of wine?"

"Yes." As always when his tone grew seductive, she felt herself practically melting toward him. "I'd like that a lot."

If only they were alone, sitting in front of the fireplace, sipping wine and talking, the way they had so many evenings during the past two months. He'd slip his arm around her shoulder and pull her closer, while the fire died down and the night heated up.

Dillon's second kiss brought her back to reality. Jessy almost sighed aloud when he left the kitchen. Then she set about putting the finishing touches on the meal while her mind wandered through the time since Dillon had come back into her life. Their time together had been so much like a honeymoon that sometimes she wanted to pinch herself to see if she was dreaming.

Then she remembered that there could be no real honeymoon without a wedding first, and so far, Dillon had yet to mention the subject of commitment. In fact, since their return to Austin from San Antonio nearly two months earlier, Dillon hadn't even been seen in public with her.

Not that she really minded. Each morning he went his way and she went hers. Each evening he stopped by his place to check his messages and pick up a change of clothes before arriving at her apartment, where they stayed until the next morning.

When he said that he wanted to keep her all to himself for as long as possible, she knew how he felt. Their time together was so special, so complete, that she never missed the rest of the world. But that special time was coming to an end. Tonight was only the first crack in the wall Dillon had erected around them.

Any day now, the swimsuit issue she had done the shots for in November would be on the stands. And on the heels of that, the magazine fashion layout she and Dillon had posed for in San Antonio would be released. Their private time was almost gone, and with it, as much as she hated to think about it, their future together could be gone, as well.

Lifting the fettuccine, Jessy forced a smile to cover her heavy heart and left the kitchen. As she entered the dining room her steps slowed. Dillon stood at one end of the table. His eyes were narrowed and almost coal black. His cheeks were a deeper bronze than normal, and the muscles of his jaw stood out like ropes. Standing in the double doorway leading to the living room, his grandfather twirled his wineglass and smiled, first at Dillon, then at Jessy.

"It's so nice to have you join us, Jessy. The conversation was beginning to wear a little thin with just the two of us in here. Don't you think so, Dillon?"

"Practically transparent," Dillon answered through gritted teeth, then turned away and refilled his wineglass before he returned to the table and held Jessy's chair for her to sit down.

His hands didn't linger at her shoulders and his lips didn't brush her hair as they normally did whenever he was so near. Even without a crystal ball, she knew there had been an argument and she had been the topic. Whatever Harlan had said had left Dillon shaken, shaken enough that he was partially angry with her because of it, and that was enough to bring the icy chill creeping back into the pit of her stomach.

"You know, I'm amazed that we haven't become acquainted before this, Jessy," Harlan said, taking his place at the table across from her. "I believe we were even at the same party last year in Houston."

"Oh, really?" Jessy forced a smile.

She knew the kind of party he meant, the kind where only the wealthiest and most elite society gathered in honor of some charity or annual tradition, Texas style. The kind where only a few selected outsiders were sprinkled into the mix for added spice, and beautiful women, especially models, were the most popular additions of all. Over the years Jessy had received quite a few invitations to such parties and, recognizing them for what they were, she had attended only the best.

"Tinka Grant's spring gala to kick off the racing season," Harlan said. "I'm sure you were there."

Jessy's smile remained in place. "Along with about three hundred and fifty others. I didn't stay very long. Some of us decided we'd rather go sailing."

"Ah. You were part of that group that left with Conrad, then."

"Yes. I know his daughter, Bethany. She dated my brother in college."

"How interesting." He sounded anything but interested.

"Small world," Jessy answered, dismissing the subject as she turned her attention to Dillon, who had cooled to a low simmer. She had almost forgotten what it was like to see the smoldering anger in his eyes directed toward her, and she liked the feeling even less now than she had when they first met.

"I'm doubly surprised you and Dillon hadn't met before," Harlan said. "Both of you living here in Austin, and traveling in the same circles the way you do."

"Maybe it's because we both spend a lot of time out of town," Jessy said with the barest glance toward Harlan before returning her worried gaze to Dillon. She didn't like his stony silence.

She could almost feel the barometer in the room plummet while the storm clouds rolled in, and Harlan wasn't helping at all. But then, of course, he wasn't trying to. Whatever he had said to put Dillon into such a temper was a wound Harlan was still rubbing salt into with each parry of his seemingly innocent conversation.

"You know," Jessy said with a burst of inspiration, "I think a little music would be nice with dinner. Why don't you pick some out, Dillon, while I see if I can entice your grandfather into having a little more of my fettuccine?"

She smiled broadly as she lifted the platter of pasta and waited. Dillon returned her gaze with a suspicious frown.

Moving with obvious reluctance, he laid his napkin on the table. "Would classical be all right?"

"I think it would be wonderful." Still smiling, she waited, platter in hand, while he pushed his chair away from the table with more force than was necessary and stalked into the living room.

Then Jessy leaned toward Harlan with the pasta and said very softly, "I don't know what you said to upset him so much, but I invited you into my home for the evening with the understanding that you were a gentleman and would conduct yourself accordingly."

She plunked the platter down in front of Harlan. "Now, I'm not having my dinner table turned into a war zone, so you can either stop pushing Dillon's buttons right now, or this meal is over."

A cold smile spread over the old man's face, never reaching his eyes, and Jessy was reminded of the lunch she had almost shared with his daughter, who had the same ice blue eyes.

"I admire your style, young lady. That was done with so much feeling, I could almost believe you meant it. When you get tired of Dillon, why don't you give me a call?"

He stroked her hand with cold, steely fingers, and Jessy recoiled with an anger that was almost nauseous. "If you were anyone but Dillon's grandfather, I'd—"

"What would you do, dear?" He rose languidly, unmoved by her passion. "Toss wine in my face? Slap me?" He laughed quietly. "The dinner was really quite good. I'm sorry I can't stay longer."

Practically frothing, Jessy grabbed the platter of fettuccine and stormed into the kitchen. One more second in that snake's company was more than she could bear, but however horrid he was—and he *was* horrid—he was still Dillon's grandfather, and a certain amount of respect had to be shown, whether it was earned or not.

Standing at the kitchen island, she drew in deep breaths and counted slowly to ten, something she hadn't done since she was a child. But she couldn't remember the last time she had felt this out of control. Then, in a dying effort to keep up appearances, she turned and went back into the dining room.

Dillon stood in the living room, his back to her. Harlan stood in front of him, his attention riveted on Dillon.

"She'll ruin you. She'll take you for everything she can get, and then she'll leave you with your life in tatters. I can tell you men she's done it to." Harlan shook the manila folder that he clutched in his hand. "I have the names in here, and stories that'll curl your hair."

"Lies!" Dillon grabbed the folder and threw it as far as he could, sending papers spiraling across the room. "What kind of schoolboy do you take me for? Do you think I don't know that you'd pay people to lie for you?"

"What about these?" His grandfather took a magazine from the coffee table and flipped through the pages. "Pictures don't lie." He found what he was looking for and held it out to Dillon. "Not that I blame you. Looking at these I could even be tempted myself."

Harlan tossed the magazine onto the sofa, and in its brief flight through the air Jessy recognized the swimsuit on the cover. It was the one she had worn for the surf shots. Somehow Harlan had gotten an advance copy of the swimsuit issue and was trying to turn it into something it wasn't.

"She's just a woman, Dillon. She's replaceable. Don't let her ruin your chances to be governor."

"I think you'd better leave now. I'll make your excuses to Jessy when she comes back."

"You fool!" Harlan spat out his venom. "I'll ruin you. I'll cut you out of my will and see to it that you lose every bit of the support my name brought you."

"I never wanted your money, or your support, and I'll tell you something else." Dillon stabbed angrily at the air between them. "I never needed them, either. You thought you could bring my mother to heel by disowning her. But it didn't work with her, and it *won't* work with *me.*"

Shaking his head, he walked to the door and opened it, then stepped back for his grandfather to walk through.

"I feel sorry for you," Dillon said in a voice almost devoid of anger. "You don't know the first thing about love or loyalty or any of the things in life that are really important. You may be my grandfather, but you're not welcome in my life any longer. Good night."

At the door Harlan hesitated, looking first at Dillon and then past him to where Jessy stood frozen in the kitchen doorway. "You'll regret this." He looked back to Dillon. "You'll both regret this." Then he wheeled and walked out, looking every inch the tired old man that he was.

Dillon closed the door and turned to face Jessy. "How long have you been there?"

"Awhile."

"I'm sorry. I had no idea he was going to do this."

"I may have started it." She shook herself loose and began to walk toward the living room. "While you were putting on the music, I told him to straighten up or leave."

A weak but genuine smile crossed Dillon's face. "You told him that? I'll bet that must have shocked him." He reached down to retrieve one of the papers that had fallen from the manila folder, then followed the paper trail across the living room until he had retrieved them all.

"What is that?" Jessy stopped at the back of the couch and pointed to the collection he held in his hands.

"A dossier."

"On me?"

"On you." With a vicious tug, Dillon ripped it in half. "Intended to expose you, and to bring me to my senses." He ripped it again, into fourths.

"What was in it?" She tried to think back over her life to anything she had done worthy of exposing.

"Lies and half-truths." He tossed the shredded folder and its contents onto the coffee table. "Pictures I saw years ago."

"Pictures?"

"You, lounging in a bedroom, wearing a little piece of lace and not much else and giving the camera a come-hither look with just that touch of baby-doll innocence you do so well. The kind of catalog shots that convinced me you were a notorious woman and kept me fantasizing about you for years before I ever met you."

"That was all?"

"That and the testimonials of half a dozen men who've had you for their mistress." Quiet as his voice was, a blaze of anger burned in Dillon's eyes.

"One at a time, I hope." Flippancy wasn't the answer, but it was all she could come up with to hold her tears at bay. Until this moment she hadn't comprehended the frightening extent of one man's power.

"I didn't read that closely," Dillon said with quiet fury.

"He really could ruin your career, couldn't he? Lies and half-truths are enough if you give them to the right people. I can't let that happen to you, Dillon, and I don't know how to stop it."

"It won't happen."

"Maybe not, but it could." She remembered the stand-off she had walked in on earlier. "Something he said carried enough truth to upset you. What was it?"

Dillon nodded to the magazine on the sofa. "Have you seen that?"

"I just pose," she said with a quick shake of her head. "They pick which shots get printed."

"You're on the cover."

She glanced down. The picture was a good one. A cold, wet, irritable woman and a tired, determined photographer had managed to beat the sunset and create one frozen moment in time that was better than them both.

"Some models work their whole lives and never get a cover shot." She should be elated, but she couldn't feel anything except a hollow, gnawing fear that her world was crumbling around her feet and there was nothing she could do to stop it.

"The first time I saw you was on the cover of a magazine Stephen had. You looked so sweet, and pure, and wholesome that I just knew you had to be hell on wheels."

In spite of her sense of impending doom, Jessy laughed. "You were right, you know. Maybe not in the way you meant, but you were right. My mother used to tell people that I came out running and never slowed down."

Still wound tight, he relaxed enough to let his lips twitch in a half smile. "I can believe that. There aren't a lot of people who've stood up to my grandfather, especially to his face."

Dillon left the spot he had been rooted to. His gaze was locked on Jessy as he moved closer. "Harlan may not be able to respect that in you, but I do," he said quietly. Reaching out to her, Dillon pulled her into his arms. "He won't hurt you, Jessy. I won't let him. And I won't let him come between us, no matter what he does."

She wished she could believe him, but an uneasy doubt remained. "That may not be an easy promise to keep."

"You let me worry about that. I'll figure something out."

"What do we do until then?" She nodded toward the sofa. "That magazine's only the beginning. I'm surprised he didn't have an advance copy of the other one, too."

"I'm sure he does. But this was the one he knew would get to me."

"Why?" She turned away and picked up the magazine, but Dillon took it from her and tossed it aside.

"Not now," he said, pulling her back into his arms. "I've had enough of all this for tonight."

"I don't like to have things hanging over me, Dillon," Jessy insisted. "If there's a problem, I want to know what it is." She twisted in his arms to see where the magazine had landed.

"It's not the pictures. It's what they represent." He pulled her closer again and pressed her head against his chest. His cheek gently brushed her hair as he said, "It's all the faceless men who are going to be picking up that magazine and having the kind of thoughts about you that *I* used to have."

"Oh, good grief, Dillon." Exasperated, she struggled free of his restraining arms and stepped back to challenge him. "Do you think that women don't see your picture and lust after you? I've sat in powder rooms all over Austin and listened to women salivate over you."

"That's different."

"Why is it different?" His answer only incensed her more. "Because it's you, instead of me? Or because you're a man, and for men the rules are different?"

"The rules *are* different," he said with a scowl settling over his features.

Jessy drew herself up stiffly. "I beg your pardon?"

"Maybe they shouldn't be," he insisted, "but they are. I know I have a reputation as a ladies' man, but it's never hurt my career for a minute. For women, the reverse just isn't true. That's not fair, and it's not right, but it's the way things are."

Her chin lifted another notch, and she looked him in the eye. "I've always lived life by my own rules, Dillon." Her tone carried the warning that she wasn't about to change now.

He smiled. "I had pretty much figured that out."

"I'm not going to run and hide just because there might be a spotlight turned on me. People have thought the wrong thing about me before."

Jessy threw her arm into the air and stopped herself an instant before she was about to turn and pace. Dampening her anger, she said calmly, "I've had to deal with it practically since I was in diapers. And I admit I was wild, but I wasn't bad. I was just independent.'' Her voice rose steadily as she talked, but she resisted the continuing urge to pace. ''And I'm getting pretty tired of having to defend myself against people who don't seem to understand the difference.''

''Jessy, I'm not asking you to change.''

''Aren't you? It sounds to me like you want me to apologize for those pictures.'' She jabbed a stiff finger toward the magazine, which had landed on the coffee table. Another seductive pose similar to the one on the cover stared up at her from an inside page.

''What else do you want, Dillon?'' she asked, turning back to face him. ''Because I don't make a practice of apologizing for things I'm not sorry for, and I've spent half my life telling people to go to hell when they tried to get me to.''

Her stance was combative and her eyes flashed fire as Dillon stepped up, almost nose to nose with her and jabbed an equally stiff finger toward the coffee table. ''You can almost see right through one of your swimsuits in there.''

Making each word distinct, Jessy said, ''That's how I make my living.''

''Well, you're *my* woman now, damn it. And I don't want other men looking at you like that.''

''And what am I supposed to do? Quit working so you can stick me in an ivory tower and have me all to yourself?''

Still so close that his chest brushed hers with each breath they took, Dillon suddenly lowered his voice seductively. ''Would that be so bad, Jessy? Would that really be so bad?'' His hands hovered inches from her arms, but he didn't touch her.

''No.'' When he looked at her like that, when he talked to her like that, she melted. Struggling to hold on to her last shred of resistance, she said, ''But I've got to have more than that, Dillon. I've got to *be* more than that.''

''You are, Jessy. Don't you know that?''

"And what about tomorrow? What about when I become the weapon that people can use against you? How are you going to feel then?"

"It won't happen." His hand touched her wrist and slid up her forearm.

She fought the feelings he brought to life and struggled to hold on to the argument she had pieced together from the shadowy fears that haunted her.

"Yesterday I might have believed you, but not now. Not after that old man and his dossier paid us a visit. Dillon, what if I hadn't been a virgin? What if you didn't *know* there weren't any other men before you?"

"Jessy, sweetheart." Dillon took her hands in his and gazed down at her with his heart in his eyes. "I spent ten years tormenting myself with your other lovers, and I still wanted you in a way I never wanted any other woman. I know there'll always be people who see you the way I used to, and it doesn't matter. You're mine now, and I'll fight the devil himself to keep you."

His words only reminded her of why she was afraid, and Jessy shuddered. "Judging from your grandfather's threats, you may have to."

"Forget him," Dillon said and pulled her to him. "He's history." Wrapping his arms around her, Dillon brushed his cheek against her hair and kissed her temple. "If it's any consolation to you," he said, "Harlan Siddons isn't going to do *anything* that could bring public embarrassment to his own name. He's supported me too publicly for too long to risk slinging mud at me now. There are too many chances it could backfire on him, especially since I was dead serious when I said I didn't need his support to stay in office."

Jessy lifted her head from his chest and drew back far enough to look up at him. "You really don't?"

"Everything I stand for, every issue I was elected on, is in direct opposition to what Harlan Siddons and his fat-cat powermongering stand for. I have had to remind people at every turn that I am not a product of his money. I'm a product of the barrio. That's where I came from, and when I leave office that's what I'm going back to." Dillon brushed his thumb over the soft skin at the edge of her mouth. "And I hope to hell that when the time comes you'll be going with me."

Jessy tried to smile, uncertain of what he was asking. "Keep hanging around with me, and that time may come a lot sooner than you'd planned."

He shook his head. "It doesn't matter. There comes a time in every man's life when he needs to settle down and devote himself to making babies." He ran his fingers through her hair and gently pulled her face closer. His lips parted in a teasing grin. "As long as he's got the right woman to work with, that's all that matters."

His lips were almost to hers when Jessy uttered a moan and jerked away. It was hopeless, and to go on kidding herself, it would just prolong the torture. She was never the right woman for Dillon, and no amount of time would change that.

"Jessy!" He reached out for her, and she backed away.

"No, Dillon," she said, shaking her head as she retreated toward the bedroom. "This is never going to work. I'll never be right for you."

Thunderstruck, Dillon held out his hands and started toward her. "Jessy."

"No." She held up her hand to stop him. "I'm just a face in a magazine, and you're trying to make me into something that I'm not."

"What did I say?"

"It doesn't matter." At the bedroom door she paused. "I'm sorry, Dillon. I never meant for it to go this far. I just couldn't seem to say goodbye." A heartbeat away from tears, she turned and closed the door behind her.

Alone in the room, she went to the closet and stopped with her hand on the doorknob, wondering what to do next. She could always go to visit Rebecca just long enough for this awful pain in her heart to ease. At their lowest times she and her sister had always been there for each other. Except that Rebecca was nine months pregnant and didn't need anybody else's problems right now.

Jessy leaned her head against the closet door and closed her eyes tight against the tears that were seconds away from brimming over. She wouldn't cry. Drawing in a deep breath, she let it out with a huff and banged the side of her closed fist against the door. She never cried. But then, she'd never given up the only man she'd ever loved before, either.

Quiet as a whisper, soft as a petal, Dillon slipped his arms around her from behind and asked, "Jessy, baby, what is it? Was it something I said, sweetheart?" He brushed her hair aside and kissed her cheek. "Baby, I love you with all my heart. I'd never do anything to hurt you like this. If you'll just tell me what I did," he begged.

As badly as she hurt, Jessy's heart did a somersault. Finally, he'd said he loved her. When she had made up her mind to let him go, when she had made up her mind that nothing would stop her, Dillon had finally said that he loved her, and it wasn't enough anymore.

She could never give him the things that he wanted, and she could cost him everything that he had worked so many years to achieve. He was a man whose life had been filled with sacrifices, and she wouldn't ask him to make one more. He deserved a woman who could make his house a home, cook his meals and bear his children. And she loved him enough to let him go.

He turned her around, and she gazed up at the face she adored, the bronzed, heart-stoppingly sensual face she would carry in her memories for the rest of her life.

"You're scaring me, Jessy. And that's not something that's easy to do. Please, baby, tell me anything but that you're really leaving me."

"I have to," Jessy whispered around the tears that blocked her throat. "And if I stay any longer, I don't think I'll be able to."

"Then don't," he coaxed in a husky whisper.

"Dillon." She dropped her head, unable to look at him and say what she had to say. "I can't give you the things you want."

"You've been doing a pretty good job so far."

The hoarse caress of his voice and the gentle nudging of his finger beneath her chin brought Jessy's face back into view, but her eyes remained downcast. Another nudge and her lips were in reach of Dillon's, and what words couldn't do, the gentle brush of his mouth against hers did.

The warm, soft, tenderest touch of flesh on flesh brought a moan of despair from Jessy, which he quickly silenced with a second lingering nuzzle from his barely parted lips. His hands moved over her shoulders and down her back, pressing the length of her body to his until his hands reached the curve of her waist and he stopped, content to hold her there while his mouth opened over hers and his kiss grew more insistent.

The tip of his tongue flicked over her lips, teasing and tantalizing, until she opened herself to him and he slipped inside. While his mouth made love to her with increasingly passionate hunger, Dillon's hands moved lower. His fingers spread slowly over the smooth, firm mounds of her hips until he reached their base. Then, cupping the weight in his hands, he lifted her against him and spread her legs on either side of his thighs while he pressed her back against the wall next to the closet.

A voice of warning, almost too weak to be heard, cried out in Jessy's head. She was losing the battle before a blow had been struck, but, oh, how sweet was the loss. She wrapped her arms around his shoulders and tightened her legs around his hips and surrendered for the moment to the desire that flowed through her like a tidal wave.

Sweeping her off her feet, passion carried her along too quickly for reason to catch up, too quickly for regrets to form, too quickly for anything but the pagan drumbeats of her own heart and the sensual promise of Dillon's kiss.

With Jessy still wrapped around him and with the hard press of his body still firmly against her, he lifted her away from the wall and turned toward the bed. Once there, he held her with one hand while he unfastened the top of her jumpsuit and peeled it down to her waist with the other.

Still holding her, he unbuttoned her blouse and reached inside to unhook her bra. With his arousal throbbing against her, Dillon cupped her breast in his hand. His thumb raked slowly over the swollen nub as he said, "I want to know why you were leaving. I know it wasn't because you wanted to."

"Not now," she said, unwilling to think about anything but the way he made her feel.

"Yes, now," Dillon insisted. His hand tightened on her breast, crushing it tenderly in his grasp. "I'm not going one step further until I know." He lifted the weight in his hand and leaned to flick his tongue roughly over the tip, then drew it into his mouth and suckled, slowly, deeply, totally, before releasing it finally and lifting his head once again. "And I know you want to finish this as much as I do."

Each time he spoke, the deep, strong throb of his voice was as intoxicating as his touch. Jessy drew a shaky breath and tried to clear her head.

"Okay," she agreed finally, "but you'll have to put me down. I can't talk like this."

"Fair enough." Dillon leaned over the bed and spread her out full-length across it. Then he grasped her jumpsuit and tugged it down over her hips.

"Wait!" Jessy bolted up and grabbed with both hands before he could go any further.

He shook his head and held on. "This has to come off. I'm not going to risk having you run away from me again before we get this hashed out."

"But, Dillon," she pleaded, while the jumpsuit slipped through her fingers and down her legs, leaving her in bikini pants, a white cotton blouse dangling open and an unfastened bra brushing the sides of her breasts each time she moved. "How am I ever going to concentrate?"

"You'll see." He dropped her jumpsuit onto the floor and straightened, stripping off his shirt and unbuckling his belt with practiced speed. Just as smoothly, he slipped out of his shoes and shed his pants. When he was down to his briefs he stopped and said, "Your turn."

She looked up at him standing tall and lean, with his powerful build and smooth bronze skin. She could think of only one thing, and conversation wasn't it. "You have no intention of talking, do you?"

"I have every intention of talking." He leaned over the bed and with the touch of a finger slid her blouse over her shoulder and down her arm, exposing one full, ripe breast to view.

"Before or after?" she asked unsteadily as he repeated the process with the other shoulder.

"Before." His voice was calm and controlled. "But we may have to talk fast." He slipped his finger under the lace band of her underwear and stroked his knuckle over the smooth skin of her stomach. "I *am* beginning to feel a little impatient." Taking a deep breath, he stood and dropped Jessy's blouse and bra onto the pile at his feet. "Maybe we should leave the rest."

He walked to the head of the bed and peeled down the covers. Jessy curled into the shelter of the sheets and pulled the covers over her while Dillon lay down beside her and slipped his arm under her. With her head on his shoulder and his arm holding her close, they lay chest to chest, legs entwined.

"Why do you want to leave me?" he asked again in a soft, sad voice that dared her to find a reason more powerful than the passion they shared.

"Dillon, there are two things about me that I've never discussed with other people," Jessy began slowly, not knowing how she would say what he wanted her to say. "One of them you discovered for yourself."

"To my great shock and dismay," he agreed, able to smile now at the memory. He held her a little closer and brushed a kiss on her brow. "If I had that to do over, sweetheart, I wouldn't wish that you were any different. I only wish that I had been different. You deserved more that night."

"I have no regrets about that night." She tilted her head back and kissed the soft skin of his neck in a lingering, tantalizing kiss that expressed the full extent of her memories from that night. Her voice was significantly huskier when she added, "Except that I didn't do it two days sooner, when I first had the chance."

Dillon sucked in a long, ragged breath and drew back to put a slender space between their heated bodies. "Jessy." He pulled in another lungful of air and expelled it in a tortured sigh. "I'm not going to let you go. Whatever the problem is, we'll work it out."

"There's nothing to work out, Dillon." Before he could argue, she gathered up her courage and plunged ahead. "You want children, and I can't have them."

"What do you mean?" He drew back to look down at her.

"I can't have children. Most women can. Some women can't. I can't."

With the determination he showed in every conflict, Dillon rose up on his elbow and asked, "How do you know, if you've never tried?"

Jessy looked away, staring at the quilt that covered them. If only it was that easy. "I know how you feel," she said when she had composed herself again. "I felt the same way when the doctor told me."

"How long have you known?" His voice was only a whisper, and stunned acceptance had taken the place of his resistance.

"I was eighteen. I'd been having a lot of problems. I'd never been normal, like other girls. The doctor ran a lot of tests before he gave me the final news."

"Eighteen," Dillon said with the quietness of thought. "Then it wasn't just Stephen, was it? This was the other reason you never got serious with another man."

"Maybe. I tried not to think about it, but maybe." She still wasn't eager to think about it. The only reason she was putting herself through this was that she owed Dillon the truth, even if she could give him nothing else.

"What did I have that nobody else had?" He turned her face toward him, touching his fingertips to her lips, stroking their softness while his eyes roamed her face with a hunger that was untouched by her confession. "Why was I the one you gave what no one else could have?"

"There's no one else like you, Dillon. I tried to leave. I tried to say no. But in the end I was battling myself, and it was a battle I couldn't win."

"And you were going to leave me because you couldn't have children?" he asked gently.

"*Your* children," she corrected while tears she couldn't hide burned in her eyes. "I never really wanted what I knew I couldn't have until I met you. I would have given anything if I could have been the woman you were looking for."

Dillon heaved an exasperated groan and sat straighter. "Why didn't you say something, Jessy? Why didn't you tell me to shut up? I was just talking. I would never have said those things if I'd known."

"But you were talking about the things that matter to you, Dillon. You're entitled to those things, and if I can't give them to you, you're entitled to a woman who can."

In spite of her impassioned plea, Dillon fought a smile. "Well, can I have you, too?" he asked tenderly. "That way I can keep you, and I can still have another woman just to bear my children."

Indignant, Jessy pushed herself upright. "Are you serious?"

"No! Of course I'm not serious." He looked at her with both laughter and tears brimming in his eyes. "This whole discussion is ridiculous. If you can't have children, fine. We won't have children. If we want them, we can adopt."

"This is not ridiculous," Jessy insisted angrily. "This is a very important issue."

He was racing too far ahead of her changing emotions, and the answers he was giving her were too easy for a question that could affect the rest of their lives. She had to make him stop and face the problem realistically.

Dillon took her face between his hands and looked deeply and sincerely into her eyes. "If you can live with it, I can live with it. The happiness you give me is more important than producing my own biological offspring. Please, Jessy, believe me."

"I think you should take some time before you make any promises. People change. Feelings change. But this—" she motioned toward her stomach "—this will never change."

"Are you sure? I mean, that this isn't a condition that could change?"

Again she saw the hope come alive in his eyes, telling her that regardless of what he said, in his heart he wished differently.

She shook her head. "I only have one functioning ovary, so I'm only fertile every other month. And the one that works doesn't work too well, so to begin with, my chances of conceiving are well under a normal person's. And then there are other complications that make it even more difficult and by the time you factor it all in, my chances of ever getting pregnant are practically zero."

"But there is a chance."

Still shaking her head, Jessy explained, "The doctor said that it is so minimal that I shouldn't consider it a possibility."

"But there *is* a chance."

"It would be in the realm of miracles," she insisted, remembering all too clearly the doctor's answers to her own identical questions.

"You don't believe there's a *chance* you could get pregnant?" Dillon asked gently.

"No," she said definitely.

She had fought this battle with herself long ago, and she wasn't going to let anyone put her through that misery again. She could live with the knowledge she would never bear a child of her own. She couldn't live with the daily hope and heartbreak of wishing for what could never be, and she couldn't watch Dillon live with it, either.

"Then I'll tell you what, sweetheart." Dillon's gaze followed her as he pressed her shoulders down onto her pillow. "We'll just see how sure you are." He pushed back the covers and gently tugged her last article of clothing over her hips and down the length of her legs.

As he tossed aside her panties and stood to shed his own, Jessy watched him with caution. The gleam in his eye seemed to issue a challenge she wasn't sure she wanted to accept. "What do you mean?"

He rejoined her in bed, quickly sliding across her and into the valley between her legs. His weight settled over her, its pressure centered in all the right places, and Jessy drew in her breath at the quick surge of desire within her.

She could feel him move against her, grinding gently, swollen with desire, as ready as she was. He shifted, sliding lower and returning slowly, throbbing and rock hard to the opening where he paused, waiting. She moved toward him and he slipped just inside and then withdrew, waiting again at the brink.

"Now?" he asked softly.

"Yes." Again she rose toward him and again he teased and then retreated.

"Are you sure?" He nudged her, then slipped inside and stroked deep once, twice, before withdrawing completely, to rise poised above her, his upper weight held aloft by his extended arms. "Think about it," he cautioned.

Puzzled by his hesitation, Jessy returned his piercing gaze with one of bewilderment until, almost without conscious thought, she realized what Dillon had not done. He had never gone near the nightstand. The part of him that pressed against her was unencumbered by the protection he never omitted.

"But, Dillon, you didn't—" she began and then stopped when she saw in his eyes that he hadn't forgotten.

"No," he said, shaking his head in confirmation, "I didn't."

Again he entered her slowly, his cool control evaporating quickly as the heat of passion transformed his features. He plunged deeper, and deeper still, before once more withdrawing almost completely. This time, not quite motionless, he remained just inside her. And the arms holding him above her trembled with the effort that it took for him to remain at the entrance, moving only enough to remind them both vividly of his presence.

Unsure whether the game he played was with her or with himself, Jessy tried to still the raging tide within her. She longed to pull him to her and end the waiting, but he had done something he never did, and she didn't know why. Again she looked toward the nightstand.

"Do you want me to go on?" he asked, seeing her glance. "You'd be the first."

"Ever?"

"Ever." Except for the faint tremor of his arms and the sheen of sweat that coated his body, all outward signs of control were restored. "Not even in high school. I wouldn't risk bringing a baby into the world by accident." The subtle grinding of his hips increased, and he moved deeper. "And I never wanted to be trapped into a marriage I wasn't ready for."

Breathless, Jessy lifted to meet him. "Like your parents?" She smoothed her hands down his sides and over his flanks, urging him on, afraid that if he stopped talking he would withdraw again and leave her suspended in agony.

His words coming in gasps, he said, "She didn't get pregnant on purpose."

"Same difference." Drawing him to her, Jessy rose higher and Dillon released a ragged moan and plunged into her harder.

"Yes," he whispered and, drawing in a haggard breath, began to slow again. "It's the same difference. And you, Jessy, you never answered me. Should I go on?"

"Yes." The word sounded more like a plea.

"You're not afraid?"

"Are you?"

"No need to be. I've never made love without it, and you never made love to anyone but me." He looked down at her with undisguised challenge in his eyes as he slowed almost to a halt. "So if you can't get pregnant, we don't need it at all, do we?"

Almost angry, she narrowed her eyes and returned his unwavering gaze. "You're testing me."

He came to a dead stop. "Should I go on?"

"Yes," she snapped.

"And if a miracle happens?" His movements began again before the sentence was ended.

"Then I guess you're just trapped, aren't you?" Jessy said almost savagely as she tightened her arms around him and pulled him hard against her.

Throwing open the gates of passion held too long at bay, Dillon brushed his lips hungrily over hers as he thrust into her with long, steady strokes that showed no sign of slowing.

"That's a chance I'm willing to take," he answered, giving in to desire pushed almost to the breaking point.

Throwing back his head, he drank in gasps of air while an avalanche of need rolled over him like none he had ever known. Sweet and pure as mountain air, intense and wrenching as the most primal jungle rite, it took him higher than he had ever been and left him replenished and at peace at the end of a wild and intoxicating ride.

Wrapping Jessy tightly in his arms, Dillon buried his face in the soft waves of her hair and whispered, "Don't ever try to leave me again."

"I don't think I could if I wanted to."

The sweet curves of her body were molded to him. He breathed a sigh of relief and whispered, "Whatever comes, I'll protect you." Then he drifted off to sleep, content.

## Chapter Eleven

What was swept away on a tidal wave of passion the night before was back stronger than ever in the bright light of day. Alone on the balcony, idly twirling her spoon in a breakfast cup of yogurt mixed with raisins and nuts, Jessy tried to find her way past the sense of desolation that had returned with the dawn.

There was no pain worse than the pain of disappointing the one you loved, and that was what she had done. Dillon might say that he understood, that it didn't matter to him, but his actions said otherwise. He wanted a child of his own, and a man of his determination didn't give up easily. Last night was only the beginning.

In time, she would see the dawning of defeat in his eyes, the realization that she could never give him all that he wanted, that what they had together wasn't enough, and when that day came she didn't know if she could survive the heartbreak.

Behind her the door slid open and Dillon stepped onto the balcony, dressed in a robe and vigorously rubbing his hair dry with a towel. "What's for breakfast?" he asked, leaning down to place an enthusiastic morning kiss on her lips. When he stood, he glanced at the cup in her hands. "Mmm, yogurt. Again?"

"Well, I could always make a stab at biscuits and gravy, but you know what happened the last time."

Dillon shuddered. "How about a bowl of cornflakes?"

In spite of the sense of loss that dragged at her, Jessy laughed. "We might even be able to find some orange juice to go with it."

He leaned closer and kissed her again, a slower, deeper kiss that said much more than good morning. "I wish I didn't have to leave today," he murmured when the kiss ended. He took her hand. "There's so much I want to talk to you about. There's so much I've never said."

Jessy all but jumped to her feet in her rush to stop him before he went any further. "Sweetheart, you're going to be late. Why don't I get your breakfast while you finish dressing?"

"All right." Reluctantly he relinquished her hand. "But there are a few things we're going to talk about before I leave here this morning."

"Are you packed?"

He nodded. "My aide's picking up the suitcases at my apartment this morning. He'll take me from the office to the airport."

Leaving Dillon in the bedroom to dress, Jessy went into the kitchen and breathed a sigh of relief. While she was trying to find the courage to give up the man who meant more to her than life, the last thing in the world she needed was for him to make it even harder for her. He had already said that he loved her. If he said any more, she didn't know if she could stand it.

If only he had been willing to go on with things the way they were, with no promises or commitments, without the expectations that could lead to disappointment and heartbreak. She would have stayed with him forever if they could have remained just the way they had been.

"Jessy?" Dillon said, obviously not for the first time. "Sweetheart?" He waved his hand in front of her face when she turned to look at him with the wide-eyed expression of someone emerging from a daze. "What in the world were you thinking about?"

"You're dressed." She hurried to the refrigerator and took out the orange juice and milk. "I'll have your breakfast ready in just a minute."

"No, that's okay." He caught up to her and set the two cartons on the counter. "I'll grab something on the way. What are you so upset about?"

"Maybe you're right. Maybe we do need to talk." Without warning, she was on the verge of tears. "Dillon, I know what I am. I don't apologize for it, and I don't feel bad about myself. I'm not perfect, but I have a lot of good qualities. I have a lot to offer someone."

"I know that."

"I'm not so sure. I'm especially not sure that you will ever really be happy with me."

Dillon reached for her, and Jessy dodged out of the way, holding up her hands to ward him off. "Let me finish. Every time we have a problem you grab me and kiss me and then nothing else matters, at least for a while. But the problems always come back again. They're there, and they're real."

Mystified, Dillon remained where he was, his hands clenched into fists at his sides. "What problems?"

"I *cannot* have children. That isn't going to change."

"I said that was okay."

"And then you tried to make me pregnant!" Jessy shouted, stiff with the anger and hurt that had been building all night. "Don't you think I wish I could be what you want, do the things you want? But I can't! Maybe you can change the rest of the world, Dillon, but I don't want to be another one of your projects. Accept me as I am, or leave me the hell alone!"

"Jessy." His face was stricken as he took a step toward her with his arms outstretched.

Again she backed away. "Don't touch me."

Obeying, he remained where he was. "This must have been building for a while," he said quietly, obviously struggling to keep his own emotions under a tight rein.

"I don't know," she said nervously. "I'm as surprised as you are."

"I always did admire your temper." A grudging smile smoothed the worried lines on his face. "You're the only woman I've ever met who could argue me to a standoff."

"I don't want to make this a contest." She sagged against the counter, her anger seeping away. This would all be so much easier if only she didn't love him so much. "Maybe it's a good thing you're going to be gone awhile. I think we both need some time apart to sort things out."

"Jessy, no, please." He held out his hands, but made no other move toward her. "Ah, Jessy, how did we come to this?"

Biting her lower lip, Jessy shook her head. "I don't know."

In an effort at compromise, he asked, "If I agree not to call the rest of this week, will you meet me at the cabin on Friday?"

Unwilling to agree outright, she countered with, "Will you think about what I've said?"

"I'm sorry, Jessy. I never meant—"

She held up her hand to stop him again. "It's okay. It's just the way we are. We can't help that."

"Will you at least kiss me goodbye?"

With all her heart she wished she could wipe out the past few minutes and pretend they had never happened. She longed to throw herself into his arms and let him chase away her doubts and fears and rebuild her life again. She had known from the beginning that even one night with

Dillon was too big a risk, that once she had a taste of the happiness he could offer, she would never walk away with her heart in one piece.

She shook her head slowly. "I don't think so." It took everything she had to reject one last touch of his lips.

His eyes clouded, but otherwise unmoved, Dillon said, "There's a spare key under the mat in case I'm not there yet. I'll mail you a map with directions."

Jessy nodded, almost certain that she wouldn't be going to the cabin, and almost equally certain that Dillon knew it. This was goodbye. Their grand passion was ending with a whimper.

"Have a safe trip," she said, just wanting him to leave so that she could get on with the business of mourning what remained of her life.

Without warning, Dillon's calm facade shattered. His face twitched with emotions that refused to be controlled and anger blazed in his eyes. "Damn you, Jessy." His voice was a hoarse growl. "It didn't have to be this way."

Turning on his heel he left her in silence, and only when the door slammed behind him did Jessy move. Stooped and aching with a pain that almost drove the breath out of her, she drew the curtains and turned out the lights before she crawled back into bed and remained there, too sick at heart to face the world.

The harsh ring of the telephone brought Jessy up out of a dreamless sleep and sent her groping toward the sound before her eyes were open.

"Hello," she croaked into the receiver. One eyelid lifted far enough for her to see that the sun was up and filling her room with a cheerful light not at all in keeping with her mood. "Who is it?"

She looked at the bedside clock with its fluorescent numerals and decided that maybe she shouldn't be so irritated. It was eight-fifteen on Saturday morning. For an instant her heart lifted at the thought that it might be Dillon's voice she was about to hear.

He had been gone since Tuesday without a phone call, just as he had promised. And if this was Dillon, he would be demanding to know why she hadn't met him in San Miguel last night.

"Hello?" Jessy demanded less forcefully. She wasn't looking forward to telling him that she wouldn't be coming, not this weekend or any other.

"Uh, I'm sorry," an unfamiliar male voice said. "I hope I didn't wake you. I was calling for a Jessy Carder."

He sounded as if his morning hadn't been exactly wonderful, either, which gained Jessy's sympathy but still left her prepared to bolt at the first sign of a sales pitch.

"What can I do for you?"

He sighed. "This is very difficult, but we're trying to locate Senator Ruiz. And, uh, he had given us your number several weeks ago."

"And you are?" She had a pretty good idea where Dillon was, and an equally good idea that no one would be able to locate him until he wanted to be located.

"Oh, I'm terribly sorry. I'm Bill Sanders, Senator Ruiz's chief aide. We've been trying to reach him since last night. I don't suppose, um, you would know where he is?"

"No, I'm sorry. When was the last time you heard from him?"

"Thursday afternoon just before his final speaking engagement. He checked out of his room later that evening, and seems to have disappeared."

"Have you tried his home in San Miguel?"

"Yes. We called there last night and again this morning. They haven't heard from him, either."

Positive now that Dillon was at the cabin, Jessy could only shrug and hope that she didn't sound as evasive as she felt. "I'm sorry. I'm sure he'll be back in the office on Monday."

"Uh, well, yes. Ahem." The man cleared his throat and plunged ahead. "Well, in the event that we were unable to locate Senator Ruiz, we were asked to contact you."

"Asked? By whom?" Fully awake now, she swung her legs over the side of the bed and sat frowning at the closet door.

"By, um, the juvenile authorities in San Miguel. It seems that—"

"Juvenile authorities?" Jessy stood, her mind a swirl of possibilities that all circled back to a small, dark-eyed boy. Dread pounded through her even as she cautioned herself that it could be about anything or anybody.

"It seems that," he repeated, "an Emilio Suarez, a juvenile, asked them to call Senator Ruiz or you, and no one else, in his behalf."

"What happened?" she practically shouted. "Where is he? Is he all right? They called you yesterday, and you're just now calling me?"

The man explained in his slow, reasonable tone, "I was instructed to call you only if—"

"Okay, okay. Fine," Jessy interrupted. "What is it?"

With only the barest huff of irritation, he continued. "It seems that this Emilio Suarez was arrested—"

"Arrested?" She whirled and paced into the living room, trailing the long cord of the telephone behind her. "For what?"

"Arrested for armed robbery, it appears." By now he sounded almost pleased to be delivering bad news.

"Armed robbery?" Jessy sank onto the arm of the sofa, suddenly calm. "He's only nine years old. There must be a mistake." She almost felt like laughing at the absurdity of the whole thing. Nine-year-olds played with water pistols. They didn't commit armed robberies.

"All I know is that he's in jail, and he's going to stay in jail until either you or Dillon get down there to get him out."

Afraid to trust something as important as Emilio's rescue to her hunch that Dillon was at the cabin, Jessy smiled into the receiver and became sweetness personified. "Tell me something, uh, Bill, wasn't it?"

"Yes." He sounded suspicious, but warmer than he had only moments earlier.

"If Dillon was handling this, and if he couldn't get there right away, is there someone he would call in San Miguel to grease some wheels for him?"

"Well, there's Judge Patterson. He's retired, but he still has some pull."

"Can you give me his phone number?"

"I'm not sure I should do that."

She could almost hear him trying to back away from the phone, and she dispensed with her smile. "Listen, Bill, when Dillon hears about this, he's going to want to know that *everyone* did *everything* they could for this little boy. Emilio is very important to Dillon. *Very* important."

"If you're wrong, I could lose my job for giving you Judge Patterson's number."

"Do us both a favor, Bill, and help me all you can."

"I'll get the number," he said with a sigh that Jessy echoed.

"Thank you."

After she hung up she called the airline and made her flight plans, then she dialed the judge's number and packed with one hand while she held the receiver in the other and explained who she was and what she needed.

The judge was much easier to deal with than Bill had been and promised that by the time she arrived Emilio would be released to her without any delays. She gave him her heartfelt thanks and left for the airport at a dead run.

By the time her plane touched down she had worn out her anger, guilt and fear and was down to determination. She was going to pick up Emilio, find out what had happened and why, make sure Angelina was all right and then find

Dillon. And if he still wasn't ready to start adoption proceedings, then *she* would.

Guilt almost edged its way back into her heart when she remembered the last time she had seen Emilio, walking away with Angelina in tow. Something had told her that day that time was running out, but she had let Dillon convince her otherwise. She wouldn't let that happen again. She might not be able to change the world, but she could change the lives of two little children who deserved something better. And in doing it, she could change her own life into something a lot better than what she had now.

But all the pep talks in the world didn't prepare her for the reality of Emilio walking out to meet her, his thin body trembling, his sad brown eyes brimming with tears he refused to shed. When she stooped down to gather him into her arms, she knew she'd fight the world for him. She didn't care if he'd done the things they said he had.

She held him, waiting for his tears to come, while she struggled to control her own. But he didn't cry. He just stood there shaking, with his little arms clinging to her as if she were his last hope on earth. And when his trembling stopped, she took him by the hand and led him outside in the sunlight.

"Are you hungry?"

He shook his head. She knew he probably was, but she wasn't going to argue.

"Do you mind if we walk for a few minutes before I take you home?"

Again he shook his head. Still holding his hand in hers, Jessy led him across the parking lot and into a square where winter had only turned the grass brown in patches. A wooden bench sat under a tree, its branches bare except for a few dead leaves that flapped with each whisper of wind that passed by.

"Why don't we sit down for a minute, and maybe you can tell me a little bit about what happened."

Still silent, Emilio sat on the bench. He knotted his hands together and jammed them between his knees and sat there looking at the ground in front of him. Jessy sat next to him, almost touching him, but giving him the space he seemed to need. Her heart ached to hold him until the coiled spring inside him came undone and all the emotions he had bottled up came rushing out.

Taking a cue from him, she clasped her hands and laid them on her lap.

"Well, I guess the first thing I really need to know is, did you do it?" she asked softly.

He nodded without looking up, and Jessy blinked in surprise. Even with him admitting it, she couldn't believe it.

"You did?"

He nodded again.

"With a gun?"

He nodded, and she unclasped her hands to lay one over the beginning swell of her breasts while she took a deep breath.

"It was a liquor store?"

"Yeah." His answer was sullen, but at least he spoke.

Jessy knew she had begun to make progress. "Why a liquor store?" She had heard news reports that even children could have problems with alcohol and drugs, but the reality of it had never hit home.

"Fewer people."

"Fewer people?" she repeated blankly, feeling totally out of her element. Whispering through her mind was the reminder that he was only nine years old.

"Yeah." He almost looked at her. "You rob a grocery store, there's too many people around. Somebody could get hurt."

"How do you know things like that?" She hoped it wasn't psychologically incorrect to sound as shocked as she felt, but she just couldn't help herself.

He shrugged, sounding more like a shriveled little old man than a child. "You hear people talking."

"About which are the best places to rob?" She couldn't believe what she was hearing.

"Sure. About lots of things."

Bringing her incredulity under control, Jessy got herself together and said sternly, "Emilio, a child your age simply shouldn't know things like that."

He twisted around just enough to look up at her and shrugged again. "You got to know how to survive out here, Jessy. Life ain't easy."

"Why did you do it, Emilio?" she demanded. "And don't give me any more of that macho song and dance. I want the truth."

He was quiet for a long time. Finally Jessy said, "Well?"

Sullen again, he said, "We were hungry."

"What about your grandmother?"

"She's sick. She can't get out of bed. We ran out of money. Angelina was scared, hungry, crying. I had to do something."

"So you robbed a liquor store? Where'd you get the gun?"

"My grandmother had it. It was in her drawer." He raised impassioned eyes to Jessy. "But I took it out to sell it. I didn't go out to steal."

"What happened?" She could feel his tough-guy wall beginning to crumble.

"I walked by the store. And I see there's just one guy in there, all alone."

"And you got a better idea."

Her disbelief was gone, leaving her with nothing but grief and a slow-motion sense of impending disaster, as if she were watching a freight train hurtle toward her while she struggled to free her foot that was trapped between the railroad ties.

"Yeah." He hung his head sadly.

"Have you ever heard the term 'credibility gap,' Emilio?"

"No." He raised his head again, looking at her with interest while he waited for her to continue.

"Well, that's what happens when a little kid points a gun at a grown man who knows that he's just pushed an alarm button and the kid doesn't have a clue."

"He knew I was gonna get caught."

"And he knew you weren't going to get any of his money. That was the credibility gap. He didn't believe you, so he wasn't scared of you. You just wasted your time and got yourself in trouble for nothing. And your grandmother and Angelina are still sitting at home with no food, and *nobody* to look out for them."

When Emilio hung his head again and began to cry, Jessy almost felt ashamed of herself for being so hard on him, but at least he was a little boy again. She scooped him up and held him on her lap while he curled in her arms and cried until his tears were exhausted. When dry heaves were all he had left, she carried him to her rented car and took him home.

Along the way they stopped at a market and picked up some groceries. Then Jessy pulled in to a filling station for gas, a map and a phone call to Stephen asking him to meet her at Emilio's. With the map, she found her way to the right neighborhood, and with Emilio's help, to the rundown building where he lived with his grandmother and sister.

When they got there, Stephen was waiting. He left his parked car and came across the street to meet them. "What's going on?"

Jessy had a tight hold on Emilio, who was straining to run ahead. "No," she said, grabbing the impatient boy with both hands, "you have to wait for me. I've never been here before."

"Hurry!" he urged, still tugging.

"Your grandmother's going to need the doctor."

"Is somebody hurt?" Stephen fell into step beside Jessy, who was being dragged along behind Emilio.

"His grandmother's been sick for quite a while. I think she's going to need you."

Jessy was about to explain that she would also need Stephen to take charge of the grandmother for a while when Emilio plunged into a dark doorway and she plunged in behind him. She twisted around to make sure Stephen was following and almost tripped over debris strewn across the floor. Her hand slipped off Emilio, who darted ahead.

"Stop! I won't be able to find you." She could see him several yards ahead and disappearing fast, a dark blob in the gloom of the unlit hallway.

"I'll come back for you," Emilio called out, still running.

"No, you won't! You stop right there, damn it. It's time you started minding *somebody!*" To her amazement he stopped, and she hurried to catch up before he changed his mind. "Stephen, are you still here?" she called over her shoulder once she had Emilio's hand in hers again.

"I'll be right there."

"Are all the buildings around here like this?" she asked when she could hear Stephen close behind her.

"Most of them." He followed as they began to climb a staircase that was so dark they had to feel their way. "This is the building where Dillon and I delivered that baby last fall. I didn't know this was where Emilio lived."

"Neither did I." If she had, she wouldn't have had a decent night's sleep since. At the image of Angelina sitting behind one of these doors, hungry and alone with a woman too old and sick to take care of her, a terrible sense of urgency swept over Jessy, leaving her weak in the knees after the steep climb. "How much farther, Emilio?"

"There!"

She could feel his body lunge, and she let him go. As impatient as she was, she knew he was feeling ten times worse. His whole world was waiting behind a door halfway down the corridor, and if anything had happened to them in the day he had been gone, she knew he would never forgive himself.

A dim rectangle of light appeared in the gloom, and Emilio's small figure darted inside. Hurrying after him, Jessy could hear an excited exchange in Spanish. An adult female spoke first in scolding tones that were softened by relief. Emilio answered, his voice clearly worried, and a little girl began to cry in a high wail. Lost in the din, Jessy could barely hear a weak, quavery voice repeating Emilio's name.

The commotion had calmed by the time Jessy and Stephen entered to find Emilio kneeling beside his grandmother's bed and Angelina sitting beside him on the floor, tugging at his shirt and jabbering between ragged sobs. A middle-aged woman stood in the middle of the room, staring at the tableau and wringing her hands. When she saw Stephen, she began gesturing toward the bed and talking in rapid-fire Spanish.

"What is it?" Jessy demanded.

"Rosa, his grandmother, is very sick." He started toward the bed. "Señora Estevez has been here since last night, when she came to investigate Angelina's crying."

Señora Estevez caught Jessy's hands and, gazing into her eyes, poured out her worries. Profoundly grateful that this woman had stepped in to help when she did, Jessy summoned up her paltry store of Spanish and said, *"Gracias."* She squeezed the woman's hands and poured all the feelings of her heart into her eyes. *"Muchas gracias."* Then she spread her hands in a gesture of helplessness and shrugged. *"No hablo español."*

Señora Estevez smiled, and Jessy turned toward the bed. Emilio watched worriedly while Stephen examined their grandmother. Angelina peeked around her brother and smiled when she caught Jessy's eye.

"Emilio," Jessy called softly. "Come here a minute." She knew that the neighbor had contributed her time and probably her food in caring for Angelina and Rosa, and

Jessy wanted to reimburse her, but not if money would be considered insulting.

With a last hesitant glance at the frail figure on the bed, Emilio hung his head and slowly made his way toward Jessy. Angelina followed with her tiny fist clenched around her brother's shirttail. Her dark, luminous eyes brimmed with unshed tears, while her shy smile lit up her face each time she peeked around Emilio to look at Jessy.

Emilio stopped in front of Jessy, but refused to raise his head. "What's wrong?" she asked, leaning toward him.

"Everyone knows," he mumbled. Angelina wrapped her arms around his waist and peered up at Jessy from under his arm.

"Knows what?" Jessy stooped in front of him and looked up at his stricken face as she slid her hands under his, palm against palm.

"What I did. I've disgraced my family." His voice dropped to a whisper.

"Who said that?"

"She did." His gaze darted toward Señora Estevez's feet and then back to his own.

"Emilio, what you did, you did for love. It may not have been smart, but it wasn't shameful." She caught his chin and lifted his face until it was level with her own. "Sometimes the worst mistakes come from the best intentions. The wise man learns from his mistakes and moves on. That's what I want you to do."

From his frown and blank stare, Jessy realized she may have gone over his head just the littlest bit. "Let's put it this way," she said. "If you had it to do over again, would you do the same thing?"

"No," he said with a vigorous shake of his head.

"Why?"

He looked at her as if she'd taken leave of her senses. "I got caught."

Jessy pursed her lips to keep from smiling and tried a different tack. "How did you feel when you were standing there pointing that gun at the man?"

"Scared."

"Were a lot of things going through your mind?"

He nodded. "Yeah. Lots."

"What was the main thing?"

Emilio closed his eyes and thought a minute. Then he opened his eyes and said definitely, "I wished I wasn't doing it."

"Do you think there could ever be anything that would make you try something like that again?"

Sad eyes, older than his years, looked back at her as Emilio slowly shook his head.

Jessy smiled and gathered him into her arms. Angelina wormed her way into the hug, climbing on Jessy's lap and almost toppling her. Emilio's hand on Jessy's shoulder helped steady her as she held him close.

"Sometimes mistakes, even big ones, teach us things," she said, looking at him to make sure he could understand what she meant. "If we learn not to make the same mistake again, then we can take a bad thing and we can get good things out of it. That's what I want you to do. But I don't want you to be ashamed. Okay?"

He still frowned, but he nodded, willing to agree even if he didn't fully understand what he was agreeing to. At that moment Angelina's tiny hands clamped onto Jessy's cheeks and pulled her face around.

"Hi!" Shining brown eyes smiled at her. "'Member me?"

Surprised that the little girl spoke at all, much less in English, Jessy laughed. "Why, yes, sweetheart. How could I forget you? I just have one more thing to ask your brother. Is that okay?"

Angelina's head bobbed up and down in an exaggerated nod, and Jessy turned back to Emilio, whispering. "Find out if Señora Estevez spent any money taking care of Angelina and your grandmother and tell me if I need to pay her back. Can you do that?''

No longer afraid to look at the other woman, Emilio lifted his head and spat out a stream of Spanish, which brought forth an answering burst. When it ended he said to Jessy, "She fed them last night and again this morning, but it was food left over from what she fed her own family. It was kindness and she expects nothing in return.''

"Would she be insulted if I gave her something, anyway?''

Emilio rolled his eyes and shook his head in disbelief, and Jessy realized she had asked a very silly question. "Hand me my purse, would you?'' She pointed to where she had laid it, and he trotted over to retrieve it. She fished out enough bills to make the little boy's eyes grow round.

"Give this to her and thank her. Tell her we'll never forget her kindness.'' As his fingers closed around the bills, Jessy caught his hand in hers and squeezed gently. "And make it sound sincere. Without Señora Estevez, we don't know what might have happened to your grandmother and Angelina while you were gone. And I, for one, am grateful that we'll never have to know.''

She released him and Emilio walked over to Señora Estevez while Jessy stood and carried Angelina with her to the bed. "How is she?''

"It could be pneumonia.'' Stephen turned away from the old woman to look at Jessy over his shoulder. "How long has she been like this, and when was the last time they had a decent meal around here?''

"I'm not sure.'' She felt the hot sting of tears behind her eyes, part guilt, part sympathy. "I think she's been sick for a while, and I think they've been without much of anything for most of that time.''

"Well, she can't stay here with just two kids to look after her. She's too sick.''

"Uh, well—" Suddenly uncomfortable with what she was about to ask, Jessy shifted Angelina to the other hip. "That brings me to the other reason I wanted you here."

Stephen's eyes narrowed with mounting suspicion. "What?"

"Well, I have to find Dillon."

"I can't stay here. I could maybe find a neighbor."

"No." Gearing up for a battle of wills if necessary, Jessy twisted around and tried to hand Angelina to Emilio, but the little girl wrapped herself around Jessy like a monkey and clung, emitting a high-pitched wail each time they tried to dislodge her. "Okay, fine."

With Angelina firmly attached, Jessy gave up and turned back to Stephen. "I have to take Emilio to Dillon, and Angelina should be with Emilio."

Stephen chuckled. "Well, if you plan on leaving them there and taking off, you'd better have a crowbar with you."

"No." She stroked the soft black curls that covered the little girl's head. "I'm not planning to leave them. Not if I can help it. But we won't be able to take care of her." Jessy's gaze indicated the grandmother. "Not until she's better. Right now she needs you."

"There's no room at the clinic for—"

"I think Dillon's room would be a good place for her."

"At the house? Florence would never—"

"I don't really have time to argue about this, Stephen." She sounded more tired than emphatic but there was nothing she could do about it. Stephen was too sweet a guy to get tough with, but she didn't have time to confront Florence herself.

"Look, if Dillon was here," Jessy said, "he'd take care of it, but he's not, so I'm doing the best I can. Rosa needs food. She needs a doctor's care. And she needs a decent home for as long as it takes to get well."

Warming to her subject, Jessy began to find it easier to get tough. "As soon as Rosa can travel, I'll take her with me, but until then, she's going with you. And if Florence doesn't like it, she can just go whistle Dixie because the house belongs to Dillon, and Florence has no right to refuse.''

"Do you seriously expect me to repeat that?"

"All I know is that Emilio is in serious trouble, and we have to find Dillon right now. Today." She took a step closer to Stephen and lowered her voice. "And that little boy has enough to feel guilty about without having to worry about his grandmother dying while he's trying to get out of a jam he shouldn't have gotten into in the first place."

"I agree."

"Then you'll do it?"

"Yes. I don't think Lita will require much persuading, and she can handle her mother. Where can I reach you if I need you?"

Jessy sighed at the thought of one more hurdle. "You can't. There's no phone where I'm going, but we have to be back in court on Monday, so I'll call you then if not sooner."

"This all sounds pretty mysterious, Jessy." With a nod toward Emilio, Stephen asked, "Did he really do what they say he did?"

"Yes. But the gun wasn't loaded."

Stephen smiled. "That makes a *big* difference. I hope Dillon can straighten it out."

"No child should ever have to get that hungry."

"Or be that proud. Everybody knows Dillon would stand good for anything Emilio ever needed."

"The problem is that nobody bothered to tell Emilio that. He thought he was on his own, and he just got lost for a minute."

A light slowly dawned in Stephen's eyes. He pulled Jessy toward him, wrapping his arm around her shoulder as he lightly kissed her cheek. "And I always thought Rebecca was the one with the big heart. I guess you just save yours for special causes, don't you?"

Not knowing what to say, Jessy just sniffed back the tears that threatened and patted his hand. "Don't get gushy on me. I still have a lot to do today. Emilio, why don't you pack a few clothes for you and your sister? We're going to have to leave in a minute."

"Pack? In what?"

The moment of emotion was safely behind her. Jessy turned in surprise. "You don't have a suitcase?"

"I got a paper bag," Emilio offered helpfully.

"Fine. Pack it." She turned back to Stephen. "So, you'll take care of their grandmother?"

"No problem. I'll take her down to the clinic and check her out while Lita gets things ready at home. It'll be a breeze."

Impulsively Jessy returned Stephen's kiss on the cheek. "Thank you. You'd have made a great brother-in-law."

"Maybe I still can be."

With his words ringing in her ears, Jessy shepherded her charges outside and drove off in search of a cabin somewhere east of San Miguel. After a snack of bananas and milk, Angelina drifted off to sleep in the back seat while Emilio sat in the front and helped Jessy navigate her way out of town.

He wasn't much help, but he was better than she would have been on her own. She had made the trip to the cabin only twice four months ago and hadn't paid much attention either time. Nor had she paid much attention to the map Dillon had mailed to her before she had thrown it away to avoid temptation. Trying to remember the way to the cabin now was like trying to find her way to the land of Oz, but she had to get there, and not just for Emilio's sake.

Earlier in the week she hadn't been ready to hear the promises Dillon wanted to make. She was too full of her own doubts, her own fears, to risk putting her heart on the line any more than it already was. She was willing to have him halfway rather than not have him at all, so she wouldn't let him say what he wanted to say. She was even willing to risk losing him by staying away this weekend, and all out of fear.

"Where are we?" Emilio asked.

His high-pitched voice held an edge of panic and yanked Jessy out of her daydreams. She glanced around, uncertain if the road they were on looked familiar or not. "I have no idea. Are you getting tired?"

"Angelina's asleep."

"I know. Do you want to take a nap?"

"What if you get lost?"

"I'm already lost, sweetheart, but you don't have to worry. If this isn't the right road, I'll just turn around and go back to the highway and try the next exit. It's going to be one of these roads, and once I find the right one I'll be able to find the cabin."

"What if Dillon's not there?"

"We'll have some supper, get some rest and look for him again tomorrow." She reached over and patted his hand. "Is there anything else you're worried about? Like your grandmother, maybe?"

"Maybe. A little."

"You know Dr. Barlow's a good doctor. He'll take care of her. He said she'd be fine in a couple of days, and she'll be in Dillon's house where she'll be safe. Have you ever been there?"

Emilio shook his head.

"It's a very nice house." Jessy looked around carefully. She had been driving on this road for over forty-five minutes and should have already passed the turnoff to the cabin. She hadn't seen any other landmarks she recognized, either.

"Is where we're going a nice house, too?"

"Well, it's small and it's pretty old, but I think it's very nice." Memories swirled to the surface of her mind. Memories of a potbellied stove and a creaking old bed and a claw-foot tub barely big enough for two. With a sigh, Jessy slowed the car to a crawl and pulled off onto the shoulder of the road before steering the car into a tight U-turn.

"Why are we turning around?"

"Because this isn't the right road, honey." Accelerating, she checked her watch and wondered how many more false starts she could get in before dark made the search even harder. Again she patted Emilio's hand, and found it clenched tightly with his other hand in his lap. "What is it, Emilio? There's something else bothering you. Do you want to tell me about it?"

"Do we have to go see Dillon?"

"This is more than I can handle alone, little one. We need Dillon. *You* need Dillon. Why wouldn't you want to see him?"

"He's gonna be so mad at me."

"Oh—" Jessy started to protest and then stopped herself. With Dillon's temper, there was no way he wouldn't hit the ceiling. She had had hours to get her emotions under control before she confronted Emilio. Dillon wouldn't have that luxury, and the guilt he would undoubtedly feel would make his anger even worse. "Well," she finally said, "maybe with Angelina there, he won't get too upset."

"Yeah," Emilio agreed, perking up instantly. "And you'll be there, too." His fingers tightened on Jessy's.

She lifted her hand and brushed his cheek. "Don't worry, little one. I'm not going to let anything happen to you. Now why don't you get some rest so you'll feel better when we get where we're going?"

By the time she got back to the highway, both children were sleeping, and Jessy was alone with her own thoughts down the second country lane that turned out to be a wild-goose chase. Checking her watch and hurrying back to the highway for one more try, she watched a tall bank of dark clouds move in from the west, shutting out the sun and turning an already dismal afternoon into a truly oppressing one.

On her third try, with lightning flashing in her rearview mirror and her stomach tying itself into tighter and tighter knots, she finally saw a sign that looked familiar. Soon after that was a row of fencing and a pond beside a stand of trees, all of which she was sure she had seen before. When her headlights fell on the posts of a rickety gate and the sign dangling from a rusty chain beside a single-lane dirt road that led off at a right angle to the one she was on, Jessy stopped the car and offered up a brief but sincere prayer of thanks. She had found it.

And at the end of this long and winding rutted road, Dillon waited. Whether he waited for her, she didn't know, but at least she could lay her burden on his shoulders. Once Emilio's problems had been taken care of, there would be enough time to find out if Dillon still wanted her, on any terms, or if she had unwisely given him time to come to his senses.

Mustering her courage, Jessy turned onto the dirt lane and made her way slowly and carefully over the remaining miles to the cabin. When she was within sight, the cabin stood out as a low, dark lump against what little light was left in the eastern sky. No light glowed from inside. No windows stood open.

Letting the children sleep, Jessy parked the car and went to the front door alone. She knocked and stood there waiting, wondering what she would say when he opened the door, wondering if he would be happy to see her. When there was no answer, she knocked again and waited, and when there was still no answer, she turned the doorknob and stepped back while the door slowly swung open.

"Dillon?" Jessy stepped over the threshold of the dark cabin and listened. "Dillon?" She peered into the shadows and realized with a sinking heart that she was alone.

She was relieved the children were asleep because her own disappointment was enough for her to bear. She had been so sure he would be here waiting for her, angry maybe, but still waiting for her. Heartsick, she felt her way to the lamp at the end of the couch and turned the switch.

The yellow glow of a low-wattage bulb filled the room with a soft, indistinct light. Jessy walked on into the kitchen and turned on the light there. A small cluster of dirty dishes had been abandoned next to the sink. On the stove an almost empty pan of soup sat congealing.

She lifted the pan and carried it to the sink to run water into it. Then she went to the refrigerator, which was stocked with enough food for at least the weekend. Shaking her head with puzzlement, Jessy left the light on in the kitchen and went across the living room to the loft staircase.

Dillon had clearly been here. If she could find a suitcase, maybe that would show he would be back, if not tonight, then tomorrow. Either way, life had to go on. After she checked the loft she would bring the children in and feed them, then get them ready for bed.

If Dillon was back by tomorrow, fine. If not, she would figure out what to do then. At the top of the staircase she flicked on another small lamp. Pale lemon light bled across the room. On the bed a figure stirred, lifting a hand to ward off the light.

Under a tousled mop of black hair, dark, hollowed eyes opened and a papery-thin voice called, "Jessy?"

"Dillon!"

## Chapter Twelve

Jessy flew across the room as Dillon rose onto his elbow and reached toward her.

"Jessy, is it you?"

His words sounded like the dry rattle of an autumn wind. If she hadn't been in the same room with him, she wasn't sure she could have heard him. With three brothers, she'd seen a lot of hangovers in her day, but she'd never seen one pack a wallop like this.

As she reached him, his strength gave out and he toppled forward into her arms. With one hand on his shoulder to guide him and one arm across his back to support his almost dead weight, Jessy helped soften his fall as he collapsed back against the pillow. Even through his shirt she could feel the feverish heat of his skin. His glazed eyes stared up at her with a child's trust, making her ashamed of her first assumption.

"Dillon," she whispered as she brushed his damp hair away from his face. "What's wrong? How long have you been like this?"

His head rolled loosely from side to side. "Don't know. Day? Two?" His tongue raked across his dry lips while the look in his eyes turned to unmasked adoration. "Knew you'd come." His mouth spread in a painful attempt at a smile that came closer to a grimace. "Knew it."

"Oh, Dillon." Jessy cradled him to her and almost cried to think how close she had come to not showing up at all.

At the thought of Dillon lying alone and sick, waiting for her to arrive and care for him, all the excuses in the world ceased to matter. If anything happened to him, she would never forgive herself.

"Sweetheart, think." She tilted his head back and stared down into his flushed, feverish face. "This is Saturday. When did you get here?"

"Don't know." He pulled away from her restraining hand and snuggled against her, wrapping his arms around her waist as he nestled his cheek against her breast.

"It was either Thursday night or Friday morning. Was it dark or light?" she asked.

His breathing seemed shallow but clear, and the longer she held him, the less life threatening his fever felt. He was probably suffering from the results of a not-so-mild case of food poisoning, or else he just had an old-fashioned virus.

"Dark," he mumbled into her breast. "Very dark." With each word, his breath burned a warm path across her skin.

"And you brought groceries," Jessy coaxed, "so you couldn't have been sick then. Do you remember getting up the next morning?"

He nuzzled closer. "Sick. Couldn't eat. Cold. All day." He shivered again at the memory.

"Do you ache?"

He felt so good in her arms. She had never seen him weak or sick. He had always seemed invincible. Until this moment she had never imagined he could really need her.

Dillon nodded, and she rubbed her cheek against his head. "Have you taken any medicine?"

He shook his head, and Jessy could feel the constant friction of his movements against her breast beginning to spark life in all the wrong places, or the right places at the wrong time. She shifted her position and took a deep, soothing breath. He was far too sick for the thoughts or feelings that were stirring inside her.

"When did you eat last?"

His cheek rubbed against her in a half nuzzle, half shake of his head, and Jessy clasped his head in both her hands to hold him still against her.

"Talk, don't shake," she ordered.

"Don't know."

"Was it soup?" she asked.

His head began to rock again, indicating a yes, and Jessy tightened her grip. "Talk!"

"Yes." His hot breath passed through the soft cotton of her sweater and warmed the patch of skin beneath his mouth.

"That was probably yesterday," she said, remembering the congealed remnants in the pot downstairs.

Unable to stand the sweet torture of cosseting him any longer, Jessy released her hold on Dillon and began to slip away. His arms tried to tighten around her, but he was too weak to stop her.

"You stay here," Jessy said as she spread the covers over him. "I've got to find some aspirin and get some food down you."

A quick check of the bathroom at the end of the loft yielded a bottle of tablets for pain and fever. Jessy set them on the dresser and checked Dillon again. He was almost asleep. As she touched his cheek, he turned toward her hand and brushed his lips across her palm, then sagged into the bed and was asleep.

She stood a minute longer, listening to him breathe, before she leaned to kiss his brow. "Be safe, my love," she whispered. "Please, please, be safe."

Then she straightened and tiptoed from the room and down the stairs. Through the kitchen window she saw Dillon's car tucked in behind the cabin. The children were waiting in her rented car, and she hoped they were still asleep. She found soup in the pantry and put two cans on to heat, enough to satisfy Dillon's minimal appetite and to fill the children when she brought them in.

Next she poured three glasses of orange juice and made two sandwiches. With Emilio to watch over Angelina, Jessy hoped she would be able to leave them in the kitchen eating while she took Dillon's soup and juice up to him. Continuing through her mental list of things yet to do before she could rest, she decided that after she helped Dillon wash and got him settled for the night, she could give the children their baths and put them to bed on a pallet in the living room, close to the fire.

"Oh, gosh," she said aloud and raced to the door of the living room to stare at the potbellied stove, standing cold and unused. Beyond that was the door to the outside, still standing open.

In a flash of consternation, Jessy thought of Rebecca as a new mother, alone and starting life over again in a little cabin in the middle of nowhere, hustling from one chore to the next, busy, happy and fulfilled.

On Jessy's frequent visits, she would stand on the sidelines, amazed and admiring, but certain—absolutely certain—that she would never have a life like that because she and Rebecca were such drastically different people with such starkly different life-styles and totally different needs.

Smiling at the tricks life plays, Jessy turned and went through the kitchen to the back of the house where the firewood was stacked just outside the door. As she carried the wood back to the living room she began to chuckle, and while she struggled to light the fire that stubbornly resisted

her, she actually laughed aloud. When a small blaze finally caught, held and began to grow stronger, tears glistened on Jessy's lashes, and she felt much less tired than she
had earlier.

As the fire grew stronger, so did her confidence. She
stayed on her knees a few minutes longer, watching the
flames. Then she closed the door of the stove and stood.
Brushing the dust from her knees she turned toward the
front door and found Emilio standing there, watching her.

Rubbing his eyes, he asked, "What are you laughing
at?" He sounded tired despite his nap.

"At the tricks adults sometimes play on themselves,
sweetheart. I just realized that I've been playing one on
myself for years."

He frowned and dropped his hand to his side. "Why are
you happy?"

"I'm happy to find out I was wrong," she explained, still
smiling broadly. "I'm very happy. Are you hungry?"

"Angelina is."

"Is she awake?"

"Almost."

Jessy walked over to the door and smoothed the rebel-
lious hair away from his face. "Why don't you go bring her
in? I've got a little snack fixed."

He was gone before she finished talking, and in the few
seconds she had to spare, Jessy ran up the stairs to check on
Dillon again. Satisfied that he was sleeping peacefully and
that his fever wasn't rising, she tucked the covers in around
him and went back down to the kitchen to feed the children.

While they hungrily devoured everything she put in front
of them and asked for seconds, Jessy gathered up all the
blankets and quilts she could find and made a pallet on the
living-room floor.

With the covers that were left, she added another layer
to Dillon and woke him long enough to give him his juice
and two of the tablets she had found. Then while he drifted

off to sleep again she bathed the children and put them down to sleep.

Once they were resting quietly she fed Dillon his soup and washed his face and chest with a warm rag, leaving a more thorough washing for the morning, when he would be stronger and the cabin would be warmer. The remainder of Jessy's night was spent catching catnaps between quieting a restive Dillon, whose fever rose again during the night, adding logs to the fire and rocking Angelina back to sleep after recurring nightmares.

At dawn, after coaxing liquids down Dillon and tucking the quilts in around him one more time, Jessy laid the back of her hand against his forehead and was relieved to find his fever had broken. She went downstairs then, took a quick bath and curled up between the children to rest for just a minute before fixing breakfast. The ceiling above her weary head swam as she closed her eyes. The next sound she heard was the irate bellow of a wounded bull.

"What the hell!"

Startled into instant alertness, Jessy opened her eyes to find the sun well up and flooding the room with light. Raising her head to check her watch, she found herself held down by the dead weight of a sleeping child on each arm. Not able to move more than her head, she twisted to the side to find Dillon clinging to the banister at the bottom of the staircase.

"Shh," she hissed.

"Jessy?"

He sounded much too surprised. With a sense of foreboding Jessy carefully slipped her arms out from under the children and rose to confront him in a whisper. "Keep your voice down."

"Who is that?" he demanded, looking past her to the children.

Since he wouldn't lower his voice, Jessy hurried to meet him. "Emilio and Angelina," she said, still whispering.

"What are they doing here? What are *you* doing here? What's today?" In full voice he shot the questions at her rapid-fire.

"Sunday."

"Well, you sure took your sweet time, didn't you?" Suddenly what little color was in his face drained, and he sank onto a step at the bottom of the staircase. "What's wrong with me?"

She leaned toward him, hesitant to get too close for fear of setting off another full-volume volley from his vile temper. "A virus, maybe. I'm not sure. You weren't making a lot of sense yesterday."

With his head resting in his hands, he mumbled, "You've been here since yesterday?"

"You don't remember?"

"Nothing," he answered without looking up.

"Do you remember when you got sick?"

"Friday, about midday."

He sounded almost normal again, and Jessy breathed a sigh of relief. "You're lucky you didn't kill yourself," she said gently. "When I got here, there was no heat in the cabin. You were lying on top of the covers, and your clothes were damp with sweat. I don't think you'd had anything to eat or drink for about a day." She reached out and touched the cloth covering his shoulder. It was wet. "You're going to get sick all over again. We need to get you back upstairs."

Instead of arguing, Dillon draped his arm over her shoulder and let Jessy guide him back to the bed. While he stripped out of his wet shirt, she looked through his closet.

"Don't you have any pajamas here?"

"Jessy, sweetheart," he asked softly, "have you ever seen me sleep in pajamas?"

"Come to think of it, no." She glanced over her shoulder and saw him sitting on the edge of the bed, wan and bedraggled, but still the most handsome man she'd ever known.

"I've got some sweats in the dresser," he said. "Why don't you just bring me those? A long soak in a hot tub and a good meal ought to be all I need to get me back on my feet."

"A long soak in a hot tub ought to be all you'd need to put you out again for the afternoon, but it'd probably be good for you." She stopped in front of him. Sweatpants dangled from one hand and a sweat top from the other. "I think what you need now is lots of food and rest. You're probably dehydrated."

Dillon looked up at her and smiled. He took the clothes from her hands and laid them aside. "Tell you what, nurse Nancy. I'll be a good little boy if, uh..." He wrapped his arms around her hips and twisted to the side, bringing her down onto the bed next to him as he rolled onto his elbows above her.

He brushed his cheek against her breast. "Oh, man, I've missed you," he said with a heartfelt sigh. His mouth twitched in a playful grin. "I'd sure like to kiss you, but I know I must smell awful."

Jessy stroked the soft skin of his shoulders. "You smell wonderful to me." She loved him with all her heart. She loved him so much it scared her.

Dillon lifted his head and looked deep into her eyes. His smile was gone. "You weren't coming, were you?" he asked softly.

Caught by surprise, she could only look back at him and know that her eyes had already given her away.

"I waited for you," he said in that same soft, sad voice, "getting sicker and sicker, until I finally realized you weren't coming. So I unbolted the door and went back to bed. I figured if I didn't get better, at least they wouldn't have to break the door down to get to my body."

With a half smile that held no humor, he released her and sat up. Alone on the bed, Jessy shivered as a cold chill passed through her. If she hadn't arrived to cover him and feed him and watch over him while he fought his way through the worst of his illness, Dillon might not have gotten better.

Another chill went through her, shaking the bed, and Dillon turned. "Are you getting sick?"

Jessy bolted upright, driven into his arms by terror multiplied by guilt. She had let him think she would join him at the cabin when she had no intention of doing it, and her betrayal had almost cost him his life.

If she had left Dillon to die alone in the middle of nowhere, her grief would have haunted her until the day she died, and to think of how close she had come filled her with a horror beyond description. Clasping her arms around his bare torso, she buried her face against his chest and clung as if her very soul depended on it.

"Sweetheart?" Dillon stroked her back. "I've tried, but I just don't understand any of this. What's wrong? What did I do?"

"I'm sorry," she gasped, forcing the words out past the tears she fought to contain. "I didn't know what I wanted. I thought I did, but I was wrong. I was so wrong," she whispered in the throes of a sorrow too strong to contain.

"Jessy," he said softly, "you're not making any sense. What are you talking about?"

"I wanted to. I wanted to so bad, but I just couldn't." Her words were starting to crumble into hiccups, but she held the tears at bay.

"Wanted to *what?*"

She took a deep gulp of air and stammered, "Y-y-you were better off without me."

"Oh." His brow arched sharply, and his voice went flat. "Never mind what *I* wanted. You decided you knew better, and you were going to stay away for my own good."

Jessy drew in a long, staggered breath and nodded, then buried her face against his chest again.

"Jessy, look, if it's about the modeling, I don't care," Dillon said fervently. "If you need it for money, or independence, or self-worth, then do it. I'll adjust."

"No." She struggled to get the pitch of her voice down below a pitiful whine. "I don't really like it. I never have."

"Then what is it? My grandfather? The publicity? The pregnancy thing?"

She shook her head no, no, then nodded.

"But, damn it, Jessy," he exploded. "I *told* you I didn't care. What does it take to get through to you?"

Jessy slowly lifted her head and gazed into his dark eyes, overflowing with love, anger and frustration. She smiled and shrugged. "It seemed terribly important at the time."

"And now?" he demanded.

"After the scare you gave me last night—" Her voice broke and a shudder ran through her at the thought of how close she had come to losing him for good.

Dillon tightened his arms around her. "Shh," he whispered. "Everything's going to be all right now." He cradled her against him as he rocked back and forth, soothing their wounded spirits with his quiet words. "From now on we're going to talk things through. No more fighting, no more running away and no more making decisions for the other person. Okay?"

Jessy nodded, burrowing deep against his chest, so grateful just to have him alive and stronger that she would agree to anything. But he was right, and she knew it. If heartbreak came in the end, so be it. Until then, for now and for as long as he wanted her, she was Dillon's, and she would never deny it again.

"We can always get children if we want children, sweetheart," Dillon said. He brushed his cheek against her hair. "Children are no problem."

"Oh." At the memory of why she was here, Jessy's head popped up and she drew back, smiling weakly, to look at Dillon head-on. "Don't be so sure of that."

"What?" He sounded instantly suspicious. "Does it have anything to do with—"

She put her fingers over his mouth and gently shushed him, wanting to put off the bad news for as long as possible. "We can get to all that later. Right now I need to start breakfast. I think a nice, hearty bowl of oatmeal would do everyone a lot of good."

"Ugh," he said, wincing. "What's the matter? You didn't bring any yogurt with you?"

Jessy smiled. "I'll get your bath started downstairs, and I think by the time you're through there, you'll be glad to see that oatmeal."

She began to stand, and Dillon took her by the wrist, bringing her back onto the bed beside him.

"Why are the kids here?"

"Well, among other things—" she reached past him to retrieve his sweats from the nightstand where he had laid them "—their grandmother's sick, and I didn't want to leave them with anybody else."

She handed the sweats to him, and Dillon laid them behind him on the bed, then turned his attention back to Jessy. "Among what other things?"

She grimaced and heaved a sigh of irritation. He was the only person she'd ever met who was even more stubborn than she was. "Okay, if you insist, I'll tell you now. But you can't get upset. Remember your promise to talk things through."

"This buildup isn't helping any, Jessy." His voice rumbled ominously. "What is it?"

She took a deep breath and said, "Emilio got into some trouble."

"What kind of trouble?" Dillon shot back before she'd even put the period on her sentence.

"Armed robbery." She braced for an explosion.

*"Armed ro—"*

Before Dillon could finish shouting, Jessy lunged toward him and clapped her hand over his mouth.

"Now you listen to me," she said in deadly earnest. "You haven't got the strength to get upset, so just cut it out. And Emilio is so scared of what you'll say he didn't even want to come here yesterday. But I promised him that you would understand.''

Without releasing her hold on Dillon, she glared into his eyes. "And you will, won't you?" He glared back as she slid her hand away. "Well?"

Through gritted teeth he asked, "Who'd he rob?"

"A liquor store." Forestalling his next question, she added, "With a gun, and don't you dare yell."

"And I suppose," Dillon asked with care, "that you weren't at all upset when you heard any of this?"

"Luckily I had time to compose myself before I saw Emilio. He spent twenty-four hours in jail, Dillon. They couldn't find you, and nobody called me until Saturday morning. And if it makes you feel any better, Emilio didn't exactly stroll out of there whistling a happy tune."

With a sigh Dillon released the death grip he had on his temper. "Why did he do it?"

"His grandmother had been sick and was getting sicker. Angelina was crying from hunger and there was no money. He found the gun in his grandmother's dresser and was going to take it out and sell it. I don't think he'd eaten for days. He probably wasn't thinking very clearly, and when he passed the liquor store he got a very bad idea. A nine-year-old brandishing a rusty old gun apparently didn't impress the liquor store owner very much."

Dillon closed his eyes. "Damn."

"And if you're asking yourself why he didn't call you, all I can say is that I asked myself the same thing. He knew enough to have them call you in Austin after he was arrested. He knew enough to have them find me if you weren't available. So why didn't he know enough to call one of us before he robbed someone? You'd come a lot closer to guessing the answer than I would."

"Pride," Dillon said, half to himself. The eyes he lifted to her held nothing but sorrow and resignation. "He didn't want to come here yesterday?"

Jessy smiled softly and brushed aside the lock of hair that fell across his forehead. "You're a pretty scary dude when you get angry."

He caught her hand and held it against his cheek, welcoming the silent solace she offered. "When is Emilio due back in court?"

"Tomorrow at eleven."

Dillon frowned, lowering her hand as he began to plan. "That doesn't give us much time." Then a new thought occurred to him. "How did you get him released? Have you already got an attorney?"

"Judge Patterson took care of the release for me, but I came running to you for everything else."

"Judge Patterson?"

A long string of silent questions danced across Dillon's face, and Jessy smiled. "I can be very resourceful when I need to be."

"You'll have to tell me more about that someday."

"Someday," she agreed, still smiling. "Do you think it's safe for me to go fix the oatmeal now? You're not going to get upset all over again once I leave you alone, are you?"

"You know, there's one good thing that's come out of all of this."

"What's that?"

A slow smile crept across his face. "You're already starting to sound like a wife."

A warm rush of happiness swept through Jessy at the meaning of his words. He was all but proposing. Maybe everything would be all right, after all. Maybe—

An unexpected shriek from below cut through her half-formed thought and turned her attention in another direction as it brought her bounding to her feet.

"The children are awake, dear." She smiled down at Dillon's shocked face.

"What in the world?"

"Angelina," Jessy explained as she started toward the stairs. "She's been having nightmares. I don't know if it's just this last week, or if this is a regular thing. I'll start your bath. Will you be down in a minute?''

"Yeah, I'll just grab a quick shave up here first.''

Halfway across the room she turned back. "Don't overdo it now. You're not as well as you think you are. You're probably going to be weak off and on for days."

Dillon rose from the bed. "Yes, dear." He unzipped his jeans and hooked his thumbs inside the waistband, while a tempting grin played at the corners of his mouth. "Are you going downstairs, or do you want to stay for the show?" he asked while he edged the tight jeans lower on his lean hips.

She stood mesmerized by the widening triangle of flesh revealed as his pants eased ever lower. A second shriek made her decision for her, and Jessy turned and scampered down the stairs to the sound of Dillon's low chuckle.

Downstairs, Angelina waited with arms outstretched and tears flowing. Jessy scooped up the little girl and held her close, murmuring softly until the first wild burst of crying eased. Emilio, who had been trying to quiet his sister, lay back down, apparently in no hurry to be up.

"You okay?" Jessy asked when Angelina's sobs had quieted.

He nodded.

"Did Angeline wake you, or have you been awake for a while?"

"Little while."

"Why don't you come on into the kitchen with me? I'm going to fix oatmeal for breakfast."

Emilio made a face, but dutifully arose and followed her. With Angelina on her hip, Jessy put water on to heat for the oatmeal and then went into the bathroom to begin filling the claw-foot tub for Dillon, with Emilio still following closely behind her.

"Did you hear us talking?" she asked with the water from the tub muffling her question from ears other than their own.

Emilio nodded.

"Dillon was only upset for a minute." She smiled and led Emilio back into the kitchen. "I'm sure you were upset, too, when it first happened."

Emilio hung his head, but he laughed.

"He's not mad at you, sweetheart." She poured in the oatmeal and began to stir. "He's just worried because he doesn't want anything bad to happen to you, and he's upset with himself because he wasn't there to take care of you this time."

"It's *my* fault."

"Well, yes, it is," she agreed. "You're the one who did it, and you're the one who'll have to pay for it one way or another."

The oatmeal began to bubble, and Jessy lowered the flame. When she turned away from the stove with Angelina still on her hip and Emilio by her side, she saw Dillon standing in the doorway.

His hair, wet and gleaming black, was combed away from his face. The two-day stubble was gone. His cheeks were smooth and only a little paler than normal. He wore his sweatpants and carried the top, and though his stomach might be more concave than normal, none of the rest of him appeared to have suffered from deprivation.

"Hi," Jessy said and ran a hand through her own messy locks. She suddenly remembered the water running in the bathroom. "Oh, your tub!"

"I'll do it," Emilio offered and darted into the next room.

Dillon's gaze roamed over Jessy and then flickered to Angelina, who was contentedly grafted to Jessy's hip. "I had no idea there were so many sides of you I still hadn't seen."

"This is pretty virgin territory here. Even *I* haven't seen me like this before." She tried to smile, but it wouldn't come.

Her arm tightened protectively around Angelina, and once again Jessy realized how much she wanted these children. She only prayed that Dillon wouldn't make her choose in order to hold on to one or the other.

"It looks pretty good on you," Dillon said. Something much stronger than mere approval shone in his ebony eyes.

"You think so?"

"I sure do."

Letting out the breath she had been holding, she could smile finally. "I'm glad. You'd better hurry, or the oatmeal's going to get cold," she said, reluctantly sending him on his way while she returned to the unaccustomed press of duty.

While Dillon bathed, she fed the children and then sorted through their meager belongings for enough clothes to get them through the day. After they were dressed she gathered up the remainder and met Dillon when he was coming out of the bathroom.

"Do you have a washer and dryer here?"

He stepped back into the bathroom and pushed aside a folding door to reveal a stacking washer and dryer.

"Great. I'm going to put these in to wash, and while you eat I'm going to change the sheets on the bed. You shouldn't have to sleep on those another night."

Dillon caught her arm after she emptied her burden into the washer and pulled her closer. "We," he corrected. "I'm not spending another night in that bed alone."

While her heart pounded, Jessy tried to hold on to her sense of reason. As much as she wanted to, it just wasn't possible. "You're far too sick," she said, trying to put conviction into her voice, "and then there're the children. What if—"

"Shh." It was his turn to silence her with the touch of his fingertip to her lips. "I'm not saying we have to do anything. I know the bed squeaks, but you're at least going to sleep next to me even if neither one of us can sleep a wink all night. I love you, Jessy. And we've got a lot more to talk about before tomorrow."

"What?" she asked as her stomach did a somersault.

He'd said it again. He'd said he loved her. Surely, if he really loved her, he'd let her keep the children if he knew how much it meant to her. Dillon had even said he wanted Emilio himself once upon a time.

"Patience." Dillon ran a finger down the side of her neck and across her collarbone. As his finger started into the valley between her breasts, he stopped and sighed. "I have to go over some things with Emilio now. Can you take Angelina upstairs with you while you change the bed?"

"Sure."

Almost relieved to have more time to work out all the complications still facing them, Jessy agreed without hesitation. Besides, every time they spent more than a few minutes together alone they came closer and closer to doing things that shouldn't be done in Dillon's weakened condition.

"Good. Send Emilio into the kitchen," Dillon said.

After a lingering kiss on her lips, he led her out of the bathroom. He went to the stove and took up a dish of oatmeal while she went on into the living room. No longer silent or clinging, Angelina jabbered in a mixture of Spanish and English that was charming but hard to understand as she scrambled up the staircase to the loft.

Jessy tried to pay attention and respond appropriately, but her mind raced ahead to the discussion Dillon had promised. She was afraid to get her hopes too high. He'd never actually mentioned marriage. She'd just assumed that he was considering it. And even though she was more than ready to make the commitment now, there was no guarantee he was, or that he was ready for the addition of the two troubled and troublesome waifs she had taken under her wing with no intention of relinquishing.

Swinging Angelina into her arms, Jessy cuddled the little girl close while her heart swelled with a protective love far different from what she felt for Dillon. As much as she adored him, she wouldn't let these children go. She just couldn't.

The soft, scuffing sound of footsteps on the staircase drew her attention, and Jessy turned to wait. Moments later Dillon appeared, breathing heavily. Emilio's head came into sight immediately after. His slender arms were around Dillon's waist, lending support.

When they reached the loft, Dillon stopped to catch his breath. "You were right about that bath." He gave Jessy a sheepish grin, then looked down and ruffled Emilio's hair. "Maybe after I've had a nap, you and I'll be able to finish that talk."

"That's okay." Emilio seemed anything but heartbroken by the postponement.

"We're still going to have it," Dillon warned as they began to make their way slowly toward the bed. "I have to know everything before we go into that courtroom tomorrow."

Jessy started to put Angelina down and offer her shoulder, but Dillon and Emilio seemed to have things under control. "Did you get any of your oatmeal eaten?" she asked Dillon. She hated to sound like a nag, but he needed food to get back the strength he'd lost over the past forty-eight hours.

"The whole bowl, plus a glass of orange juice. Emilio's as bad as you are. He was shoving food at me so fast we didn't have time to talk about anything."

Jessy's gaze caught Emilio's, and she smiled. He was such a sweet, smart little survivor. She could see a lot of herself in Emilio, just as she knew that Dillon could. As the two slowly shuffled past her, she touched Emilio's cheek.

"Why don't you take Angelina back downstairs. I'll make sure Dillon gets to bed safely. Maybe while he naps, we'll take a look around outside. Then you two can take your naps."

"I don't nap," Emilio said stubbornly.

Surprised, Jessy took a longer look at him. "You don't? Why not?"

An insulted scowl pinched at his still haggard face. "I'm too old."

"Is he?" Jessy swung around to Dillon for confirmation.

Shrugging, Dillon lowered himself gingerly onto the bed. "Well, I don't think Lita's boys nap anymore."

"Well, okay." Jessy linked Emilio's hand with Angelina's and turned him toward the staircase. "But for today I think you still need to catch up on your rest. After that we'll figure out something else for you to do with your afternoons besides run wild." Jessy smiled benevolently and waved goodbye as the little boy shot her a dirty look over his shoulder and started down the stairs with his sister's hand clutched firmly in his.

Dillon stretched out on the bed with a sigh and motioned for Jessy to join him. "What did you mean by that?" he asked softly when she had.

"Well, I'm sure his grandmother's done her best, but he's practically been allowed to run wild. And every child needs discipline, especially a child as intelligent and imaginative as Emilio is. He needs structure, a sense of security, three good meals a day. He needs to stop being the head of the household at nine years of age. He needs to be a child again."

"And how are you planning to do all that?"

The moment of truth had come before she was ready. Jessy had no clever speech prepared, no well-thought-out plan. She had only raw emotion and determination. "I want him."

The simple statement carried the ring of a challenge. Her heart pounding in her ears, Jessy clenched her jaw and leveled her unflinching eyes on Dillon's.

"When did you decide this?"

"I've been toying with the idea for a long time, but yesterday I made up my mind. I can't let them go back to the way they were living."

"You can't, huh?" His finger stroked her cheek.

Jessy wanted to jerk away, to keep her head clear until after they'd talked, but she couldn't move. Her determination was unwavering, but her voice turned meltingly soft. "No."

"Have I told you that I love you?"

"You've mentioned it."

"Well, I meant it. You're the finest, purest, most wonderful woman I've ever known."

"Oh, Dillon." Jessy shook her head, preparing to argue.

"See?" He smiled and then laughed aloud as he pulled her down across his chest and wrapped his arms around her. "You think you're so tough." He laughed again and rolled, bringing her down onto the bed with him propped on his elbow beside her. "You think that because you don't take the world to your bosom the way your sister does, that you're not as good a person as she is, but you're wrong. You're the one who always watched out for her while she watched out for others. You're the one who takes care of the care givers. Jessy, you're the woman I've been waiting for my whole life."

"I am?"

"Yes, you are, and I'd have told you so the other day if you'd let me." He stroked her cheek with the backs of his fingers. "Baby, I need you. I need you so much I don't think I could go on if I didn't have you. I can't imagine my life without you in it."

"So, let me get this straight," Jessy said, calming the deafening drumbeat of her heart with sheer willpower. "You *really* love me?"

Dillon smiled and nodded. "Yes."

"That's wonderful, Dillon." Filled with joy, she seized the moment while she had it in her grasp. "Now, exactly what do you plan to do about this?"

"Do about this?"

Seeing that he needed guidance, she said, "You love me, aaand..." She drew the word out and paused, waiting for him to fill in the blank.

"Oh," he said. The light of realization dawned in his eyes. "I've never actually asked you, have I?"

"I don't believe so."

"Jessy." He swung up and out of the bed in a fluid motion that ended with him on one knee on the floor, one hand supporting hers, the other laid over his heart. "I love you more than I ever dreamed I would love any woman."

He paused while his dark eyes grew darker still. A small frown crinkled his brow while the silence stretched, and Jessy began to fear that he wouldn't continue.

"Will you please marry me, Jessy?" he asked finally in a whispery shadow of his usual baritone.

She let out her breath with a sigh. "You scared me."

"Answer me," he demanded, tightening his fingers around hers.

"Yes."

He closed his eyes and released a sigh of his own.

"Did you think I wouldn't?" She leaned toward him and laid her hand against his cheek.

"If there's one thing I've learned about you, Jessy, it's never to jump to conclusions, because you confound me every time."

"I'll try to work on that," she said, genuinely compliant possibly for the first time in her life.

He shook his head. "Don't. I'm getting used to you this way. And you'll only confuse me if you start changing now." He covered her hand with his and looked into her eyes. "Are we going to adopt them?"

"Yes."

"You're sure?"

"There's only one thing I've ever been more sure of, and that's how much I love you." The happiness inside her was so strong she thought she might burst.

Dillon gazed deeply into her eyes and moved closer inch by slow inch. "I want to make love to you," he said in a voice rich with seduction.

"You're sick, remember?" Jessy reminded him slightly breathless. "And the bed squeaks."

"Trifles." He shook his head, tossing aside her arguments. "I'm feeling stronger by the minute, and we can put the mattress on the floor."

"You're the most stubborn man I've ever met." Laughing gently, she gazed up into the face she adored, the bronzed, heart-stoppingly sensual face she would cherish each day for the rest of her life. "And I hope you never change," she said tenderly.

## Epilogue

Wearing a pale shrimp-colored kimono that was short enough to reveal her white garters and the lace tops of her sheer white stockings, Jessy clutched both sides of the bathroom door and glared at Rebecca.

"Let me get someone, please?" Rebecca coaxed.

"It's just nerves."

"You've been nervous like this every morning since I got here. Has it occurred to you that it might *not* be nerves?"

"What else could it be?" Jessy let go of the doorway and hurried to the bed, where she collapsed. "Hand me that satin pillow, would you?"

"Well, speaking as one who's had two already," Rebecca said, retrieving the pillow, "it could be a baby. Have you been using protection?"

"Why should I?" Jessy lifted her head and helped Rebecca tuck the pillow in place without messing a hair. "I can't get pregnant."

"Jessy, I was there with you. The doctor said it was highly unlikely. He never said it was impossible."

"Don't, Rebecca, please." Jessy sat up slowly and carefully, not wanting a repetition of the nausea and dizziness that had plagued her every morning for two weeks.

She caught her sister's hand and pulled her down beside her. "This is the happiest day of my life. I don't want to cast a shadow on it by getting my hopes up for something that would be a miracle if it happened. What I have is enough."

Compelled by the need to reinforce those words, Jessy rose and went to the window that overlooked the backyard of Dillon's family home. She pulled aside the curtain and peeked out at the gathering below. She could see Dillon, not yet changed into his tuxedo, talking to her brother Houston, who had flown in from Savannah with his wife, Laura. Cody, Rebecca's husband, was also there with their toddler, Matthew, close at hand and baby Susan in her carriage.

"Isn't he gorgeous?" With his dark, dramatic looks, Dillon stood out from the crowd around him. Jessy knew there would always be that hint of the untamed in him that called out to her, that promise of passion unchained if she would only come with him to the secret place that was theirs alone.

Rebecca joined her at the window. "He sure is."

At the dreamy quality of her sister's voice, Jessy turned to her and smiled. "You're looking at Cody."

"Dillon's nice, too." Rebecca danced away laughing. "Come on, everyone's going to be leaving for the church soon, and you're not even dressed."

"The thought of squeezing *this* stomach into *that* corset really fills me with dread." Jessy rubbed her tender tummy and tried to banish the mental image of her dashing down the aisle in search of a bathroom while Dillon stood waiting at the altar and the organist played on and on and on.

"Jessy, you're marrying into a family with two doctors. Don't you think one of them could give you something that would get you through the ceremony?"

"I think maybe I'd better lie down again. Just for a minute."

The door opened and Laura Carder swept in, a vision of Southern loveliness in her bridesmaid gown of palest peach. "Hi. How are we coming in here? Why is she lying down, Rebecca?"

"Because she's *not* pregnant, and she can't quit throwing up," Rebecca said sweetly.

"You know, the older we get, the more you sound like me," Jessy complained from her prone position on the bed. "Hi, Laura. Are you dressed yet? Come around here and let me see you."

Laura walked around to the other side of the bed, where Jessy's long legs dangled, ending in white satin heels.

"Oh," Jessy exclaimed when her sister-in-law came into view, "those dresses turned out so nice. You just look wonderful."

"Well, thank you, but you look kind of pale, Jessy." Laura moved closer and felt Jessy's forehead. "Are you really pregnant?"

"No."

"Oh, well, that's a shame." Laura touched her stomach and smiled. "Because maybe we could have had ours at the same time."

"Laura?" Jessy and Rebecca spoke at the same time.

"Really?" Jessy asked. She rose slowly while Rebecca left the other side of the bed and came around to where Laura was.

"We've been trying since we were married," Laura said at the end of hugs all around, "and we just found out before we left Savannah that it's finally going to happen."

Gingerly Jessy sank back onto the bed, and Laura leaned to kiss her cheek, careful not to mar the perfect makeup that was already in place.

Still holding her sister-in-law's hand, Laura said, "We didn't want to say anything to the others until after the wedding. After all, this is your time, Jessy. But I just couldn't wait to share this with you two."

"I'm so happy for you." Taking a tissue from Rebecca, Jessy dabbed at the corners of her eyes. "I've just been so emotional lately. I don't know how I'm ever going to get through this day without breaking down and bawling."

"I don't suppose you've missed any periods recently?" Laura asked.

Jessy shrugged. "I only have one every other month. It'd be a while before I'd notice."

Shifting her thoughts away from the possibility of an impossible pregnancy, Jessy asked, "Does anybody know who's watching my little flower girl?"

She looked first at the hazel-eyed blonde her besotted brother had once likened to a porcelain doll, then to the brown-eyed brunette whose sensual beauty seemed to blossom more fully with each child she bore.

"The mothers," Rebecca answered first.

"Both of them?" Jessy cringed, hating to think of poor little Angelina being shepherded by Dillon's mother, Florence, and Jessy's own mother, Cissy, at the same time. Two more different women she couldn't imagine.

"Both of them," Laura confirmed. "They seem to be forming a real bond."

"Probably the bond of relief. Dillon's mother is relieved that I'm not as bad as she thought. And my mother's relieved that I settled down and got married without any of her worst fears coming to pass." Jessy groaned. "Speaking of worst fears," she asked, dropping her voice to a whisper, "has Dillon's grandfather arrived yet?"

"Is that the tall, distinguished looking man with the white hair and blue eyes to die for?" Laura asked, going to the window to peer out.

"Yes," Jessy answered, looking up as Rebecca came to stand over her.

"Jessy," Rebecca said sternly. "You've got to get dressed. At the rate you're going, this June wedding is going to stretch into July."

"He's out there," Laura said. "It looks like he's with, hum, I think that's Emilio. They seem to be deep in conversation."

Rising as ordered, Jessy walked over to retrieve the dreaded corset. "He's probably recruiting my own kid to spy on me now," she grumbled.

"I think that's all in the past, don't you?" Rebecca said as she opened the closet and took out the white satin and cream lace piece of froth that Jessy was to wear down the aisle. "He seems more than happy with the political mileage he's gotten out of Dillon marrying the woman he fell in love with while shooting a fashion layout. And then with your adopting two orphaned children from the barrio, and even taking in their grandmother. How's that going, by the way?"

Jessy sucked in her breath and managed to fasten all but the top hook on her corset. Her breasts simply refused to be corralled any more than they already were. "Just fine," she said, letting out a sigh of relief. "The cabin's being enlarged, and we should be able to move back in next month. What with our practically adopting Rosa, too, the state couldn't agree to let us have Emilio and Angelina fast enough."

She turned and saw Rebecca holding the wedding dress and Jessy's heart did a dive into the pit of her stomach only to turn around and soar back into her throat. "Oh, I'm so nervous," she said with her voice shaking worse than her knees were.

"It's a piece of cake," Laura said, taking her hands. "You'll be fine."

"What if I get sick?" On the edge of panic, Jessy hurried to the window. Dillon was gone. Everyone was gone. Houston and Cody would be waiting downstairs for their wives. Everyone else would be waiting at the church.

"Jessy," Rebecca said softly. "You're in your underwear."

"It's okay. There's no one down there." She turned away from the window. "I wish I could have seen Dillon one more time. With all the people coming and going, it seems like it's been forever since we were alone together."

"I thought it was very romantic of him to move out this last month," Laura said. "There are a lot of men who wouldn't dream of a separation like that, much less have come up with the idea himself."

"I can definitely think of one who wouldn't," Rebecca said, laughing as she thought of Cody, who hadn't been separated from her for a day since he had proposed, except for when she delivered Susan.

"Make that two," Laura added shyly, then blushed almost the same shade as her peach gown. "But I think Dillon is planning a really traditional honeymoon, if you know what I mean."

"Ladies, please," Jessy protested as she stepped into her dress. "I'm nervous enough already. Don't get me started thinking about the honeymoon before I've even survived the wedding."

Rebecca guided the gown carefully upward. Laura came around to take one shoulder and help Jessy into the sleeve.

"Somebody open a window," Jessy said, fanning herself with her one free arm. "I think I'm going to faint it's so stuffy in here."

"The house is air-conditioned, Jessy," Rebecca re
minded her gently. "Pretend you're on a photo shoot
Think cool, calm thoughts."

Jessy turned her head and looked at her sister over he
shoulder. "Did you, on your wedding day?"

Rebecca laughed. "No. I was a nervous wreck."

"Do you suppose Dillon's this nervous?" Jessy asked
looking out the window at the cloudless blue sky.

"Worse," Laura assured her. "The grooms are alway
worse."

"And the ring bearers," Rebecca said, carefully zippin
the back of the dress. "Emilio asked me yesterday if I wa
sure he and Angelina could stay with us in Eden while yo
were honeymooning. He said something about violating hi
probation. I thought the charges against him wer
dropped."

"They were," Jessy said.

Rebecca tugged the two sides of the dress together acros
Jessy's ribs. "Suck in."

"Yes, ma'am," Jessy said, sucking in. "But Dillon an
I put him on probation for a year, and Emilio keeps get
ting it confused with a real probation from the court. I'
have Dillon explain it to him again so he won't worry."

"Jessy, when was the last time you tried this dress on?"
Rebecca asked, tugging again.

"A couple of weeks ago." She didn't like Rebecca's tone
"Why?" Jessy asked, growing worried.

"How did it fit then?"

"Just fine," Jessy said, still worried. "Why?"

"Take a deep breath and let out all the air and then don
move," Rebecca ordered.

Not bothering to ask why again, Jessy did as she was tol
and then stood there, unmoving, while Rebecca tugged an
zipped and tugged and zipped some more until the last fe

inches were closed. Then she stepped back with a sigh of relief.

"Turn around and let me look at you," Rebecca said.

Jessy turned, feeling like a sausage in a casing that was too tight.

"You're beautiful, Jess." Tears glistened in Rebecca's eyes. "You're just beautiful. And you're going to have to move very carefully and take very small breaths because your chest has outgrown that dress, and that zipper's about to blow. And, Jessy dear, nerves don't make your breasts swell."

"No," Jessy scoffed, turning to the full-length mirror on the closet door. A vision looked back at her, a vision in shimmering satin and antique lace.

Moving closer, she checked the low-cut satin bustline, saved from boldness only by the creamy lace that went all the way to her collarbone. But the amount of flesh revealed beneath the lace was more than had been there before, and the fullness encased in satin was more obvious than it had been before.

"I still don't believe it," she said softly and turned away from the mirror.

"Well, it's time to go," Rebecca said, opening the bedroom door. "Your limo awaits, princess."

Jessy closed her eyes and drew in as deep a breath as she could, then let it out with a sigh. "Wish me luck," she said, looking from Laura to Rebecca.

"Luck," Laura said, smiling.

"Luck." Rebecca caught Jessy by the shoulders and hugged her soundly, then ushered her out the door with Laura coming behind.

"And later this year," Rebecca said, just above a mutter, as they proceeded to the staircase, "when your stomach's protruding outrageously from some unknown cause, and you start getting *really* bad cramps you can time with a watch, promise me you'll stop arguing and just go to the hospital."

"I am *not* pregnant," Jessy said as she walked carefully down the stairs, taking shallow breaths and wondering with a growing smile if she just might be a walking miracle, after all.

\*     \*     \*     \*     \*

# Take 4 bestselling love stories FREE

## Plus get a FREE surprise gift!

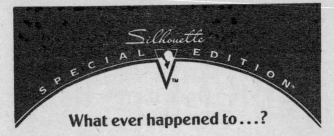

*Silhouette*

SPECIAL EDITION™

## What ever happened to...?

Have you been wondering when a much-loved character will finally get their own story? Well, have we got a lineup for you! Silhouette Special Edition is proud to present a *Spin-off Spectacular!* Be sure to catch these exciting titles from some of your favorite authors.

**TRUE BLUE HEARTS** (SE #805 April) *Curtiss Ann Matlock* will have you falling in love with another Breen man. Watch out for Rory!

**FALLING FOR RACHEL** (SE #810 April) *Those Wild Ukrainians* are back as *Nora Roberts* continues the story of the Stanislaski siblings.

**LIVE, LAUGH, LOVE** (SE #808 April) *Ada Steward* brings you the lovely story of Jessica, Rebecca's twin from *Hot Wind in Eden* (SE #759).

**GRADY'S WEDDING** (SE #813 May) In this spin-off to her *Wedding Duet, Patricia McLinn* has bachelor Grady Roberts waiting at the altar.

**THE FOREVER NIGHT** (SE #816 May) *Myrna Temte's* popular *Cowboy Country* series is back, and Sheriff Andy Johnson has his own romance!

**WHEN SOMEBODY WANTS YOU** (SE #822 June) *Trisha Alexander* returns to Louisiana with another tale of love set in the bayou.

**KATE'S VOW** (SE #823 July) Kate Newton finds her own man to love, honor and cherish in this spin-off of *Sherryl Woods's Vows* series.

**WORTH WAITING FOR** (SE #825 July) *Bay Matthews* is back and so are some wonderful characters from *Laughter on the Wind* (SE #613).

Don't miss these wonderful titles, only for our readers—only from Silhouette Special Edition!

*New York Times* Bestselling Author

# Sandra Brown

## Tomorrow's Promise

### She cherished the memory of love but was consumed by a new passion too fierce to ignore.

For Keely Preston, the memory of her husband Mark has been frozen in time since the day he was listed as missing in action. And now, twelve years later, twenty-six men listed as MIA have been found.

Keely's torn between hope for Mark and despair for herself. Because now, after all the years of waiting, she has met another man!

**Don't miss TOMORROW'S PROMISE by SANDRA BROWN.**

**Available in June wherever Harlequin books are sold.**

A romantic collection that
will touch your heart....

# *Mother* *to* *with* *Love* *'93*

**Diana Palmer**
**Debbie Macomber**
**Judith Duncan**

As part of your annual tribute to
motherhood, join three of Silhouette's
best-loved authors as they celebrate the
joy of one of our most precious gifts—
mothers.

Available in May at your favorite retail outlet.

Only from ▼ *Silhouette*®

—where passion lives.